Dulcibel: A Tale of Old Salem

Henry Peterson

Illustrated by Howard Pyle

DULCIBEL

A Tale of Old Salem

BY

HENRY PETERSON

Author of

"Pemberton, or One Hundred Years Ago"

Illustrations by

HOWARD PYLE

1907

She stood up serene but heroic

CONTENTS.

Illustrations

CHAPTER I.

Dulcibel Burton.

In the afternoon of a sunny Autumn day, nearly two hundred years ago, a young man was walking along one of the newly opened roads which led into Salem village, or what is now called Danvers Centre, in the then Province of Massachusetts Bay.

The town of Salem, that which is now the widely known city of that name, lay between four and five miles to the southeast, on a tongue of land formed by two inlets of the sea, called now as then North and South Rivers. Next to Plymouth it is the oldest town in New England, having been first settled in 1626. Not till three years after were Boston and Charlestown commenced by the arrival of eleven ships from England. It is a significant fact, as showing the hardships to which the early settlers were exposed, that of the fifteen hundred persons composing this Boston expedition, two hundred died during the first winter. Salem has also the honor of establishing the first New England church organization, in 1629, with the Reverend Francis Higginson as its pastor.

Salem village was an adjunct of Salem, the town taking in the adjacent lands for the purpose of tillage to a distance of six miles from the meeting-house. But in the progress of settlement, Salem village also became entitled to a church of its own; and it had one regularly established at the date of our story, with the Reverend Samuel Parris as presiding elder or minister.

There had been many bickerings and disputes before a minister could be found acceptable to all in Salem village. And the present minister was by no means a universal favorite. The principal point of contention on his part was the parsonage and its adjacent two acres of ground. Master Parris claimed that the church had voted him a free gift of these; while his opponents not only denied that it had been done, but that it lawfully could be done. This latter view was undoubtedly correct; for the parsonage land was a gift to the church, for the perpetual use of its pastor, whosoever he might be. But

Master Parris would not listen to reason on this subject, and was not inclined to look kindly upon the men who steadfastly opposed him.

The inhabitants of Salem village were a goodly as well as godly people, but owing to these church differences about their ministers, as well as other disputes and lawsuits relative to the bounds of their respective properties, there was no little amount of ill feeling among them. Small causes in a village are just as effective as larger ones in a nation, in producing discord and strife; and the Puritans as a people were distinguished by all that determination to insist upon their rights, and that scorn of compromising difficulties, which men of earnest and honest but narrow natures have manifested in all ages of the world. Selfishness and uncharitableness are never so dangerous as when they assume the character of a conscientious devotion to the just and the true.

But all this time the young man has been walking almost due north from the meeting house in Salem village.

The road was not what would be called a good one in these days, for it was not much more than a bridle-path; the riding being generally at that time on horseback. But it was not the rather broken and uneven condition of the path which caused the frown on the young pedestrian's face, or the irritability shown by the sharp slashes of the maple switch in his hand upon the aspiring weeds along the roadside.

"If ever mortal man was so bothered," he muttered at last, coming to a stop. "Of course she is the best match, the other is below me, and has a spice of Satan in her; but then she makes the blood stir in a man. Ha!"

This exclamation came as he lifted his eyes from the ground, and gazed up the road before him. There, about half a mile distant, was a young woman riding toward him. Then she stopped her horse under a tree, and evidently was trying to break off a switch, while her horse pranced around in a most excited fashion. The horse at last starts in a rapid gallop. The young man sees that in trying to get the switch, she has allowed the bridle to get loose and over the horse's head, and can no longer control the fiery animal. Down the road towards him she comes in a sharp gallop, striving to stop the animal with her voice, evidently not the least frightened, but holding on to the pommel of the saddle with one hand while she makes desperate grasps at the hanging rein with the other.

The young Puritan smiled, he took in the situation with a glance, and felt no fear for her but rather amusement. He was on the top of a steep hill, and he knew he could easily stop the horse as it came up; even if she did not succeed in regaining her bridle, owing to the better chances the hill gave her.

"She is plucky, anyhow, if she is rather a tame wench," said he, as the girl grasped the bridle rein at last, when about half way up the hill, and became again mistress of the blooded creature beneath her.

"Is that the way you generally ride, Dulcibel?" asked the young man smiling.

"It all comes from starting without my riding whip," replied the girl. "Oh, do stop!" she continued to the horse who now on the level again, began sidling and curveting.

"Give me that switch of yours, Jethro. Now, you shall see a miracle."

No sooner was the switch in her hand, than the aspect and behavior of the animal changed as if by magic. You might have thought the little mare had been raised in the enclosure of a Quaker meeting-house, so sober and docile did she seem.

"It is always so," said the girl laughing. "The little witch knows at once whether I have a whip with me or not, and acts accordingly. No, I will not forgive you," and she gave the horse two or three sharp cuts, which it took like a martyr. "Oh, I wish you would misbehave a little now; I should like to punish you severely."

They made a very pretty picture, the little jet-black mare, and the mistress with her scarlet paragon bodice, even if the latter was entirely too pronounced for the taste of the great majority of the inhabitants, young and old, of Salem village.

"But how do you happen to be here?" said the girl.

"I called to see you, and found you had gone on a visit to Joseph Putnam's. So I thought I would walk up the road and meet you coming back."

"What a sweet creature Mistress Putnam is, and both so young for man and wife."

"Yes, Jo married early, but he is big enough and strong enough, don't you think so?"

"He is a worshiped man indeed. Have you met the stranger yet?"

"That Ellis Raymond? No, but I hear he is something of a popinjay in his attire, and swelled up with the conceit that he is better than any of us colonists."

"I do not think so," and the girl's cheek colored a deeper red. "He seems to be a very modest young man indeed. I liked him very much."

"Oh, well, I have not seen him yet. But they say his father was a son of Belial, and fought under the tyrant at Naseby."

"But that is all over and his widowed mother is one of us."

"Hang him, what does it matter!" Then, changing his tone, and looking at her a little suspiciously. "Did Leah Herrick say anything to you against me the other night at the husking?"

"I do not allow people to talk to me against my friends," replied she earnestly.

"She was talking to you a long time I saw."

"Yes."

"It must have been an interesting subject."

"It was rather an unpleasant one to me."

"Ah!"

"She wanted me to join the 'circle' which they have just started at the minister's house. She says that old Tituba has promised to show them how the Indians of Barbados conjure and powwow, and that it will be great sport for the winter nights."

"What did you say to it?"

"I told her I would have nothing to do with such things; that I had no liking for them, and that I thought it was wrong to tamper with such matters."

"That was all she said to you?" and the young man seemed to breathe more freely.

The girl was sharp-witted—what girl is not so in all affairs of the heart?—and it was now her turn. "Leah is very handsome," she said.

"Yes—everybody says so," he replied coolly, as if it were a fact of very little importance to him, and a matter which he had thought very little about.

Dulcibel, was not one to aim all around the remark; she came at once, simply and directly to the point.

"Did you ever pay her any attentions?"

"Oh, no, not to speak of. What made you think of such an absurd thing?"

"'Not to speak of'—what do you mean?"

"Oh, I kept company with her for awhile—before you came to Salem—when we were merely boy and girl."

"There never was any troth plighted between you?"

"How foolish you are, Dulcibel! What has started you off on this track?"

"Yourself. Answer me plainly. Was there ever any love compact between you?"

"Oh, pshaw! what nonsense all this is!"

"If you do not answer me, I shall ask her this very evening."

"Of course there was nothing between us—nothing of any account—only a boy and girl affair—calling her my little wife, and that kind of nonsense."

"I think that a great deal. Did that continue up to the time I came to the village?"

"How seriously you take it all! Remember, I have your promise, Dulcibel."

"A promise on a promise is no promise—every girl knows that. If you do not answer me fully and truly, Jethro, I shall ask Leah."

"Yes," said the young man desperately "there was a kind of childish troth up to that time, but it was, as I said, a mere boy and girl affair."

"Boy and girl! You were eighteen, Jethro; and she sixteen nearly as old as Joseph Putnam and his wife were when they married."

"I do not care. I will not be bound by it; and Leah knows it."

"You acted unfairly toward me, Jethro. Leah has the prior right. I recall my troth. I will not marry you without her consent."

"You will not!" said the young man passionately—for well he knew that Leah's consent would never be given.

"No, I will not!"

"Then take your troth back in welcome. In truth, I met you here this day to tell you that. I love Leah Herrick's little finger better than your whole body with your Jezebel's bodice, and your fine lady's airs. You had better go now and marry that conceited popinjay up at Jo Putnam's, if you can get him."

With that he pushed off down the hill, and up the road, that he might not be forced to accompany her back to the village.

Dulcibel was not prepared for such a burst of wrath, and such an uncovering of the heart. Which of us has not been struck with wonder, even far more than indignation, at such times? A sudden difference occurs, and the man or the woman in whom you have had faith, and whom you have believed noble and admirable, suddenly appears what he or she really is, a very common and vulgar nature. It makes us sick at heart that we could have been so deceived.

Such was the effect upon Dulcibel. What a chasm she had escaped. To think she had really agreed to marry such a spirit as that! But fortunately it was now all over.

She not only had lost a lover, but a friend. And one day before, this also would have had its unpleasant side to her. But now she felt even a sensation of relief. Was it because this very day a new vision had entered into the charmed circle of her life? If it were so, she did not acknowledge the fact to herself; or even wonder in her own mind, why the sudden breaking of her troth-plight had not left her in a sadder humor. For she put "Little Witch" into a brisk canter, and with a smile upon her face rode into the main street of the village.

CHAPTER II.

In Which Some Necessary Information is Given.

Dulcibel Burton was an orphan. Her father becoming a little unsound in doctrine, and being greatly pleased with the larger liberty of conscience offered by William Penn to his colonists in Pennsylvania, had leased his house and lands to a farmer by the name of Buckley, and departed for Philadelphia. This was some ten years previous to the opening of our story. After living happily in Philadelphia for about eight years he died suddenly, and his wife decided to return to her old home in Salem village, having arranged to board with Goodman Buckley, whose lease had not yet expired. But in the course of the following winter she also died, leaving this only child, Dulcibel, now a beautiful girl of eighteen years. Dulcibel, as was natural, went on living with the Buckleys, who had no children of their own, and were very good-hearted and affectionate people.

Dulcibel therefore was an heiress, in a not very large way, besides having wealthy relatives in England, from some of whom in the course of years more or less might reasonably be expected. And as our Puritan ancestors were by no means blind to their worldly interests, believing that godliness had the promise of this world as well as that which is to come—the bereaved maiden became quite an object of interest to the young men of the vicinity.

I have called her beautiful, and not without good reason. With the old manuscript volume—a family heirloom of some Quaker friends of mine—from which I have drawn the facts of this narrative, came also an old miniature, the work of a well-known English artist of that period. The colors have faded considerably, but the general contour and the features are well preserved. The face is oval, with a rather higher and fuller forehead than usual; the hair, which was evidently of a rather light brown, being parted in the center, and brought down with a little variation from the strict Madonna fashion. The eyes are large, and blue. The lips rather full. A snood or fillet of blue ribbon confined her luxuriant hair. In form she was rather above the usual height of women, and slender as became her age; though with a perceptible tendency towards greater fullness with increasing years.

There is rather curiously a great resemblance between this miniature, and a picture I have in my possession of the first wife of a celebrated New England poet. He himself being named for one of the Judges who sat in the Special Court appointed for the trial of the alleged witches, it would be curious if the beautiful and angelic wife of his youth were allied by blood to one of those who had the misfortune to come under the ban of witchcraft.

Being both beautiful and an heiress, Dulcibel naturally attracted the attention of her near neighbor in the village, Jethro Sands. Jethro was quite a handsome young man after a certain style, though, as his life proved, narrow minded, vindictive and avaricious. Still he had a high reputation as a young man with the elders of the village; for he had early seen how advantageous it was to have a good standing in the church, and was very orthodox in his faith, and very regular in his attendance at all the church services. Besides, he was a staunch champion of the Reverend Mr. Parris in all his difficulties with the parish, and in return was invariably spoken of by the minister as one of the most promising young men in that neighborhood.

Jethro resided with his aunt, the widow Sands. She inherited from her husband the whole of his property. His deed for the land narrated that the boundary line ran "from an old dry stump, due south, to the southwest corner of his hog-pen, then east by southerly to the top of the hill near a little pond, then north by west to the highway side, and thence along the highway to the old dry stump again aforesaid." There is a tradition in the village that by an adroit removal of his hog-pen to another location, and the uprooting and transplanting of the old dry stump, at a time when nobody seemed to take a very active interest in the adjoining land, owing to its title being disputed in successive lawsuits, Jethro, who inherited at the death of his aunt, became the possessor of a large tract of land that did not originally belong to him. But then such stories are apt to crop up after the death of every man who has acquired the reputation of being crafty and close in his dealings.

We left Jethro, after his interview with Dulcibel, walking on in order that he might avoid her further company. After going a short distance he turned and saw that she was riding rapidly homeward. Then he began to retrace his steps.

"It was bound to come," he muttered. "I have seen she was getting cold and thought it was Leah's work, but it seems she was true to her promise after all. Well, Leah is poor, and not of so good a family, but she is worth a dozen of such as Dulcibel Burton."

Then after some minutes' silent striding, "I hate her though for it, all the same. Everybody will know she has thrown me off. But nobody shall get ahead of Jethro Sands in the long run. I'll make her sorry for it before she dies, the spoiled brat of a Quaker infidel!"

CHAPTER III.

The Circle in the Minister's House.

It would, perhaps be unfair to hold the Reverend Master Parris responsible for the wild doings that went on in the parsonage house during the winter evenings of 1691-2, in the face of his solemn assertion, made several years afterwards, that he was ignorant of them. And yet, how could such things have been without the knowledge either of himself or his wife? Mistress Parris has come down to us with the reputation of a kindly and discreet woman—nothing having been said to her discredit, so far as I am aware, even by those who had a bitter controversy with her husband. And yet she certainly must have known of the doings of the famous "circle," even if she refrained from speaking of them to her husband.

At the very bottom of the whole thing, perhaps, were the West Indian slaves—"John Indias" and his wife Tituba, whom Master Parris had brought with him from Barbados. There were two children in the house, a little daughter of nine, named Elizabeth; and Abigail Williams, three years older. These very probably, Tituba often had sought to impress, as is the manner of negro servants, with tales of witchcraft, the "evil-eye" and "evil hand" spirits, powwowing, etc. Ann Putnam, another precocious child of twelve, the daughter of a near neighbor, Sergeant Putnam, the parish clerk, also was soon drawn into the knowledge of the savage mysteries. And, before very long, a regular "circle" of these and older girls was formed for the purpose of amusing and startling themselves with the investigation and performance of forbidden things.

At the present day this would not be so reprehensible. We are comparatively an unbelieving generation; and what are called "spiritual circles" are common, though not always unattended with mischievous results. But at that time when it was considered a deadly sin to seek intercourse with those who claimed to have "a familiar spirit," that such practices should be allowed to go on for a whole winter, in the house of a Puritan minister, seems unaccountable. But the fact itself is undoubted, and the

11

consequences are written in mingled tears and blood upon the saddest pages of the history of New England.

Among the members of this "circle" were Mary Walcott, aged seventeen, the daughter of Captain Walcott; Elizabeth Hubbard and Mercy Lewis, also seventeen; Elizabeth Booth and Susannah Sheldon, aged eighteen; and Mary

Warren, Sarah Churchhill and Leah Herrick, aged twenty; these latter being the oldest of the party. They were all the daughters of respectable and even leading men, with the exception of Mercy Lewis, Mary Warren, Leah Herrick and Sarah Churchhill, who were living out as domestics, but who seem to have visited as friends and equals the other girls in the village. In fact, it was not considered at that time degrading in country neighborhoods—perhaps it is not so now in many places—for the sons and daughters of men of respectability, and even of property, to occupy the position of "help" or servant, eating at the same table with, and being considered members of the family. In the case before us, Mercy Lewis, Mary Warren and Sarah Churchhill seem to have been among the most active and influential members of the party. Though Abigail Williams, the minister's niece, and Ann Putnam, only eleven and twelve years of age respectively, proved themselves capable of an immense deal of mischief.

What the proceedings of these young women actually were, neither tradition nor any records that I have met with, informs us; but the result was even worse than could have been expected. By the close of the winter they had managed to get their nervous systems, their imaginations, and their minds and hearts, into a most dreadful condition. If they had regularly sold themselves to be the servants of the Evil One, as was then universally believed to be possible—and which may really be possible, for anything I know to the contrary— their condition could hardly have been worse than it was. They were liable to sudden faintings of an unnatural character, to spasmodic movements and jerkings of the head and limbs, to trances, to the seeing of witches and devils, to deafness, to dumbness, to alarming outcries, to impudent and lying speeches and statements, and to almost everything else that was false, irregular and unnatural.

Some of these things were doubtless involuntary but the voluntary and involuntary seemed to be so mingled in their behavior, that it was difficult sometimes to determine which was one and which the other. The moral sense seemed to have become confused, if not utterly lost for the time.

They were full of tricks. They stuck concealed pins into their bodies, and accused others of doing it—their contortions and trances were to a great extent mere shams—they lied without scruple—they bore false witness, and what in many, if not most, cases they knew was false witness, against not only those to whom they bore ill will but against the most virtuous and kindly women of the neighborhood; and if the religious delusion had taken another shape, and we see no reason why it should not have done so, and put the whole of them on trial as seekers after "familiar spirits" and condemned the older girls to death, there would at least have been some show of justice in the proceedings; while, as it is, there is not a single ray of light to illuminate the judicial gloom.

When at last Mr. Parris and Thomas Putnam became aware of the condition of their children, they called in the village physician, Dr. Griggs. The latter, finding he could do nothing with his medicines, gave it as his opinion that they were "under an evil hand"—the polite medical phrase of that day, for being bewitched.

That important point being settled, the next followed of course, "Who has bewitched them?" The children being asked said, "Tituba."

CHAPTER IV.

Satan's Especial Grudge against Our Puritan Fathers.

"Tituba!" And who else? Why need there have been anybody else? Why could not the whole thing have stopped just there? No doubt Tituba was guilty, if any one was. But Tituba escaped, by shrewdly also becoming an accuser.

"Who else?" This set the children's imagination roving. Their first charges were not so unreasonable. Why, the vagrant Sarah Good, a social outcast, wandering about without any settled habitation; and Sarah Osburn, a bed-ridden woman, half distracted by family troubles who had seen better days. There the truth was out. Tituba, Sarah Good and Sarah Osburn were the agents of the devil in this foul attempt against the peace of the godly inhabitants of Salem village.

For it was a common belief even amongst the wisest and best of our Puritan fathers, that the devil had a special spite against the New England colonies. They looked at it in this way. He had conquered in the fight against the Lord in the old world. He was the supreme and undoubted lord of the "heathen salvages" in the new. Now that the Puritan forces had commenced an onslaught upon him in the western hemisphere, to which he had an immemorial right as it were, could it be wondered at that he was incensed beyond all calculation? Was he, after having Europe, Asia and Africa, to be driven out of North America by a small body of steeple-hatted, psalm-singing, and conceited Puritans? No wonder his satanic ire was aroused; and that he was up to all manner of devices to harass, disorganize and afflict the camp of his enemies.

I am afraid this seems a little ridiculous to readers nowadays; but to the men and women of two hundred years ago it was grim and sober earnest, honestly and earnestly believed in.

Who, in the face of such wonderful changes in our religious views, can venture to predict what will be the belief of our descendants two hundred years hence?

CHAPTER V.

Leah Herrick's Position and Feelings.

I have classed Leah Herrick among the domestics; but her position was rather above that. She had lived with the Widow Sands, Jethro's aunt, since she had been twelve years old, assisting in the housework, and receiving her board and clothing in return. Now, at the age of twenty, she was worth more than that recompense; but she still remained on the old terms, as if she were a daughter instead of a servant.

She remained, asking nothing more, because she had made up her mind to be Jethro's wife. She had a passion for Jethro, and she knew that Jethro reciprocated it. But his aunt, who was ambitious, wished him to look higher; and therefore did not encourage such an alliance. Leah was however too valuable and too cheap an assistant to be dispensed with, and thus removed from such a dangerous proximity, besides the widow really had no objection to her, save on account of her poverty.

Leah said nothing when she saw that Jethro's attentions were directed in another direction; but without saying anything directly to Dulcibel, she contrived to impress her with the fact that she had trespassed upon her rightful domain. For Leah was a cat; and amidst her soft purrings, she would occasionally put out her velvety paw, and give a wicked little scratch that made the blood come, and so softly and innocently too, that the sufferer could hardly take offence at it.

Between these sharp intimations of Leah, and the unpleasant revelations of the innate hardness of the young man's character, which resulted from the closer intimacy of a betrothal, Dulcibel's affection had been gradually cooling for several months. But although the longed-for estrangement between the two had at length taken place, Leah did not feel quite safe yet; for the Widow Sands was very much put out about it, and censured her nephew for his want of wisdom in not holding Dulcibel to her engagement. "She has a good house and farm already, and she will be certain to receive much more on the death of her bachelor uncle in England," said the aunt sharply. "You must strive to undo that foolish hour's work. It was only a tiff on her part, and you should have cried your eyes out if necessary."

And so Leah, thinking in her own heart that Jethro was a prize for any girl, was in constant dread of a renewal of the engagement, and ready to go to any length to prevent it.

Although a member of the "circle" that met at the minister's house, Leah was not so regular an attendant as the others; for there were no men there and she never liked to miss the opportunity of a private conversation with Jethro, opportunities which were somewhat limited, owing to the continual watchfulness of her mistress. Still she went frequently enough to be fully imbued with the spirit of their doings, while not becoming such a victim as most of them were to disordered nerves, and an impaired and confused mental and moral constitution.

CHAPTER VI.

A Disorderly Scene in Church.

If anything were needed to add to the excitement which the condition of the "afflicted children," as they were generally termed, naturally produced in Salem village and the adjoining neighborhood, it was a scene in the village church one Sunday morning.

The church was a low, small structure, with rough, unplastered roof and walls, and wooden benches instead of pews. The sexes were divided, the men sitting on one side and the women on the other, but each person in his or her regular and appointed seat.

It was the custom at that time to select a seating committee of judicious and careful men, whose very important duty it was to seat the congregation. In doing this they proceeded on certain well-defined principles.

The front seats were to be filled with the older members of the congregation, a due reverence for age, as well as for the fact that these were more apt to be weak of sight and infirm of hearing, necessitated this. Then came the elders and deacons of the church; then the wealthier citizens of the parish; then the younger people and the children.

The Puritan fathers had their faults; but they never would have tolerated the fashionable custom of these days, whereby the wealthy, without regard to their age, occupy the front pews; and the poorer members, no matter how aged, or infirm of sight or hearing are often forced back where they can neither see the minister nor hear the sermon. And one can imagine in what forcible terms they would have denounced some city meeting-houses of the present era where the church is regarded somewhat in the light of an opera house, and the doors of the pews kept locked and closed until those who have purchased the right to reserved seats shall have had the first chance to enter.

The Reverend Master Lawson, a visiting elder, was the officiating minister on the Sunday to which we have referred. The psalm had been sung after the opening prayer and the minister was about to come forward to give his sermon, when, before he could rise from his seat, Abigail Williams, the niece of the Reverend Master Parris, only twelve years old, and one of the "circle" cried out loudly:— "Now stand up and name your text!"

When he had read the text, she exclaimed insolently, "It's a long text." And then when he was referring to his doctrine, she said:—"I know no doctrine you mentioned. If you named any, I have forgotten it."

And then when he had concluded, she cried out, "Look! there sits Goody Osburn upon the beam, suckling her yellow-bird betwixt her fingers."

Then Ann Putnam, that other child of twelve, joined in; "There flies the yellow-bird to the minister's hat, hanging on the pin in the pulpit."

Of course such disorderly proceedings produced a great excitement in the congregation; but the two children do not appear to have been rebuked by either of the ministers, or by any of the officers of the church; it seeming to have been the general conclusion that they were not responsible for what they said, but were constrained by an irresistible and diabolical influence. In truth, the children were regarded with awe and pity instead of reproof and blame, and therefore naturally felt encouraged to further efforts in the same direction.

I have said that this was the general feeling, but that feeling was not universal. Several of the members, notably young Joseph Putnam, Francis Nurse and Peter Cloyse were very much displeased at the toleration shown to such disorderly doings, and began to absent themselves from public worship, with the result of incurring the anger of the children, who were rapidly assuming the role of destroying angels to the people of Salem village and its vicinity.

As fasting and prayer were the usual resources of our Puritan fathers in difficulties, these were naturally resorted to at once upon this occasion. The families to which the "afflicted children" belonged assembled the neighbors—who had also fasted—and, under the guidance of the Reverend Master Parris, besought the Lord to deliver them from the power of the Evil One. These were exciting occasions, for, whenever there was a pause in the proceedings, such of the "afflicted" as were present would break out into demoniac howlings, followed by contortions and rigid trances, which, in the words of our manuscript, were "enough to make the devil himself weep."

These village prayers, however, seeming to be insufficient, Master Parris called a meeting of the neighboring ministers; but the prayers of these also had no effect. The "children" even surpassed themselves on this occasion. The ministers could not doubt the evidence of their own reverend eyes and ears, and united in the declaration of their belief that Satan had been let loose in this little Massachusetts village, to confound and annoy the godly, to a greater extent than they had ever before known or heard of. And now that the ministers had spoken, it was almost irreligious and atheistical for others to express any doubt. For if the ministers could not speak with authority in a case of this kind, which seemed to be within their peculiar field and province, what was their judgment worth upon any matter?

CHAPTER VII.

A Conversation with Dulcibel.

As Dulcibel sat in the little room which she had furnished in a pretty but simple way for a parlor, some days after the meeting of the ministers, her thoughts naturally dwelt upon all these exciting events which were occurring around her. It was an April day, and the snow had melted earlier than usual, and it seemed as if the spring might be an exceptionally forward one. The sun was pleasantly warm, and the wind blowing soft and gently from the south; and a canary bird in the rustic cage that hung on the wall was singing at intervals a hymn of rejoicing at the coming of the spring. The bird was one that had been given her by a distinguished sea-captain of Boston town, who had brought it home from the West Indies. Dulcibel had tamed and petted it, until she could let it out from the cage and allow it to fly around the room; then, at the words, "Come Cherry," as she opened the little door of the cage, the bird would fly in again, knowing that he would be rewarded for his good conduct with a little piece of sweet cake.

Cherry would perch on her finger and sing his prettiest strains on some occasions; and at others eat out of her hand. But his prettiest feat was to kiss his mistress by putting his little beak to her lips, when she would say in a caressing tone, "Kiss me, pretty Cherry."

After playing with the canary for a little while, Dulcibel sighed and put him back in his cage, hearing a knock at the front door of the cottage. And she had just turned from the cage to take a seat, when the door opened and two persons entered.

"I am glad to see you, friends," she said calmly, inviting them to be seated.

It was Joseph Putnam, accompanied by his friend and visitor, Ellis Raymond, the young man of whom Dulcibel had spoken to Jethro Sands.

Joseph Putnam was one of that somewhat distinguished family from whom came the Putnams of Revolutionary fame; Major-General Israel Putnam, the wolf-slayer, being one of his younger children. He, the father I mean, was a man of fine, athletic frame, not only of body but of mind. He was one of the very few in Salem village who despised the whole witch-delusion from the beginning. He did not disbelieve in the existence of witches—or that the devil was tormenting the "afflicted children"—but that faith should be put in their wild stories was quite another matter.

Of his companion, Master Ellis Raymond, I find no other certain account anywhere than in my Quaker friend's manuscript. From the little that is there given of personal description I have only the three phrases "a comelie young man," "a very quick-witted person," "a very determined and courageous man," out of which to build a physical and spiritual description. And so I think it rather safer to leave the portraiture to the imagination of my readers.

"Do you expect to remain long in Salem?" asked Dulcibel.

"I do not know yet," was the reply. "I came that I might see what prospects the new world holds out to young men."

"I want Master Raymond to purchase the Orchard Farm, and settle down among us," said Joseph Putnam. "It can be bought I think."

"I have heard people say the price is a very high one," said Dulcibel.

"It is high but the land is worth the money. In twenty years it will seem very low. My father saw the time when a good cow was worth as much as a fifty-acre farm, but land is continually rising in value."

"I shall look farther south before deciding," said Raymond. "I am told the land is better there; besides there are too many witches here," and he smiled.

"We have been up to see my brother Thomas," continued Joseph Putnam. "He always has had the reputation of being a sober-headed man, but he is all off his balance now."

"What does Mistress Putnam say?" asked Dulcibel.

"Oh, she is at the bottom of all his craziness, she and that elfish daughter. Sister Ann is a very intelligent woman in some respects, but she is wild upon this question."

"I am told by the neighbors that the child is greatly afflicted."

"She came in the room while we were there," responded Master Raymond. "I knew not what to make of it. She flung herself down on the floor, she crept under the table, she shrieked, she said Goody Osburn was sticking pins in her, and wound up by going into convulsions."

"What can it all mean?—it is terrible," said Dulcibel.

"Well, the Doctor says she is suffering under an 'evil hand,' and the ministers have given their solemn opinion that she is bewitched; and brother Thomas and Sister Ann, and about all the rest of the family agree with them."

"I am afraid it will go hard with those two old women," interposed Ellis Raymond.

"They will hang them as sure as they are tried," answered Joseph Putnam. "Not that it makes much difference, for neither of them is much to speak of; but they have a right to a fair trial nevertheless, and they cannot get such a thing just now in Salem village.

"I can hardly believe there are such things as witches," said Dulcibel, "and if there are, I do not believe the good Lord would allow them to torment innocent children."

"Oh, I don't know that it will do to say there are no witches," replied Joseph Putnam gravely. "It seems to me we must give up the Bible if we say that. For the Old Testament expressly commands that we must not suffer a witch to live; and it would be absurd to give such a command if there were no such persons as witches."

"I suppose it must be so," admitted Dulcibel, with a deep sigh.

"And then again in the New Testament we have continual references to persons possessed with devils, and others who had familiar spirits, and if such persons existed then, why not now?"

"Oh, of course, it is so," again admitted Dulcibel with even a deeper sigh than before.

But even in that day, outside of the Puritan and other religious bodies, there were unbelievers; and Ellis Raymond had allowed himself to smile once or twice, unperceived by the others, during their conversation. Thus we read in the life of that eminent jurist, the Honorable Francis North, who presided at a trial for witchcraft about ten years before the period of which we are writing, that he looked upon the whole thing as a vulgar delusion, though he said it was necessary to be very careful to conceal such opinions from the juries of the time, or else they would set down the judges at once as irreligious persons, and bring in the prisoners guilty.

"I am not so certain of it," said Ellis Raymond.

"How! What do you mean, Master Raymond?" exclaimed Joseph Putnam; like all his family, he was orthodox to the bone in his opinions.

"My idea is that in the old times they supposed all distracted and insane people—especially the violent ones, the maniacs—to be possessed with devils."

"Do you think so?" queried Dulcibel in a glad voice, a light seeming to break in upon her.

"Well, I take it for granted that there were plenty of insane people in the old times as there are now; and yet I see no mention of them as such, in either the Old or the New Testament."

"I never thought of that before; it seems to me a very reasonable explanation, does it not strike you so, Master Putnam?"

"So reasonable, that it reasons away all our faith in the absolute truthfulness of every word of the holy scriptures," replied Joseph Putnam sternly. "Do you suppose the Evangelists, when they spoke of persons having 'familiar spirits,' and being 'possessed of devils,' did not know what they were talking about? I would rather believe that every insane person now is possessed with a devil, and that such is the true explanation of his or her insanity, than to fly in the face of the holy scriptures as you do, Master Raymond."

Dulcibel's countenance fell. "Yes," she responded in reverential tones, "the holy Evangelists must know best. If they said so, it must be so."

"You little orthodox darling!" thought young Master Raymond, gazing upon her beautiful sad face. But of course he did not express himself to such an effect, except by his gaze; and Dulcibel happening to look up and catch the admiring expression of two clear brown eyes, turned her own instantly down again, while a faint blush mantled her cheeks.

The young Englishman knew that in arousing such heterodox opinions he was getting on dangerous ground. For expressing not a greater degree of heresy than he had uttered, other men and even women had been turned neck and heels out of the Puritan settlements. And as he had no desire to leave Salem just at present, he began to "hedge" a little, as betting men sometimes say.

"Insane people, maniacs especially, do sometimes act as if they were possessed of the devil," he said frankly. "And no doubt their insanity is often the result of the sinful indulgence of their wicked propensities and passions."

"Yes, that seems to be very reasonable," said Dulcibel. "Every sinful act seems to me a yielding to the evil one, and such yielding becoming common, he may at least be able to enter into the soul, and take absolute possession of it. Oh, it is very fearful!" and she shuddered.

"But I find one opinion almost universal in Salem," continued Raymond, "and that is one which I think has no ground to sustain it in the scriptures, and is very mischievous. It is that the devil cannot act directly upon human beings to afflict and torment them; but that he is forced to have recourse to the agency of other human beings, who have become his worshipers and agents. Thus in the cases of these children and young girls, instead of admitting that the devil and his imps are directly afflicting them, they begin to look around for witches and wizards as the sources of the trouble."

"Yes," responded Joseph Putnam earnestly, "that false and unscriptural doctrine is the source of all the trouble. That little Ann Putnam, Abigail Williams and the others are bewitched, may perhaps be true—a number of godly ministers say so, and they ought to know. But, if they are bewitched, it is the devil and his imps that have done it. If they are 'possessed with devils'—and does not that scripture mean that the devils directly take possession of them— what is their testimony worth against others? It is nearly the testimony of Satan and his imps, speaking through them. While they are in that state, their evidence should not be allowed credence by any magistrate, any more than the devil's should."

It seems very curious to those of the present day who have investigated this matter of witch persecutions, that such a sound and orthodox view as this of Joseph Putnam's should have had such little weight with the judges and ministers and other leading men of the seventeenth century. While a few urged it, even as Joseph Putnam did, at the risk of his own life, the great majority not only of the common people but of the leading classes, regarded it as unsound and irreligious. But the whole history of the world proves that the *vox populi* is very seldom the *vox Dei*. The light shines down from the rising sun in the heavens, and the mountain tops first receive the rays. The last new truth is always first perceived by the small minority of superior minds and souls. How indeed could it be otherwise, so long as truth like light always shines down from above?

"Have you communicated this view to your brother and sister?" asked Dulcibel.

"I have talked with them for a whole evening, but I do think Sister Ann is possessed too," replied Joseph Putnam. "She fairly raves sometimes. You know how bitterly she feels about that old church quarrel, when a small minority of the Parish succeeded in preventing the permanent settlement of her sister's husband as minister. She seems to have the idea that all that party are emissaries of Satan. I do not wonder her little girl should be so nervous and excitable, being the child of such a nervous, high-strung woman. But I am going to see them again this afternoon; will you go too, Master Raymond?'

"I think not," replied the latter with a smile, "I should do harm, I fear, instead of good. I will stay here and talk with Mistress Dulcibel a little while longer."

Master Putnam departed, and then the conversation became of a lighter character. The young Englishman told Dulcibel of his home in the old world, and of his travels in France and Switzerland. And they talked of all those little things which young people will—little things, but which afford constant peeps into each other's mind and heart. Dulcibel thought she had never met such a cultivated young man, although she had read of such; and he felt very certain that he never met with such a lovely young woman. Not that she was over intelligent—one of those precociously "smart" young women that, thanks to the female colleges and the "higher culture" are being "developed" in such alarming numbers nowadays. If she had been such a being, I fancy Master Raymond would have found her less attractive. Ah, well, after a time perhaps, we of the present day shall have another craze—that of barbarism—in which the "coming woman" shall pride herself mainly upon possessing a strong, healthy and vigorous physical organization, developed within the feminine lines of beauty, and only a reasonable degree of intelligence and "culture." And then I hope we shall see the last of walking female encyclopedias, with thin waists, and sickly and enfeebled bodies; fit to be the mothers only of a rapidly dwindling race, even if they have the wish and power to become mothers at all.

I am not much of a believer in love at first sight, but certainly persons may become very much interested in each other after a few hours' conversation; and so it was in the case before us. When Ellis Raymond took up his hat, and then lingered minute after minute, as if he could not bring himself to the point of departure, he simply manifested anew to the maiden what his tones and looks had been telling her for an hour, that he admired her very greatly.

"Come soon again," Dulcibel said softly, as the young man managed to open the door at last, and make his final adieu. "And indeed I shall if you will permit me," was his earnest response.

But some fair reader may ask, "What were these two doing during all the winter, that they had not seen each other?"

I answer that Dulcibel had withdrawn from the village gatherings since the breaking of the engagement with Jethro. At the best, it was an acknowledgment that she had been too hasty in a matter that she should not have allowed herself to fail in; and she felt humbled under the thought. Besides, it seemed to her refined and sensitive nature only decorous that she should withdraw for a time into the seclusion of her own home under such circumstances.

As for the village gossips, they entirely misinterpreted her conduct. Inasmuch as Jethro went around as usual, and put a bold face upon the matter, they came to the conclusion that he had thrown her off, and that she was moping at home, because she felt the blow so keenly.

Thus it was that while the young Englishman had attended many social gatherings during the winter he had never met the one person whom he was especially desirous of again meeting.

One little passage of the conversation between the two it may be well however to refer to expressly for its bearing upon a very serious matter. Raymond had mentioned that he had not seen her recently flying around on that little jet black horse, and had asked whether she still owned it.

"Oh, yes," replied Dulcibel; "I doubt that I should be able to sell Little Witch if I wished to do so."

"Ah, how is that? She seems to be a very fine riding beast."

"She is, very! But you have not heard that I am the only one that has ever ridden her or that can ride her."

"Indeed! that is curious."

I have owned her from a little colt. She was never broken to harness; and no one, as I said, has ever ridden her but me. So that now if any other person, man or woman, attempts to do so, she will not allow it. She rears, she plunges, and finally as a last resort, if necessary, lies down on the ground and refuses to stir. "Why, that is very flattering to you, Dulcibel," said Raymond smiling. "I never knew an animal of better taste."

"That may be," replied the maiden blushing; "but you see how it is that I shall never be able to sell Little Witch if I desire to do so. She is not worth her keep to any one but me."

"Little Witch! Why did you ever give her a name like that?"

"Oh, I was a mere child—and my father, who had been a sea-captain, and all over the world, did not believe in witches. He named her "Little Witch" because she was so black, and so bent on her own way. But I must change her name now that people are talking so about witches. In truth my mother never liked it."

CHAPTER VIII.

An Examination of Reputed Witches.

Warrants had been duly issued against Sarah Good, Sarah Osburn, and the Indian woman Tituba, and they were now to be tried for the very serious offence of bewitching the "afflicted children."

One way that the witches of that day were supposed to work, was to make images out of rags, like dolls, which they named for the persons they meant to torment. Then, by sticking pins and needles into the dolls, tightening cords around their throats, and similar doings, the witches caused the same amount of pain as if they had done it to the living objects of their enmity.

In these cases, the officers who executed the warrants of arrest, stated "that they had made diligent search for images and such like, but could find none."

On the day appointed for the examination of these poor women, the two leading magistrates of the neighborhood, John Hathorne and Jonathan Corwin, rode up the principal street of the village attended by the marshal and constables, in quite an imposing array. The crowd was so great that they had to hold the session in the meeting-house The magistrates belonged to the highest legislative and judicial body in the colony. Hathorne, as the name was then spelt, was the ancestor of the gifted author, Nathaniel Hawthorne—the alteration in the spelling of the name probably being made to make it conform more nearly to the pronunciation. Hathorne was a man of force and ability—though evidently also as narrow-minded and unfair as only a bigot can be. All through the examination that ensued he took a leading part, and with him, to be accused was to be set down at once as guilty. Never, among either Christian or heathen people, was there a greater travesty of justice than these examinations and trials for witchcraft, conducted by the very foremost men of the Massachusetts colony.

The accounts of the examination of these three women in the manuscript book I have alluded to, are substantially the same as in the official records, which are among those that have been preserved. I will give some quotations to show how the examinations were conducted:—

"Sarah Good, what evil spirit are you familiar with?"

She answered sharply, "None!"

"Have you made no contracts with the Devil?"

"No!"

"Why then do you hurt these children?"

"I do not hurt them. I would scorn to do it."

"Here the children who were facing her, began to be dreadfully tormented; and then when their torments were over for the time, again accused her, and also Sarah Osburn.

"Sarah Good, why do you not tell us the truth? Why do you thus torment them?"

"I do not torment them."

"Who then does torment them?"

"It may be that Sarah Osburn does, for I do not."

"Her answers," says the official report, "were very quick, sharp and malignant."

It must be remembered in reading these reports, that the accused were not allowed any counsel, either at the preliminary examinations, or on the trials; that the apparent sufferings of the children were very great, producing almost a frenzied state of feeling in the crowd who looked on; and that they themselves were often as much puzzled as their accusers, to account for what was taking place before their eyes.

In the examination of Sarah Osburn, we have similar questions and similar answers. In addition, however, three witnesses alleged that she had said that very morning, that she was "more like to be bewitched herself." Mr. Hathorne asked why she said that. She answered that either she saw at one time, or dreamed that she saw, a thing like an Indian, all black, which did pinch her in the neck, and pulled her by the back part of the head to the door of the house. And there was also a lying spirit.

"What lying spirit was this?"

"It was a voice that I thought I heard."

"What did it say to you?"

"That I should go no more to meeting; but I said I would, and did go the next Sabbath day."

"Were you ever tempted further?"

"No."

"Why did you yield then to the Devil, not to go to meeting for the last three years?"

"Alas! I have been sick all that time, and not able to go."

Then Tituba was brought in. Tituba was in the "circle" or an attendant and inspirer of the "circle" from the first; and had marvelous things to tell. How it was that the "children" turned against her and accused her, I do not know; but probably she had practised so much upon them in various ways, that she really was guilty of trying to do the things she was charged with.

"Tituba, why do you hurt these children?"

"Tituba does not hurt 'em."

"Who does hurt them then?"

"The debbil, for all I knows.'

"Did you ever see the Devil?" Tituba gave a low laugh. "Of course I've seen the debbil. The debbil came an' said, 'Serb me, Tituba.' But I would not hurt the child'en."

"Who else have you seen?"

"Four women. Goody Osburn and Sarah Good, and two other women. Dey all hurt de child'en."

"How does the Devil appear to you?"

"Sometimes he is like a dog, and sometimes like a hog. The black dog always goes with a yellow bird."

"Has the Devil any other shapes?"

"Yes, he sometimes comes as a red cat, and then a black cat."

"And they all tell you to hurt the children?"

"Yes, but I said I would not."

"Did you not pinch Elizabeth Hubbard this morning?"

"The black man brought me to her, and made me pinch her."

"Why did you go to Thomas Putnam's last night and hurt his daughter Ann?"

"He made me go."

"How did you go?"

"We rode on sticks; we soon got there."

"Has Sarah Good any familiar?"

"Yes, a yeller bird. It sucks her between her fingers. And Sarah Osburn has a thing with a head like a woman, and it has two wings."

("Abigail Williams, who lives with her uncle, the Rev. Master Parris, here testified that she did see the same creature, and it turned into the shape of Goody Osburn.")

"Tituba further said that she had also seen a hairy animal with Goody Osburn, that had only two legs, and walked like a man. And that she saw Sarah Good, last Saturday, set a wolf upon Elizabeth Hubbard."

("The friends of Elizabeth Hubbard here said that she did complain of being torn by a wolf on that day.")

"Tituba being asked further to describe her ride to Thomas Putnam's, for the purpose of tormenting his daughter Ann, said that she rode upon a stick or pole, and Sarah Good and Sarah Osburn behind her, all taking hold of one another. Did not know how it was done, for she saw no trees nor path, but was presently there."

These examinations were continued for several days, each of the accused being brought at various times before the magistrates, who seem to have taken great interest in the absurd stories with which the "afflicted children" and Tituba regaled them. Finally, all three of the accused were committed to Boston jail, there to await their trial for practising witchcraft; being heavily ironed, as, being witches, it was supposed to be very difficult to keep them from escaping; and as their ability to torment people with their spectres, was considered lessened in proportion to the weight and tightness of the chains with which they were fettered. It is not to be wondered at, that under these inflictions, at the end of two months, the invalid, Sarah Osburn, died. Tituba, however, lay in jail until, finally, at the expiration of a year and a month, she was sold in payment of her jail fees. One account saying that her owner, the Rev. Master Parris, refused to pay her jail fees, unless she would still adhere to what she had testified on her examination, instead of alleging that he whipped and otherwise abused her, to make her confess that she was a witch.

CHAPTER IX.

One Hundred and Fifty More Alleged Witches.

Ah this was bad enough, but it was but the beginning of trouble. Tituba had spoken of two other women, but had given no names. The "afflicted children" were still afflicted, and growing worse, instead of better. The Rev. Master Noyes of Salem town, the Rev. Master Parris of Salem village, Sergeant Thomas Putnam, and his wife,—which last also was becoming bewitched, and had many old enmities—and many other influential people and church members, were growing more excited, and vindictive against the troubles of their peace, with every passing day.

"Who are they that still torment you in this horrible manner?" was the question asked of the children and young women, and they had their answers ready.

There had been an old quarrel between the Endicotts and the Nurses, a family which owned the Bishop Farm, about the eastern boundary of said farm. There had been the quarrel about who should be minister, in which the Nurses had sided with the determined opponents of Mistress Ann Putnam's reverend brother-in-law. The Nurses and other families were staunch opposers of Master Parris's claim to ownership of the Parsonage and its grounds. And it was not to be wondered at, that the accusations should be made against opponents rather than against friends.

Besides, there were those who had very little faith in the children themselves, and had taken a kind of stand against them; and these too, were in a dangerous position.

"Who torments you now?" The answer was ready: Martha Corey, and Rebecca Nurse, and Bridget Bishop, and so on; the charges being made now against the members, often the heads, of the most reputable families in Salem town and village and the surrounding neighborhoods. Before the coming of the winter snows probably one hundred and fifty persons were in prison at Salem and Ipswich and Boston and Cambridge. Two-thirds of these were women; many of them were aged and venerable men and women of the highest reputation for behavior and piety. Yet, they were bound with chains, and exposed to all the hardships that attended incarceration in small and badly constructed prisons.

A special court composed of the leading judges in the province being appointed by the Governor for the trial of these accused persons, a mass of what would be now styled "utter nonsense" was brought against them. No wonder that the official record of this co-called court of justice is now nowhere to be found. The partial accounts that have come down to us are sufficient to brand its proceeding with everlasting infamy. Let us recur to the charges against some of these persons:

The Rev. Cotton Mather, speaking of the trial of Bridget Bishop, says: "There was one strange thing with which the Court was *newly entertained*. As this woman was passing by the meeting-house, she gave a look towards the house; and immediately a demon, invisibly entering the house, tore down a part of it; so that, though there was no person to be seen there, yet the people, at the noise, running in, found a board, which was strongly fastened with several nails, transported into another quarter of the house."

A court of very ignorant men would be "entertained" now with such a story, in a very different sense from that in which the Rev. Cotton Mather used the word. The Court of 1692, doubtless swallowed the story whole, for it was no more absurd than the bulk of the evidence upon which they condemned the reputed witches.

One of the charges against the Rev. Master Burroughs, who had himself been a minister for a short time in the village, was, that though a small, slender man, he was a giant in strength. Several persons witnessed that "he had held out a gun of seven foot barrel with one hand; and had carried a barrel full of cider from a canoe to the shore." Burroughs said that an Indian present at the time did the same, but the answer was ready. "That was the black man, or the Devil, who looks like an Indian."

Another charge against Master Burroughs was, that he went on a certain occasion between two places in a shorter time than was possible, if the Devil had not assisted him. Both Increase Mather, the father, and his son Cotton, two of the most prominent and influential of the Boston ministers, said that the testimony as to Mr. Burroughs' giant strength was alone sufficient rightfully to convict him. It is not improbable that the real animus of the feeling against Master Burroughs was the belief that he was not sound in the faith; for Master Cotton Mather, after his execution, declared to the people that he was "no ordained minister," and called their attention to the fact that Satan often appeared as an angel of light.

CHAPTER X.

Bridget Bishop Condemned to Die.

Salem, the habitation of peace, had become, by this time a pandemonium. The "afflicted children" were making accusations in every direction, and Mistress Ann Putnam, and many others, were imitating their example.

To doubt was to be accused; but very few managed to keep their heads sufficiently in the whirlwind of excitement, even to be able to doubt. With the exception of Joseph Putnam, and his visitor, Ellis Raymond, there were very few, if any, open and outspoken doubters, and indignant censurers of the whole affair. Dulcibel Burton also, though in a gentler and less emphatic way, sided naturally with them, but, although she was much less violent in her condemnation, she provoked even more anger from the orthodox believers in the delusion.

For Joseph Putnam, as belonging to one of the most influential and wealthy families in Salem, seemed to have some right to have an opinion. And Master Raymond was visiting at his house, and naturally would be influenced by him.

Besides, he was only a stranger at the best; and therefore, not entirely responsible to them for his views. But Dulcibel was a woman, and it was outrageous that she, at her years, should set up her crude opinions against the authority of the ministers and the elders.

Besides, Joseph Putnam was known to be a determined and even rather desperate young man when his passions were aroused, as they seldom were though, save in some just cause; and he had let it be known that it would be worth any person's life to attempt to arrest him. It was almost the universal habit of that day, to wear the belt and sword; and Messrs. Putnam and Raymond went thus constantly armed. Master Putnam also kept two horses constantly saddled in his stable, day and night, to escape with if necessary, into the forest, through which they might make their way to New York. For the people of that province, who did not admire their Puritan neighbors very much, received all such fugitives gladly, and gave them full protection.

As for Master Raymond, although he saw that his position was becoming dangerous, he determined to remain, notwithstanding the period which he had fixed for his departure had long before arrived. His avowed reason given to Joseph Putnam, was that he was resolved to see the crazy affair through. His avowed reason, which Master Putnam perfectly understood, was to prosecute his suit to Dulcibel, and see her safely through the dangerous excitement also.

"They have condemned Bridget Bishop to death," said Master Putnam, coming into the house one morning from a conversation with a neighbor.

"I supposed they would," replied Master Raymond. "But how nobly she bore herself against such a mass of stupid and senseless testimony. Did you know her?"

"I have often stopped at her Inn. A fine, free-spoken woman; a little bold in her manners, but nothing wrong about her."

"Did you ever hear such nonsense as that about her tearing down a part of the meeting-house simply by looking at it? And yet there sat the best lawyers in the colony on the bench as her judges, and swallowed it all down as if it had been gospel."

"And then those other stories of her appearing in people's bed-rooms, and vanishing away suddenly; and of her being responsible for the illness and death of her neighbors' children; what could be more absurd?"

"And of the finding of puppets, made of rags and hogs' bristles, in the walls and crevices of her cellar! Really, it would be utterly contemptible if it were not so horrible."

"Yes, she is to be executed on Gallows Hill; and next week! I can scarcely believe it, Master Raymond. If I could muster a score or two of other stout fellows, I would carry her off from the very foot of the gallows."

"Oh, the frenzy has only begun, my friend," replied Raymond. "You know whose trial comes on next?"

"How any one can say a word against Mistress Nurse—that lovely and venerable woman—passeth my comprehension," said Joseph Putnam's young wife, who had been a listener to the conversation, while engaged in some household duties.

"My sister-in-law, Ann Putnam, seems to have a spite against that woman. I went to see her yesterday, and she almost foams at the mouth while talking of her."

"The examination of Mistress Nurse before the magistrate comes off to-day. Shall we not attend it?"

"Of course, but be careful of thy language, Friend Raymond. Do not let thy indignation run away with thy discretion."

Raymond laughed outright, as did young Mistress Putnam. "This advice from you, Master Joseph! who art such a very model of prudence and cold-bloodedness! If thou wilt be only half as cautious and discreet as I am, we shall give no offence even to the craziest of them."

CHAPTER XI.

Examination of Rebecca Nurse.

When they arrived at the village, the examination was in progress. Mistress Rebecca Nurse, the mother of a large family; aged, venerable, and bending now a little under the weight of years, was standing as a culprit before the magistrates, who doubtless had often met her in the social gatherings of the neighborhood.

She was guarded by two constables, she who needed no guarding. Around, and as near her as they were allowed to stand, stood her husband and her grown-up sons and daughters.

One of the strangest features of the time, as it strikes the reader of this day, was the peaceful submission to the lawful authorities practised by the husbands and fathers, and grown-up sons and brothers of the women accused. Reaching as the list of alleged witches did in a short time, to between one hundred and fifty and two hundred persons—nearly the whole of them members of the most respectable families—it is wonderful that a determined stand in their behalf was not the result. One hundred resolute men, resolved to sacrifice their lives if need be, would have put a stop to the whole matter. And if there had been even twenty men in Salem, like Joseph Putnam, the thing no doubt would have been done.

And in the opinion of the present writer, such a course would have been far more worthy of praise, than the slavish submission to such outrages as were perpetrated under the names of law, justice and religion. The sons of these men, eighty years later, showed at Lexington and Concord and Bunker Hill, that when Law and Peace become but grotesque masks, under which are hidden the faces of legalized injustice and tyranny, then the time has come for armed revolt and organized resistance.

But such was the darkness and bigotry of the day in respect to religious belief, that the great majority of the people were mentally paralyzed by the accepted faith, so that they were not able in many respects to distinguish light from darkness. When an estimable man or woman was accused of being a witch, for the term was indifferently applied to both sexes, even their own married partners, their own children, had a more or less strong conviction that it might possibly be so. And this made the peculiar horror of it.

In at least fifty cases, the accused confessed that they were witches, and sometimes accused others in turn. This was owing generally to the influence of their relatives, who implored them to confess; for to confess was invariably to be acquitted, or to be let off with simple imprisonment.

But to return to poor Rebecca Nurse, haled without warning from her prosperous, happy home at the Bishop Farm, carried to jail, loaded with chains, and now brought up for the tragic farce of a judicial examination. In this case also, the account given in my friend's little book is amply confirmed by other records. Mistress Ann Putnam, Abigail Williams (the minister's niece), Elizabeth Hubbard and Mary Walcott, were the accusers.

"Abigail Williams, have you been hurt by this woman?" said magistrate Hathorne.

"Yes," replied Abigail. And then Mistress Ann Putnam fell to the floor in a fit; crying out between her violent spasms, that it was Rebecca Nurse who was then afflicting her.

"What do you say to those charges?" The accused replied: "I can say before the eternal Father that I am innocent of any such wicked doings, and God will clear my innocence."

Then a man named Henry Kenney rose, and said that Mistress Nurse frequently tormented him also; and that even since he had been there that day, he had been seized twice with an amazed condition.

"The villain!" muttered Joseph Putnam to those around him, "if I had him left to me for a time, I would have him in an amazed condition!"

"You are an unbeliever, and everybody knows it, Master Putnam," said one near him. "But we who are of the godly, know that Satan goes about like a roaring lion, seeking whom he may devour."

"Quiet there!" said one of the magistrates.

Edward Putnam (another of the brothers) then gave in his evidence, saying that he had seen Mistress Ann Putnam, and the other accusers, grievously tormented again and again, and declaring that Rebecca Nurse was the person who did it.

"These are serious charges, Mistress Nurse," said Squire Hathorne, "are they true?"

"I have told you that they are false. Why, I was confined to my sick bed at the time it is said they occurred."

"But did you not send your spectre to torment them?"

"How could I? And I would not if I could."

Here Mistress Putnam was taken with another fit. Worse than the other, which greatly affected the whole people. Coming to a little, she cried out: "Did you not bring the black man with you? Did you not tell me to tempt God and die? Did you not eat and drink the red blood to your own damnation?"

These words were shrieked out so wildly, that all the people were greatly agitated and murmured against such wickedness. But the prisoner releasing her hand for a moment cried out, "Oh, Lord, help me!"

"Hold her hands," some cried then, for the afflicted persons seemed to be grievously tormented by her. But her hands being again firmly held by the guards, they seemed comforted.

Then the worthy magistrate Hathorne said, "Do you not see that when your hands are loosed these people are afflicted?"

"The Lord knows," she answered, "that I have not hurt them."

"You would do well if you are guilty to confess it; and give glory to God."

"I have nothing to confess. I am as innocent as an unborn child."

"Is it not strange that when you are examined, these persons should be afflicted thus?"

"Yes, it is very strange."

"The Lord knows that I haven't hurt them"

"Do you believe these afflicted persons are bewitched?"

"I surely do think they must be."

Weary of the proceedings and the excitement, the aged lady allowed her head to droop on one side. Instantly the heads of the accusers were bent the same way.

Abigail Williams cried out, "Set up Mistress Nurse's neck, our necks will all be broken." The jailers held up the prisoner's neck; and the necks of all the accused were instantly made straight again. This was considered a marvelous proof; and produced a wonderful effect upon the magistrates and the people. Mistress Ann Putnam went into such great bodily agony at this time, charging it all upon the prisoner, that the magistrates gave her husband permission to carry her out of the house. Only then, when no longer in the sight of the prisoner, could she regain her peace.

"Mistress Nurse was then recommitted to the jail in Salem, in order to further examination."

"What deviltry is coming next?" said Joseph Putnam to his friend.

Many of those around glared on the speaker, but he was well known to all of them as a daring—and when angered even a desperate young man—and they allowed him to say with impunity, freely what no one else could even have whispered. His son in after years, looked not into the wolf's eyes in the dark den with a sterner gaze, than he looked into the superstitious and vengeful wolves' eyes around him.

"To think that a godly old woman like Mistress Nurse, should be tormented by this Devil's brood of witches, led on by that she-devil sister of mine, Ann Putnam."

Many around heard him, but none cared to meet the young man's fierce eyes, as they blazed upon those that were nearest.

"Do control yourself, my friend," whispered Master Raymond. "Preserve yourself for a time when your indignation may do some good."

Then the constable brought in a little girl of about five years of age, Dorcas Good, a daughter of Sarah Good, who had been arrested on the complaint of Edward and Jonathan Putnam.

The evidence against this little girl of five was overwhelming. Mistress Ann Putnam, Mercy Lewis, and Mary Walcott were the accusers—charging the innocent and pretty little creature with biting, pinching and choking them—the little girl smiling while they were giving their testimony. She was not old enough to understand what it was all about, and that even her life was in danger from these demoniacs. They absolutely pretended to show the marks of her little teeth in their arms. Then, after going through the usual convulsions, they shrieked out that she was running pins into them; and the pins were found on examination sticking into their bodies.

The little girl was, as I have said, at first inclined to laugh at all the curious proceedings, and the spasms and contortions of the witnesses, but at last, seeing everyone so solemn and looking so wickedly at her, she began to cry; until Joseph Putnam went up to her and gave her some sweet cake to eat, which he had provided for his own luncheon and then, looking into his kind face, she began to smile again.

The Magistrates frowned upon Master Putnam, as he did this, but he paid no attention to their frowns. And when the little girl was ordered back to jail as a prisoner to await her trial, he bent down and kissed her before she was led away by the constable.

This was the end of the proceedings for that day and the crowd began to disperse.

"This is a pretty day's work you have made of it, sister-in-law," said Joseph Putnam, striding up to his brother's wife. "You say that you are tormented by many devils, and I believe it. Now I want to give you, and all the Devil's brood around you, fair warning that if you dare to touch with your foul lies any one belonging to my house including the stranger within my gates, you shall answer it with your lives, in spite of all your judges and prisons."

So saying, he glared at his two brothers, who made no reply, and walked out of the meeting-house in which this ungodly business had been transacted.

"Oh, it is only Joe," said Thomas Putnam; "he always was the spoiled child of the family."

His wife said nothing, but soon a hard, bitter smile took the place of the angry flush that the young man's words had produced. Dulcibel Burton was not one of his household, nor within his gates.

CHAPTER XII.

Burn Me, or Hang Me, I Will Stand in the Truth of Christ.

After the trial and conviction of Bridget Bishop, the Special Court of seven Judges—a majority of whom were leading citizens of Boston, the Deputy Governor of the Province, acting as Chief-Justice— decided to take further counsel in this wonderful and important matter of the fathers of the church. So the Court took a recess, while it consulted the ministers of Boston and other places, respecting its duty in the case. The response of the ministers, while urging in general terms the importance of caution and circumspection, recommended the earnest and vigorous carrying on of the war against Satan and his disciples.

Among the new victims, one of the most striking cases was that of George Jacobs and his grand-daughter Margaret. The former was a venerable-looking man, very tall, with long, thin white hair, who was compelled by his infirmities to support himself in walking with two staffs. Sarah Churchill, a chief witness, against him, was a servant in his family; and probably was feeding in this way some old grudge.

"You accuse me of being a wizard," said the old man on his examination; "you might as well charge me with being a buzzard."

They asked the accused to repeat the Lord's prayer. And Master Parris, the minister, who acted as a reporter, said "he could not repeat it right after many trials."

"Well," said the brave old man finally, after they had badgered him with all kinds of nonsensical questions, "Well, burn me, or hang me, I will stand in the truth of Christ!"

As his manly bearing was evidently producing an effect, the "afflicted girls" came out in full force the next day at the adjourned session. When he was brought in, they fell at once into the most grievous fits and screechings.

"Who hurts you?" was asked, after they had recovered somewhat.

"This man," said Abigail Williams, going off into another fit.

"This is the man," averred Ann Putnam; "he hurts me, and wants me to write in the red book; and promises if I will do so, to make me as well as his grand-daughter."

"Yes, this is the man," cried Mercy Lewis, "he almost kills me."

"It is the one who used to come to me. I know him by his two staffs, with one of which he used to beat the life out of me," said Mary Walcott.

Mercy Lewis for her part walked towards him; but as soon as she got near, fell into great fits.

Then Ann Putnam and Abigail Williams "had each of them a pin stuck in their hands and they said it was done by this old Jacobs."

The Magistrates took all this wicked acting in sober earnest; and asked the prisoner, "what he had to say to it?"

"Only that it is false," he replied. "I know no more of it than the child that was born last night."

But the honest old man's denial went of course, for nothing. Neither did Sarah Ingersoll's deposition made a short time afterwards; in which she testified that "Sarah Churchill came to her after giving her evidence, crying and wringing her hands, and saying that she has belied herself and others in saying she had set her hand to the Devil's book." She said that "they had threatened her that if she did not say it, they would put her in the dungeon along with Master Burroughs."

And that, "if she told Master Noyes, the minister, but once that she had set her hand to the book, he would believe her; but if she told him the truth a hundred times, he would not believe her."

The truth no doubt is that Master Noyes, Master Parris, Cotton Mather, and all the other ministers, with one or two exceptions, having committed themselves fully to the prosecution of the witches, would listen to nothing that tended to prove that the principal witnesses were deliberate and malicious liars; and that, so far as the other witnesses were concerned, they were grossly superstitious and deluded persons.

No charity that is fairly clear-sighted, can cover over the evidence of the "afflicted circle" with the mantle of self-delusion. Self-delusion does not conceal pins, stick them into its own body, and charge the accused person with doing it, knowing that the accusation may be the prisoner's death. This was done repeatedly by Mistress Ann Putnam, and her Satanic brood of false accusers.

Sarah Churchill was no worse than the others, judging by her remorse after she had helped to murder with her lying tongue her venerable master and we have in the deposition of Sarah Ingersoll, undoubted proof that she testified falsely.

When Ann Putnam, Mercy Lewis and Mary Walcott all united in charging little Dorcas Good—five years old!—with biting, pinching and almost choking them; "showing the marks of her little teeth on their arms, and the pins sticking in their bodies, where they had averred she was piercing them"—can any sane, clear-minded man or woman suppose it was an innocent delusion, and not a piece of horribly wicked lying?

When in open court some of the "afflicted" came out of their fits with "their wrists bound together, by invisible means," with "a real cord" so that "it could hardly be taken off without cutting," was there not only deception, but undeniable collusion of two or more in deception?

When an iron spindle was used by an alleged "spectre" to torture a "sufferer," the said iron spindle not being discernible by the by-standers until it became visible by being snatched by the sufferer from the spectre's hand, was there any self-delusion there? Was it not merely wicked imposture and cunning knavery?

I defy any person possessing in the least a judicial and accurate mind, to investigate the records of this witchcraft delusion without coming to the conclusion that the "afflicted girls," who led off in this matter, and were the principal witnesses, continually testified to what they knew to be utterly false. There is no possible excuse for them on the ground of "delusion." However much we may recoil from the sad belief that they testified in the large majority of cases to what they knew to be entirely false, the facts of the case compel us with an irresistible force to such an unhappy conclusion. When we are positively certain that a witness, in a case of life or death, has testified falsely against the prisoner again and again, is it possible that we can give him or her the benefit of even a doubt as to the animus of the testimony? The falsehoods I have referred to were cases of palpable, unmistakable and deliberate lying. And the only escape from considering it *wilful* lying, is to make a supposition not much in accord with the temper of the present times, that, having tampered with evil spirits, and invoked the Devil continually during the long evenings of the preceding winter, the prince of powers of the air had at last come at their call, and ordered a legion of his creatures to take possession of the minds and bodies that they had so freely offered to him. For certainly there is no way of explaining the conduct of the "afflicted circle" of girls and women, than by supposing either that they were guilty of the most enormous wickedness, or else that they were "possessed with devils."

CHAPTER XIII.

Dulcibel in Danger.

The terrible excitement of these days was enough to drive the more excitable portion of the inhabitants of Salem almost crazy. The work of the house and of the farm was neglected; a large number of suspected persons and their relatives were sunk in the deepest grief, the families of some of the imprisoned knew not where to get their daily food; for their property was generally taken possession of by the officers of the law at the time of the arrest, the accused being considered guilty until they were proved to be innocent. Upon conviction of a capital offence the property of the condemned was attainted, being confiscated by the state; and the constables took possession at once, in order that it might not be spirited away.

And no one outside of the circle of the accusers knew whose turn might come next. Neither sex, nor age, nor high character, as we have seen, was a bar against the malice, or the wantonness of the "afflicted." The man or woman who had lived a righteous life for over eighty years, the little child who wondered what it all meant, the maiden whose only fault might be to have a jealous rival, all were alike in danger.

Especially were those in peril, however, who dared to take the side of any of the accused, and express even the faintest disbelief in the justice of the legal proceedings, or the honesty of the witnesses. These would be surely singled out for punishment. Again and again, had this been done until the voices of all but the very boldest were effectually silenced. Those arrested now, as a general thing, would confess at once to the truthfulness of all the charges brought against them, and even invent still more improbable stories of their own, as this mollified the accusers, and they often would be let off with a solemn reprimand by the magistrates.

Joseph Putnam and his male servants went constantly armed; and two horses were kept saddled day and night, in his stable. He never went to the village unaccompanied; and made no secret of his determination to resist the arrest of himself or, as he had phrased it, "any one within his gates," to the last drop of his blood.

Living with the Goodman Buckley who had leased the Burton property, was a hired man named Antipas Newton. He was a good worker though now getting old, and had in one sense been leased with the place by Dulcibel's father.

Antipas's history had been a sad one. Adopted when left an orphan by a benevolent farmer who had no children, he managed by diligence and strict economy to acquire by the age of thirty, quite a comfortable property of his own. Then the old couple that he called Father and Mother became converts to Quakerism. Fined and imprisoned, deprived of their property, and, after the expiration of their term of imprisonment, ordered to leave the colony, they had been "harbored" by the man for whom they had done so much in his early years.

Antipas was a person of limited intelligence, but of strong affections and wide sympathies. Again and again, he harbored these persecuted ones, who despite their whippings and banishment would persist in returning to Salem. Finally, Antipas himself was heavily fined, and his property sold to pay the fines. His wife had died early, but a young daughter who kept his house in order, and who had failed in her attendance at the church which was engaged in persecuting her father, was also fined heavily. As her father's property was all gone, and she had no money of her own, she could not pay the fine, and was put in prison, to be sent to Barbados, and sold as a slave, that thus the fine might be collected. But the anguish, and the exposure of her prison, were too much for the young girl; and she died before means of transportation could be found.

As a result of these persecutions, Antipas became demented. As his insanity grew evident, the prosecutions ceased; but he was still in danger of starvation, so few would give him employment, both on account of his impaired mind, and of the odium which attached to any friend of the abhorred Quakers.

Captain Burton, Dulcibel's father, came to the village at this time. He had been one of the sea-captains who had indignantly refused to take the Southwick children, or any other of the Salem children, to Barbados; and he pitied the poor insane man, and gave him employment. Not only did he do this, but, as we have said, made it an article of the lease of his property, that the Buckleys should also keep Antipas as a farm servant.

Antipas, to the general surprise of the villagers had proved to be an excellent servant, notwithstanding his insanity. Only on training days and other periods of excitement, did his insanity obtrude itself. At all other times he seemed to be a cheerful, simple-hearted, and very capable and industrious "hand."

To Dulcibel, as was natural, Antipas always manifested the greatest devotion. Her little black mare was always groomed to perfection, he never being satisfied until he took a white linen handkerchief that he kept for the purpose, and, passing it over the mare's shining coat, saw that no stain or loose black hair remained on it.

"You think that Mistress Dulcibel is an angel, do you not?" said one of the female servants to him about this time, a little scornfully.

"No, I know what she is," he replied. "Shall I tell you—but if I do, you will not believe"—and he looked at the girl a little doubtfully.

"Oh, yes, I will," said the girl.

"Come here then and I will whisper it to you. I heard the minister read about her once, she is the woman that is 'clothed with the sun and has the moon under her feet, and upon her head a crown of twelve stars.'"

"That is wicked, Antipas. If Master Parris heard that you said things like that, he would have you whipped and put in the stocks."

"Master Parris? you mean Beelzebub! I know Beelzebub when I see him." And Antipas gave one of his unnatural, insane laughs, which were getting very frequent of late.

For the general excitement was proving too much for Antipas. Fie stopped frequently in his work, and muttered to himself; and then laughed wildly, or shed tears. He talked about the witches and the

Devil and evil spirits, and the strange things that he saw at night, in the insane fashion that characterized the "afflicted children."

As for Dulcibel in these times, she kept pretty much to herself, going out very little. As she could not sympathize with the general gossip of the neighborhood, she remained at home, and consequently had very few visitors. Joseph Putnam called whenever he came to the village, which, as I have stated, was but seldom; and Ellis Raymond came every few days.

Yes, it was a courtship, I suppose; but one of a very grave and serious character. The conversation generally turned upon the exciting events continually occurring, some new arrest, some new confession, some new and outrageously absurd charges.

Master Raymond's hand, if anyone accosted him suddenly, instinctively sought the hilt of his rapier. He was better skilled in the use of that weapon than was usual, and had no fear that he should be unable to escape from the constables, if not taken at a disadvantage. Still, as that would compel him to fly into the woods, and as it would separate him from Dulcibel, he had been very careful not to express in public his abhorrence of all the recent proceedings. I am afraid that he was guilty of considerable dissimulation, even paying his court to some of the "afflicted" maidens when he had the opportunity, with soft words and handsome presents; and trying in this way to enlist a party in his behalf, in case he or any of his friends should need supporters.

Joseph Putnam censured him one day for his double dealing, which was a thing not only out of Master Joseph's line, but one which his frank and outspoken nature rendered it very difficult for him to practise. But Raymond with his references to King David's behavior towards Achish, King of Gath, and to certain other scripture, especially Paul's being "all things to all men that he might save all," was rather too weighty for Joseph, whose forte was sensible assertion rather than ingenious argument. And so Master Raymond persevered in his course, feeling no more compunction in deceiving the Salemites, as he said to himself, than he would in deceiving and cheating a pack of savage wolves, who were themselves arrayed in sheep's clothing.

Jethro Sands had of late shown a disposition to renew his attentions to Dulcibel; but, after two or three visits, in the last of which he had given the maiden the desired opportunity, she had plainly intimated to him that the old state of affairs between them could never be restored.

"I know the reason too," said Jethro, angrily "it is all owing to that English popinjay, who rides about as if we colonists were not fit to dust his pretty coat for him."

"He is a gentleman, and a friend of mine," replied Dulcibel warmly.

"Why do you not say a lover of yours, at once?"

"You have no right to talk to me in that manner. I will not endure it."

"You will not—how will you help it?" He was now thoroughly angry, and all his native coarseness came to the surface.

"I will show you," said Dulcibel, the Norse blood of her father glowing in her face. "Good evening, Sir!" and she left the room.

Jethro had not expected such a quiet, but effective answer. He sat twirling his thumbs, for awhile, hoping that she would return. But realizing at last that she would not, he took his departure in a towering anger. Of course this was the last of his visits. But Dulcibel had made a deadly enemy.

It was unfortunate, for the maiden already had many who disliked her among the young people of the village. She was a superior person for one thing, and "gave herself airs," as some said. To be superior, without having wealth or an acknowledged high social position, is always to be envied, and often to be hated. Then again, Dulcibel dressed with more richness and variety of costume than was usual in the Puritan villages. This set many of the women, both young and old, against her. Her scarlet bodice, especially, was a favorite theme for animadversion; some even going so far as to call her ironically "the scarlet woman." It is curious how unpopular a perfectly amiable, sweet-tempered and sweet-tongued maiden may often become, especially with her own sex, because of their innate feeling that she is not, in spite of all her courteous endeavors, really one of them. It is an evil day for the swan when she finds herself the only swan among a large flock of geese.

Dulcibel's antecedents also were not as orthodox as they might be. Her mother, it was granted, was "pious," and of a "godly" connection; but her father, as he had himself once said, "had no religion to speak of." He had further replied to the question, asked him when he first came to Salem, as to whether he was "a professor of religion," that he was "only a sea captain, and had no other profession." And a certain freedom of thought characterized Dulcibel, that she could scarcely have derived from her pious mother. In fact, it was something like the freedom of the winds and of the clouds, blowing where they liked; and had been probably caught up by her father in his many voyages over the untrammeled seas.

At first Dulcibel had been rather impressed by the sermons of Master Parris and Master Noyes and the other ministers, to the effect that Satan was making a deadly assault upon the "saints," in revenge for their interference with his hitherto undisputed domination of the new world. But the longer she thought about it, the more she was inclined to adopt Joseph Putnam's theory, that his sister-in-law and niece and the other "afflicted" persons were possessed by devils.

She inclined to this view in preference even to what she knew was Ellis Raymond's real conviction, that they were a set of hysterical and vicious girls and women who had rendered themselves half-insane by tampering for a whole winter with their nervous and spiritual organizations; until they could scarcely now distinguish the true from the untrue, the real from the unreal, good from evil, or light from darkness.

"They have become reprobates and given over to an evil mind," said Master Raymond to her one day; clothing his thought as nearly as he could in scriptural language, in order to commend it to her.

"Yes, this seems to be a reasonable explanation of their wicked conduct," replied Dulcibel. "But I think after all, that it amounts to about the same thing as Joseph Putnam says, only that his is the stronger and more satisfactory statement."

And thinking of it, Master Raymond had to come to the same conclusion. His own view and that of his friends were about the same, only they had expressed themselves in different phrases.

CHAPTER XIV.

Bad News.

The blow fell at last, and where they might have expected it. As Joseph Putnam said afterwards, "Why did I not bring them out to my house? They would not have dared to take them from under my roof, and they could not have done it if they had dared."

One of his servants had been sent to the village on an errand; he had not performed his errand, but he had hurried back at once with the news. Dulcibel Burton had been arrested the previous evening, about nine o'clock, on the charge of being a witch. Antipas Newton had also been arrested. Both had been taken to prison, and put in irons.

A desperate, determined look came into the faces of the two men as they gathered every word the servant had to tell. Young Mistress Putnam burst into tears. But the men dashed a tear or two from their eyes, and began to collect their thoughts. It was not weeping but stern daring, that would be needed before this thing was through.

The prisoners were to be brought up that afternoon for examination. "I have my two men, who will follow wherever I lead them," said Master Putnam. "That makes four of us. Shall we carry her off from under their very eyes?" And his face glowed—the fighting instinct of his race was very strong within him.

"It might not succeed, those men are neither cowards nor babies," answered his guest. "Besides, it would lead probably to your banishment and the confiscation of your property. No, we must have the wisdom of the serpent, as well as the boldness of the lion."

"The result of the examination may be favorable, so young and good and beautiful as she is," said Mistress Putnam.

"They lap their tongues in the blood of lambs, and say it is sweet as honey," replied her husband, shaking his head. "No, they will show no mercy; but we must try to match them."

"Yes, and with as little hazard and cost to you, my noble friend, as possible," said Master Raymond. "Let me act, and take all the risk. They cannot get hold of my property; and I would just as lief live in New York or Philadelphia or England as among this brood of crazy vipers."

"That is wise counsel, Joseph," said his wife.

"Oh, I suppose it is," he answered emphatically. "But I hate wise counsel."

"Still, my good friend, you must admit that, as Dulcibel betrothed herself to me only two days ago, I am the one to take the greatest risk in this matter."

"Indeed!" said Mistress Putnam. "I knew it would be so; and I told Joseph it would be, only yesterday."

"I give you joy of such a mistress!" cried Master Putnam, grasping his friend's hand. "Yes, I grant now your right of precedence in this danger, and I will follow your lead—yes, to the death!"

"I hold you to that," said Master Raymond. "Remember you are pledged to follow my lead. Now, whatever I do, do not wonder, much less express any wonder. For this is war, and I have a right to meet craft with craft, and guile with guile. Depend upon it, I will save her, or perish with her."

CHAPTER XV.

The Arrest of Dulcibel and Antipas.

The arrest of Dulcibel had been entirely unexpected to herself and the Buckleys. Dulcibel indeed had wondered, when walking through the village in the morning, that several persons she knew had seemed to avoid meeting her. But she was too full of happiness in her recent betrothal to take umbrage or alarm at such an unimportant circumstance. A few months now, and Salem, she hoped, would see her no more forever. She knew, for Master Raymond had told her, that there were plenty of places in the world where life was reasonably gay and sunny and hopeful; not like this dull valley of the shadow of death in which she was now living. Raymond's plan was to get married; sell her property, which might take a few months, more or less; and then sail for England, to introduce his charming wife to a large circle of relatives.

Dulcibel had been reading a book that Raymond had brought to her—a volume of Shakespeare's plays—a prohibited book among the Puritan fathers, and which would have been made the text for one of Master Parris's most denunciatory sermons if he had known that it was in the village. Having finished "Macbeth" she laid the book down upon the table and began playing with her canary, holding it to her cheek, putting its bill to her lips, and otherwise fondling it. While she was thus engaged, she began to have the uncomfortable feeling which sensitive persons often have when some one is watching them; and turning involuntarily to the window which looked out on a garden at the side of the house, she saw in the dim light that dark faces, with curious eyes, seemed nearly to fill up the lower half of the casement. In great surprise, and with a sudden tremor, she rose quickly from the seat; and, as she did so, the weird faces and glistening eyes disappeared, and two constables, attended by a crowd of the villagers, entered the room. One of these walked at once to her side, and seizing her by the arm said, "I arrest you, Dulcibel Burton, by the authority of Magistrate Hathorne. Come along with me."

"What does all this mean, friend Herrick?" said Goodman Buckley, coming into the room.

"It means," said the constable, "that this young woman is no better than the other witches, who have been joining hand with Satan against the peace and dignity of this province." Then, turning to Dame Buckley, "Get her a shawl and bonnet, goodwife; if you do not wish her to go out unprotected in the night's cold."

"A witch—what nonsense!" said Dame Buckley.

"Nonsense, is it?" said the other constable. "What is this?" taking up the book from the table. "A book of plays! profane and wicked stage plays, in Salem village! You had better hold your peace, goodwife; or you may go to prison yourself for harboring such licentious devices of Satan in your house."

Goodwife Buckley started and grew pale. A book of wicked stage-plays under her roof! She could make no reply, but went off without speaking to pack up a bundle of the accused maiden's clothing.

"See here!" continued the constable, opening the book, "All about witches, as I thought! He-cat and three other witches!

'Round about the cauldron go:
In the poisoned entrails throw.'

It is horrible!"

"Put the accursed book in the fire, Master Taunton," said Herrick.

There was a small fire burning on the hearth, for the evening was a little cool, and the other constable threw the book amidst the live coals; but was surprised to see that it did not flame up rapidly.

"That is witchcraft, if there ever was witchcraft!" said Jethro Sands, who was at the front of the crowd. "See, it will not burn. The Devil looks out for his own."

"Yes, we shall have to stay here all night, if we wait for that book to burn up," said Master Herrick. "Now if it had been a Bible, or a Psalm-book, it would have been consumed by this time."

"My father told me," said one of the crowd, "that they were once six weeks trying to burn up some witch's book in Holland, and then had to tear each leaf separately before they could burn it."

"Where is the yellow bird—her familiar—that she was sending on some witch's errand when we were watching at the window?" said another of the crowd.

"Oh, it's not likely you will find the yellow bird," replied Herrick. "It is halfway down to hell by this time."

"No, there it is!" cried Jethro Sands, pointing to a ledge over the door, where the canary-bird had flown in its fright.

"Kill it! kill the familiar! Kill the devil's imp!" came in various voices, the angry tones being not without an inflection of fear.

Several pulled out their rapiers. Jethro was the quickest. He made a desperate lunge at the little creature, and impaled it on the point of his weapon.

Dulcibel shook off the hold of the constable and sprang forward. "Oh, my pretty Cherry," she cried, taking the dead bird from the point of the rapier. "You wretch! to harm an innocent little creature like that!" and she smoothed the feathers of the bird and kissed its little head.

"Take it from her! kill the witch!" cried some rude women in the outer circles of the crowd.

"Yes, mistress, this is more than good Christian people can be expected to endure," said constable Herrick, sternly, snatching the bird from her and tossing it into the fire. "Let us see if the imp will burn any quicker than the book."

"Ah, she forgot to charm it," said the other constable, as the little feathers blazed up in a blue flame.

"Yes, but note the color," said Jethro. "No Christian bird ever blazed in that color."

"Neither they ever did!" echoed another, and they looked into each other's faces and shook their heads solemnly.

At this moment Antipas Newton was led to the door of the room, in the custody of another officer. The old man seemed to be taking the whole proceeding very quietly and patiently, as the Quakers always did. But the moment he saw Dulcibel weeping, with Herrick's grasp upon her arm, his whole demeanor changed.

"What devil's mischief is this?" cried the demented man; and springing like an enraged lion upon Master Herrick, he dashed him against the opposite wall, tore his constable's staff from his hands and laying the staff around him wildly and ferociously cleared the room of everybody save Dulcibel and himself in less time than I have taken to tell it.

Jethro stepped forward with his drawn rapier to cover the retreat of the constables; but shouting, "the sword of the Lord and of Gideon!" the deranged man, with the stout oaken staff, dashed the rapier from Jethro's hand, and administered to him a sounding whack over the head, which made the blood come. Then he picked up the rapier and throwing the staff behind him, laughed wildly as he saw the crowd, constable and all, tumbling out of the door of the next room into the front garden of the house as if Satan himself in very deed, were after them.

"I will teach them how they abuse my pretty little Dulcibel," said the now thoroughly demented man, laughing grimly. "Come on, ye imps of Satan, and I will toast you at the end of my fork," he cried, flourishing Jethro's rapier, whose red point, crimson with the blood of the canary-bird, seemed to act upon the mind of the old man as a spark of fire upon tow.

"Antipas," said Dulcibel, coming forward and gazing sadly into the eyes of her faithful follower, "is it not written, 'Put up thy sword; for he that takes the sword shall perish by the sword'? Give me the weapon!"

The old man gazed into her face, at first wonderingly; then, with the instinct of old reverence and obedience, he handed the rapier to her, crossed his muscular arms over his broad breast, bowed his grisly head, and stood submissively before her.

"You can return now safely," Dulcibel called out to the constables. They came in, at first a little warily. "He is insane; but the spell is over now for the present. But treat him tenderly, I pray you. When he is in one of these fits, he has the strength of ten men."

The constables could not help being impressed favorably by the maiden's conduct; and they treated her with a certain respect and tenderness which they had not previously shown, until they had delivered her, and the afterwards entirely humble and peaceful Antipas, to the keeper of Salem prison.

But the crowd said to one another as they sought their houses: "What a powerful witch she must be, to calm down that maniac with one word." While others replied, "But he is possessed with a devil; and she does it because her power is of the devil."

They did not remember that this was the very course of reasoning used on a somewhat similar occasion against the Savior himself in Galilee!

CHAPTER XVI.

Dulcibel in Prison.

In the previous cases of alleged witchcraft to which I have alluded, the details given in my manuscript volume were fully corroborated, even almost to the minutest particulars, by official records now in existence. But in what I have related, and am about to relate, relative to Dulcibel Burton, I shall have to rely entirely upon the manuscript volume. Still, as there is nothing there averred more unreasonable and absurd than what is found in the existing official records, I see no reason to doubt the entire truthfulness of the story. In fact, it would be difficult to imagine grosser and more ridiculous accusations than were made by Mistress Ann Putnam against that venerable and truly devout and Christian matron, Rebecca Nurse.

When Dulcibel and Antipas, in the custody of four constables, reached the Salem jail, it was about eleven o'clock at night. The jailor, evidently had expected them; for he threw open the door at once. He was a stout, strong-built man, with not a bad countenance for a jailer; but seemed thoroughly imbued with the prevailing superstition, judging by the harsh manner in which he received the prisoners.

"I've got two strong holes for these imps of Satan; bring 'em along!"

The jail was built of logs, and divided inside into a number of small rooms or cells. In each of these cells was a narrow bedstead and a stone jug and slop bucket. Antipas was hustled into one cell, and, after being chained, the door was bolted upon him. Then Dulcibel was taken into another, though rather larger cell, and the jailor said, "Now she will not trouble other people for a while, my masters."

"Are you not going to put irons on her, Master Foster?" said Herrick.

"Of course I am. But I must get heavier chains than those to hold such a powerful witch as she is. Trust her to me, Master Herrick. She'll be too heavy to fly about on her broomsticks by the time I have done with her."

Then they all went out and Dulcibel heard the heavy bolt shoot into its socket, and the voices dying away as the men went down the stairs.

She groped her way to the bed in the darkness, sat down upon it and burst into tears. It was like a change from Paradise into the infernal regions. A few hours before and she had been musing in an ecstasy of joy over her betrothal, and dreaming bright dreams of the future, such perhaps as only a maiden can dream in the rapture of her first love. Now she was sitting in a prison cell, accused of a deadly crime, and her life and good reputation in the most imminent danger. One thing alone buoyed her up—the knowledge that her lover was fully aware of her innocence; and that he and Joseph Putnam would do all that they could do in her behalf. But then the sad thought came, that to aid her in any way might be only to bring upon themselves a similar accusation. And then, with a noble woman's spirit of self-sacrifice, she thought: "No, let them not be brought into danger. Better, far better, that I should suffer alone, than drag down my friends with me."

Here she heard the noise of the bolt being withdrawn, and saw the dim light of the jailer's candle.

As the jailer entered he threw down some heavy irons in the corner of the room. Then, he closed the door behind him, and came up to the unhappy girl. He laid his hand upon her shoulder and said:

"You little witch!"

Something in the tone seemed to strike upon the maiden's ear as if it were not unfamiliar to her; and she looked up hastily.

"Do you not remember me, little Dulcy? Why I rocked you on my foot in the old Captain's house in Boston many a day."

"Is it not uncle Robie?" said the girl. She had not seen him since she was four years old.

The jailer smiled. "Of course it is," he replied, "just uncle Robie. The old captain never went to sea that Robie Foster did not go as first mate. And a blessed day it was when I came to be first mate of this jail-ship; though I never thought to see the old captain's bonnie bird among my boarders."

"And do you think I really am a witch, uncle Robie?"

"Of course ye are. A witch of the worst kind," replied Robie, with a chuckle. "Now, when I come in here tomorrow morning nae doobt I will find all your chains off. It is just sae with pretty much all the others. I cannot keep them chained, try my best and prettiest."

"And Antipas?"

"Oh, he will just be like all the rest of them, doobtless. He is a powerful witch, and half a Quaker, besides."

"But do you really believe in witches, uncle Robie?"

"What do these deuced Barebones Puritans know about witches, or the devil, or anything else? There is only one true church, Mistress Dulcibel. I have sa mooch respect for the clergy as any man; but I don't take my sailing orders from a set of sourfaced old pirates."

Then, leaving her a candle and telling her to keep up a stout heart, the jailer left the cell; and Dulcibel heard the heavy bolt again drawn upon her, with a much lighter heart, than before. Examining the bundle of clothes that Goodwife Buckley had made up, she found that nothing essential to her comfort had been forgotten, and she soon was sleeping as peacefully in her prison cell as if she were in her own pretty little chamber.

CHAPTER XVII.

Dulcibel before the Magistrates.

The next afternoon the meeting-house at Salem village was crowded to its utmost capacity; for Dulcibel Burton and Antipas Newton were to be brought before the worshipful magistrates, John Hathorne and Jonathan Corwin. These worthies were not only magistrates, but persons of great note and influence, being members of the highest legislative and judicial body in the Province of Massachusetts Bay.

Among the audience were Joseph Putnam and Ellis Raymond; the former looking stern and indignant, the latter wearing an apparently cheerful countenance, genial to all that he knew, and they were many; and especially courteous and agreeable to Mistress Ann Putnam, and the "afflicted" maidens. It was evident that Master Raymond was determined to preserve for himself the freedom of the village, if complimentary and pleasant speeches would effect it. It would not do to be arrested or banished, now that Dulcibel was in prison.

When the constable, Joseph Herrick, brought in Dulcibel, he stated that having made "diligent search for images and such like," they had found a "yellow bird," of the kind that witches were known to affect; a wicked book of stage-plays, which seemed to be about witches, especially one called "he-cat"; and a couple of rag dolls with pins stuck into them.

"Have you brought them?" said Squire Hathorne.

"We killed the yellow bird and threw it and the wicked book into the fire."

"You should not have done that; you should have produced them here."

"We can get the book yet; for it was lying only partly burned near the back-log. It would not burn, all we could do to it."

"Of course not. Witches' books never burn," said Squire Hathorne.

"Here are the images," said a constable, producing two little rag-babies, that Dulcibel was making for a neighbor's children.

The crowd looked breathlessly on as "these diabolical instruments of torture" were placed upon the table before the magistrates.

"Dulcibel Burton, stand up and look upon your accusers," said Squire Hathorne.

Dulcibel had sunk upon a bench while the above conversation was going on—she felt overpowered by the curious and malignant eyes turned upon her from all parts of the room. Now she rose and faced the audience, glancing around to see one loved face. At last her eyes met his; he was standing erect, even proudly; his arms crossed over his breast, his face composed and firm, his dark eyes glowing and determined. He dared not utter a word, but he spoke to her from the inmost depths of his soul: "Be firm, be courageous, be resolute!"

This was what Raymond meant to say; and this is what Dulcibel, with her sensitive and impassioned nature, understood him to mean. And from that moment a marked change came over her whole appearance. The shrinking, timid girl of a moment before stood up serene but heroic, fearless and undaunted; prepared to assert the truth, and to defy all the malice of her enemies, if need be, to the martyr's death.

And she had need of all her courage. For, before three minutes had passed—Squire Hathorne pausing to look over the deposition on which the arrest had been made—Mistress Ann Putnam shrieked out, "Turn her head away, she is tormenting us! See, her yellow-bird is whispering to her!" And with that, she and her little daughter Ann, and Abigail Williams and Sarah Churchill and Leah Herrick and several others, flung themselves down on the floor in apparent convulsions.

"Oh, a snake is stinging me!" cried Leah Herrick.

"Her black horse is trampling on my breast!" groaned Sarah Churchill.

"Make her look away; turn her head!" cried several in the crowd. And one of the constables caught Dulcibel by the arm, and turned her around roughly.

"This is horrible!" cried Thomas Putnam—"and so young and fair-looking, too!"

"Ah, they are the worst ones, Master Putnam," said his sympathetic friend, the Rev. Master Parris.

"She looks young and pretty, but she may really be a hundred years old," said deacon Snuffles.

Quiet at last being restored, Magistrate Hathorne said:

"Dulcibel Burton, why do you torment Mistress Putnam and these others in this grievous fashion?"

"I do not torment them," replied Dulcibel calmly, but a little scornfully.

"Who does torment them, then?"

"How should I know—perhaps Satan."

"What makes you suppose that Satan torments them?"

"Because they tell lies."

"Do you know that Satan cannot torment these people except through the agency of other human beings?"

"No, I do not."

"Well, he cannot—our wisest ministers are united upon that. Is it not so, Master Parris?"

"That is God's solemn truth," was the reply.

"Who is it that torments you, Mistress Putnam?" continued Squire Hathorne, addressing Mistress Ann Putnam, who had sent so many already to prison and on the way to death.

Mistress Putnam was angered beyond measure at Dulcibel's intimation that she and her party were instigated and tormented directly by the devil. And yet she could not, if she would, bear falser witness than she already had done against Rebecca Nurse and other women of equally good family and reputation. But at this appeal of the Magistrate, she flung her arms into the air, and spoke with the vehemence and excitement of a half-crazy woman.

"It is she, Dulcibel Burton. She was a witch from her very birth. Her father sold her to Satan before she was born, that he might prosper in houses and lands. She has the witch's mark—a snake—on her breast, just over her heart. I know it, because goodwife Bartley, the midwife, told me so three years ago last March. Midwife Bartley is dead; but have a jury of women examine her, and you will see that it is true."

At this, as all thought it, horrible charge, a cold thrill ran through the crowd. They all had heard of witch-marks, but never of one like this—the very serpent, perhaps, which had deluded Eve. Joseph Putnam smiled disdainfully. "A set of stupid, superstitious fools!" he muttered through his teeth. "Half the De Bellevilles had that mark."[1]

"I will have that looked into," said Squire Hathorne. "In what shape does the spectre come, Mistress Putnam?"

"In the shape of a yellow-bird. She whispers to it who it is that she wants tormented, and it comes and pecks at my eyes."

Here she screamed out wildly, and began as if defending her eyes from an invisible assailant.

"It is coming to me now," cried Leah Herrick, striking out fiercely.

"Oh, do drive it away!" shrieked Sarah Churchill, "it will put out our eyes."

There was a scene of great excitement, several men drawing their swords and pushing and slashing at the places where they supposed the spectral bird might be.

Leah Herrick said the spectre that hurt her came oftenest in the shape of a small black horse, like that which Dulcibel Burton was known to keep and ride. Everybody supposed, she said, that the horse was itself a witch, for it was perfectly black, with not a white hair on it, and nobody could ride it but its mistress.

Here Sarah Churchill said she had seen Dulcibel Burton riding about twelve o'clock one night, on her black horse, to a witches' meeting.

Ann Putnam, the child, said she had seen the same thing. One curious thing about it was that Dulcibel had neither a saddle nor a bridle to ride with. She thought this was very strange; but her mother told her that witches always rode in that manner.

Here the two ministers of Salem, Rev. Master Parris and Rev. Master Noyes, said that this was undeniably true, that it was a curious fact that witches never used saddles nor bridles. Master Noyes explaining further that there was no necessity for such articles, as the familiar was instantly cognizant of every slightest wish or command of the witch to whom he was subject, and going thus through the air, there being no rocks or gullies or other rough places, there was no necessity of a saddle. Both the magistrates and the people seemed to be very much instructed by the remarks of these two godly ministers.

That "pious and excellent young man," Jethro Sands, here came forward and testified as follows: He had been at one time on very intimate terms with the accused; but her conduct on one occasion was so very singular that he declined thereafter to keep company with her. Hearing one day that she had gone to Master Joseph Putnam's, he had walked up the road to meet her on her return to the village. He looked up after walking about a mile, and saw her coming towards him on a furious gallop. There seemed to have been a quarrel of some kind between her and her familiar, for it would not stop all she could do to it. As she came up to him she snatched a rod that he had cut in the woods, out of his hand, and that moment the familiar stopped and became as submissive as a pet dog. He could not understand what it meant, until it suddenly occurred to him that the rod was a branch of witch-hazel!

Here the audience drew a long breath, the whole thing was satisfactorily explained. Every one knew the magical power of witch-hazel.[2]

Jethro further testified that Mistress Dulcibel freely admitted to him that her horse was a witch; never speaking of the mare in fact but as a "little witch." As might be expected, the horse was a most vicious animal, worth nothing to anybody save one who was a witch himself. He thought it ought to be stoned, or otherwise killed, at once.

The Rev. Master Noyes suggested that if it were handed over to his reverend brother Parris, he might be able, by a course of religious exercises, to cast out the evil spirit and render the animal serviceable. The apostles and disciples, it would be remembered, often succeeded in casting out evil spirits; though sometimes, we are told, they lamentably failed.

The magistrates here consulted a few minutes, and Squire Hathorne then ordered that the black mare should be handed over to the Rev. Master Parris for his use, and that he might endeavor to exorcise the evil spirit that possessed it.

Dulcibel had regarded with calm and serious eyes the concourse around her while this wild evidence was being given. Notwithstanding the peril of her position, she could not avoid smiling occasionally at the absurdity of the charges made against her; while at other times her brow and cheeks glowed with indignation at the maliciousness of her accusers. Then she thought, how could I ever have injured these neighbors so seriously that they have been led to conspire together to take my life? Oh, if I had never come to Salem, to a place so overflowing with malice, evil-speaking and all uncharitableness! Where there was so much sanctimonious talk about religion, and such an utter absence of it in those that prated the most of its possession. Down among the despised Quakers of Pennsylvania there was not one-half as much talking about religion but three times as much of that kindly charity which is its essential life.

"Dulcibel Burton," said Squire Hathorne, "you have heard what these evidence against you; what answer can you make to them?"

Blood will assert itself. The daughter of the old sea-captain, himself of Norse descent on the mother's side, felt her father's spirit glowing in her full veins.

"The charges that have been made are too absurd and ridiculous for serious denial. The 'yellow bird' is my canary bird, Cherry, given me by Captain Alden when we lived in Boston. He brought it home with him from the West Indies. Ask him whether it is a familiar. My black horse misbehaved on that afternoon Jethro Sands tells of, as I told him at the time; simply because I had no whip. When he gave me his switch, the vixenish animal came at once into subjection to save herself a good whipping. It was not a hazel switch, his statement is false, and he knows it, it was a maple one."

"And you mean to say, I suppose," shrieked out Mistress Ann Putnam, "that you have no witch-mark either; that you do not carry the devil's brand of a snake over your heart?"

"I have some such mark, but it is a birth-mark, and not a witch-mark. It is a simple curving line of red," and the girl blushed crimson at being compelled to such a reference to a personal peculiarity. But she faltered not in her speech, though her tones were more indignant than before. "It is not a peculiarity of mine, but of my mother's family. Some say that a distant ancestor was once frightened by a large snake coming into her chamber; and her child was born with this mark upon her breast. That is all of it. There is no necessity of any examination, for I admit the charge."

"Yes," screamed Mistress Putnam again, "your ancestress too was a noted witch. It runs in the family. Go away with you!" she cried striking apparently at something with her clenched hand. "It is her old great grandmother! See, there she is! Off! Off! She is trying to choke me!" endeavoring seemingly to unclasp invisible hands from her throat.

The other "afflicted" ones joined in the tumult. With one it was the "yellow bird" pecking at her eyes, with another the black horse rearing up and striking her with its hoofs. Leah Herrick cried that Dulcibel's "spectre" was choking her.

"Hold her hands still!" ordered Squire Hathorne, and a constable sprang to each side of the accused maiden and held her arms and hands in a grasp of iron.

Joseph Putnam made an exclamation that almost sounded like an oath, and made a step forward; but a firm hand was laid upon his shoulder. "Be patient!" whispered Ellis Raymond, though his own mouth was twitching considerably. "We are the anvil now; wait till our turn comes to be sledgehammer!"

Such a din and babel as the "afflicted" kept up! By the curious power of sympathy it affected the crowd almost to madness. If Dulcibel looked at them, they cried she was tormenting them. If she looked upward in resignation to Heaven, they also stared upwards with fixed, stiff necks. If she leaned her head one side they did the same, until it seemed as if their necks would be broken; and the jailers forced up Dulcibel's neck with their coarse, dirty hands.

Dulcibel had not attended any of the other examinations, but similar demonstrations on the part of the "afflicted" had been described to her. It was very different, however, to hear of such things and to experience them in her own person. And if she had been at all a nervous and less healthy young woman, she might have been overcome by them, and even led to admit, as so many others had admitted under similar influences, that she really was a witch, and compelled by her master, the devil, could not help tormenting these poor victims.

"Why do you not cease this?" at last cried Squire Hathorne, sternly and wrathfully.

"Cease what?" she replied indignantly.

"Tormenting these poor, suffering children and women!"

"You see I am not tormenting them. Bid these men unloose my hands, they are hurting me."

"They say your spectre and your familiar are tormenting them."

"They are bearing false witness against me."

"Who does hurt them then?"

"Their master, the devil, I suppose and his imps."

"Why should he hurt them?"

"Because they are liars, and bear false witness; being hungry for innocent blood."

The spirit of the free-thinking, free-spoken old sea-captain— nurtured by the free winds and the free waves for forty years—was fully alive now in his daughter. A righteous, holy indignation at the abominable farce that was going on with all its gross lying and injustice had taken possession of her, and she cared no longer for the opinions of any one around her, and thought not even of her lover looking on, but only of truth and justice. "Yes, they are possessed with devils—being children of their father, the devil!" she continued scornfully. "And they shall have their reward. As for you, Ann Putnam, in seven years from this day I summon you to meet those you have slain with your wicked, lying tongue, at the bar of Almighty God! It shall be a long dying for you!" Then, seeing Thomas Putnam by his wife's side, "And you, Thomas Putnam, you puppet in a bad woman's hands, chief aider and abettor of her wicked ways, you shall die two weeks before her, to make ready for her coming! And you," turning to the constables on each side of her, "for your cruel treatment of innocent women, shall die by this time next year!"

The constables loosened their grasp of her hands and shrank back in dismay. The "afflicted" suddenly hushed their cries and regained their composure, as they saw the accused maiden's eyes, lit up with the wildness of inspiration, glancing around their circle with lightning flashes that might strike at any moment.

Even Squire Hathorne's wine-crimsoned face paled, lest she would turn around and denounce him too. Even if she were a witch, witches it was known sometimes spoke truly. And when she slowly turned and looked upon him, the haughty judge was ready to sink to the floor.

"As for you, John Hathorne, for your part in these wicked doings," here she paused as if waiting to hear a supernatural voice, while the crowded meeting-house was quiet as a tomb—"No! you are only grossly deluded; you shall not die. But a curse shall be upon you and your descendants for a hundred years. They shall not prosper. Then a Hathorne shall arise who shall repudiate you and all your wicked works, and the curse shall pass away!"

Squire Hathorne regained his courage the instant she said he should not die, little he cared for misfortunes that might come upon his descendants.

"Off with the witch to prison—we have heard enough!" he cried hoarsely. "Tell the jailer to load her well with irons, hands and feet; and give her nothing to eat but bread and water of repentance. She is committed for trial before the special court, in her turn, and at the worshipful judges' convenience."

[1] "Most part of this noble lineage carried upon their body for a natural birth-mark, from their mother's womb, a snake." —*North*.

[2] This and many other passages, as the reader will notice, are quoted verbatim from the manuscript volume.

CHAPTER XVIII.

Well, What Now?

The crowd drew long breaths as they emerged from the meeting-house. This was the first time that the accused had fully turned upon the accusers. It was a pity that it had not been done before; because such was the superstition of the day, that to have your death predicted by one who was considered a witch was no laughing matter. The blood ran cold even in Mistress Ann Putnam's veins, as she thought of Dulcibel's prediction; and the rest of the "afflicted" inwardly congratulated themselves that they had escaped her malediction, and resolved that they would not be present at her trial as witnesses against her, if they could possibly avoid it. But then that might not be so easy.

Even the crowd of beholders were a little more careful in the utterance of their opinions about Dulcibel than they had been relative to the other accused persons. Not that they had much doubt as to the maiden's being a born witch—the serpent-mark seemed to most of them a conclusive proof of that—but what if one of those "spectres," the "yellow bird" or the uncontrollable "black mare" should be near and listening to what they were even then saying?

"What do I think about it?" said one of the crowd to his companion. "Why I think that if he who sups with the devil should have a long spoon, he who abuses a witch should be certain her yellow bird is not listening above his left shoulder," and he gave a quick glance in the direction alluded to, while half of those near him, as they heard his warning words, did the same. And there was not much talking against Dulcibel after this, among that portion of the villagers.

Ellis Raymond had heard this speech as he walked silently out of the meeting-house with Joseph Putnam, and a grim smile flitted over his face. He felt prouder than ever of his beautiful betrothed. He was not a man who admired amazons or other masculine women, such, as in these days, we call "strong-minded;" he liked a woman to keep in her woman's sphere, such as the Creator had marked out for her by making her a woman; but circumstances may rightly overrule social conventions, and demand action suitable to the emergency. Standing at bay, among a pack of howling wolves, the heroic is a womanly as well as manly quality; and the gun and the knife as feminine implements, as the needle and the scissors. Dulcibel had never reasoned about such things; she was a maiden who naturally shrank from masculine self-assertion and publicity; but, called to confront a great peril, she was true to the noble instincts of her family and her race, and could meet falsehood with indignant denial and contempt. How she had been led to utter those predictions she never fully understood—not at the time nor afterwards. She seemed to herself to be a mere reed through which some indignant angel was speaking.

"Well," said Joseph Putnam, as they got clear of the crowd, "brother Thomas and sister Ann have wakened up the tiger at last. They will be "afflicted" now in dead earnest. Did you see how sister Ann, with all her assurance, grew pale and almost fainted? It serves her right; she deserves it; and Thomas too, for being such a dupe and fool."

"Do you think it will come true?" said Master Raymond.

"Of course it will; the prediction will fulfill itself. Thomas is superstitious beyond all reasonableness; and good Mistress Ann, my pious sister-in-law, is almost as bad as he is, notwithstanding her lies and trickery. Do you know what I saw that Leah Herrick doing?"

"What was it?"

"In her pretended spasms, when bending nearly double, she was taking a lot of pins out of the upper edge of her stomacher with her mouth, preparatory of course, to making the accusation that it was Dulcibel's doings."

"But she did not?"

"No, it was just before the time that Dulcibel scared them so with the predictions; and Leah was so frightened, lest she also should be predicted against, that she quietly spit all the pins into her hand again."

"Ah, that was the game played by a girl about ten years ago at Taunton-Dean, in England. Judge North told my father about it. One of the magistrates saw her do it."

"Well, now, what shall we do? They will convict her just as surely as they try her."

"Undoubtedly!"

"Shall we attack and break open the jail some dark night, sword in hand? I can raise a party of young men, friends of the imprisoned, to do it; they only want a leader."

"And all of you go off into perpetual banishment and have all your property confiscated?"

"I do not care. I am ready to do it."

"If you choose to encounter such a risk for others, I have no objection. I believe myself that if the friends and relatives of the accused persons would take up arms in defense of them, and demand their release, it would be the very manliest and most sensible thing they could do. But the consciences of the people here make cowards of them. They are all in bondage to a blind and conceited set of ministers, and to a narrow and bigoted creed."

"Then what do you plan?"

"Dulcibel's escape. You know that I managed to see her for a few minutes early this morning. She has a friend within the prison. Wait till we get on our horses, and I will explain it all to you."

CHAPTER XIX.

Antipas Works a Miracle.

The next morning Antipas Newton was brought before the Magistrates for examination. Antipas seemed so quiet and peaceful in his demeanor, that Squire Hathorne could hardly credit the story told by the constables of his violent behavior on the night of the arrest.

"I thought you were a Quaker," said he to the prisoner.

"No, only half Quaker; the other half gospeller," replied the old man meekly.

Mistress Ann was not present; her husband brought report that she was sick in bed. Probably she did not care to come, the game being too insignificant. Perhaps she had not quite recovered from the stunning effect of Dulcibel's prediction. Though it was not likely that a doom that was to be seven years in coming, would, after the first impression was past, be felt very keenly. There was time for so much to happen during seven years.

But the Rev. Master Parris's little niece, Abigail Williams, was present, and several other older members of the "circle," prepared to witness against the old man to any extent that seemed to be necessary.

After these had made their customary charges, and had gone through some of their usual paroxysms, Joseph Putnam, accompanied by Goodman Buckley, came forward.

"This is all folly," said Joseph Putnam stoutly. "We all know Antipas Newton; and that he has been deranged in his intellects, and of unsound mind for the last twenty years. He is generally peaceful and quiet; though in times of excitement like the present, liable to be driven into outbreaks of violent madness. Here is his employer, Goodman Buckley, who of course knows him best, and who will testify to all this even more conclusively than I can."

Then Goodman Buckley took the oath with uplifted hand, and gave similar evidence. No one had even doubted for twenty years past, that Antipas was simple-minded. He often said and did strange things; but only when everybody around him was greatly excited, was he at all liable to violent outbreaks of passion.

Squire Hathorne seemed half-convinced; but the Reverend Master Parris rose from the bench where he had been sitting, and said he would like to be heard for a few moments. Permission being accorded: "What is insanity?" said he. "What is the scriptural view of it? Is it anything but a judgment of the Lord for sin, as in the case of Nebuchadnezzar; or a possession by a devil, or devils, as in the Case of the Gadarene who made his dwelling among the tombs as told in the fifth chapter of Mark and the eighth of Luke? That these were real devils is evident—for when permission was given them to enter into the herd of swine, they entered into them, and the swine ran down a steep place into the sea and were drowned. And as there were about two thousand swine, there must have been at least two thousand devils in that one so-called insane man; which no doubt accounted for his excessive violence. After the devils had left him, we are told that his countrymen came and saw him sitting at the feet of Jesus, no longer naked, but clothed and in his right mind. Therefore it follows as a logical deduction, that his not being before in his right mind was because he was possessed with devils."

The magistrates and people evidently were greatly impressed with what Master Parris had said. And, as he sat down, Master Noyes, who was sitting beside his reverend brother, rose and said that he considered the argument they had just heard unanswerable. It could only be refuted by doubting the infallibility of the Scripture itself. And he would further add, as to the case before them, that this so-called insanity of the prisoner had not manifested itself until he had been repeatedly guilty of harboring two of that heretical and abominable sect called Quakers and had incurred imprisonment and heavy fines for so doing; to pay which fines his property had been rightfully sold. This punishment, and the death of his daughter by the decree of a just God, apparently not being sufficient to persuade him of the error of his ways, no doubt he had been given over to the devil, that he might become a sign and a warning to evil-doers. But, instead of repenting of his evil ways, he seems to have entered the service of Captain Burton, who was always known to be very loose in his religious views and observances; and who it now seems was himself a witch, or, as he might be rather more correctly termed, a wizard, and the father of the dangerous girl who was properly committed for trial yesterday. Going thus downward from bad to worse, this Antipas had at last become a witch himself; roaming around tormenting godly and unoffending people to please his mistress and her Satanic master. In conclusion he said that he fully agreed with his reverend brother, that what some of the world's people, who thought themselves wise above that which was written, called insanity, was simply, as taught in the holy scriptures, a possession by the devil.

Magistrate Hathorne nodded to Magistrate Corwin, and Magistrate Corwin nodded in turn decidedly to his learned brother. They evidently considered that the ministers had settled that point.

"Well, then," said Joseph Putnam, a little roughly to the ministers, "why do you not do as the Savior did, cast out the devils, that Antipas may sit down here in his right mind? We do not read that any of these afflicted people in Judea were cast into prison. In all cases they were pitied, not punished."

"This is an unseemly interruption, Master Putnam," said Squire Hathorne sternly. "We all know that the early disciples were given the power to cast out devils and that they exercised the power continually, but that in later times the power has been withdrawn. If it were not so, our faithful elders would cast out the spectres that are continually tormenting these poor afflicted persons."

While this discussion had been going on, Antipas had been listening to all that was said with the greatest attention. Once only had he manifested any emotion; that was when the reference had been made to the death of his daughter, who had died from her exposure to the severity of the winter season in Salem jail. At this time he put his hand to his eyes and wiped away a few tears. Before and after this, the expression of his face was rather as of one who was pleased and amused at the idea of being the center of attraction to such a large and goodly company. At the conclusion of Squire Hathorne's last remark, a new idea seemed to enter the old man's confused brain. He looked steadily at the line of the "afflicted" before him, who were now beginning a new display of paroxysms and contortions, and putting his right hand into one of his pockets, he drew forth a coil of stout leather strap. Grasping one end of it, he shouted, "I can heal them! I know what will cure them!" and springing from between the two constables that guarded him, began belaboring the "afflicted" with his strap over their backs and shoulders in a very energetic fashion.

Dividing his energies between keeping off the constable and "healing the afflicted," and aided rather than hindered by Joseph Putnam's intentionally ill-directed efforts to restrain him, the insane man managed to administer in a short time no small amount of very exemplary punishment. And, as Masters Putnam and Raymond agreed in talking over the scene afterwards, he certainly did seem to effect an instantaneous cure of the "afflicted," for they came to their sober senses at the first cut of the leather strap, and rushed pell-mell down the passage as rapidly as they could regardless of the other tormenting "spectres."

"This is outrageous!" said Squire Hathorne hotly to the constables as Antipas was at last overpowered by a host of assailants, and stood now firmly secured and panting between the two officers. "How dared you bring him here without being handcuffed?"

"We had no idea of his breaking out anew, he seemed as meek as a lamb," said constable Herrick.

"Why, we thought he was a Quaker!" added his assistant.

"I am a Quaker!" said Antipas, looking a little dangerous again.

"You are not."

"Thou liest!" said the insane man. "This is one of my off days."

Joseph Putnam laughed outright; and a few others, who were not church-members, laughed with him.

"Silence!" thundered Squire Hathorne. "Is this a time for idle levity?" and he glared around the room.

"We have heard enough," continued the Squire, after a few words with his colleague. "This is a dangerous man. Take him off again to prison; and see that his chains are strong enough to keep him out of mischief."

CHAPTER XX.

Master Raymond Goes to Boston.

Whatever the immediate effect of Dulcibel's prediction had been, Mistress Ann Putnam was now about again, as full of wicked plans, and as dangerous as ever. She knew, for everybody knew, that Master Ellis Raymond had gone to Boston. In a village like Salem at that time, such fact could hardly be concealed.

"What had he gone for?

"To see a friend," Joseph Putnam had said.

"What friend?" queried Mistress Ann. That seemed important for her to know.

She had accused Dulcibel in the first place as a means of hurting Joseph Putnam. But now since the trial, she hated her for herself. It was not so much on account of the prediction, as on account of Dulcibel's terrific arraignment of her. The accusation that her husband was her dupe and tool was, on account of its palpable truth, that which gave her perhaps the greatest offence. The charge being once made, others might see its truth also. Thus all the anger of her cunning, revengeful nature was directed against Dulcibel.

And just at this time she heard from a friend in Boston, who sent her a budget of news, that Master Raymond had taken dinner with Captain Alden. "Ah," she thought, "I see it now." The name was a clue to her. Captain Alden was an old friend of Captain Burton. He it was, so Dulcibel had said, from whom she had the gift of the "yellow bird."

She knew Captain Alden by reputation. Like the other seamen of the time he was superstitious in some directions, but not at all in others. He would not for the world leave port on a Friday—or kill a mother Carey's chicken—or whistle at sea; but as to seeing witches in pretty young girls, or sweet old ladies, that was entirely outside of the average seaman's thoughts. Toward all women in fact, young or old, pretty or ugly, every sailor's heart at that day, as in this, warmed involuntarily.

She also knew that the seamen as a class were rather inclined to what the godly called license in their religious opinions. Had not the sea-captains in Boston Harbor, some years before, unanimously refused to carry the young Quakeress, Cassandra Southwick, and her brother, to the West Indies and sell them there for slaves, to pay the fines incurred by their refusal to attend church regularly? Had not one answered for the rest, as paraphrased by a gifted descendant of the Quakers?—

"Pile my ship with bars of silver—pack with coins of Spanish gold, From keelpiece up to deck-plank the roomage of her hold, By the living God who made me! I would sooner in your bay Sink ship and crew and cargo, than bear this child away!"

And so Master Raymond, who it was rumored had been a great admirer of Dulcibel Burton, was on a visit to Boston, to see her father's old friend, Captain John Alden! Mistress Putnam thought she could put two and two together, if any woman could. She would check-mate that game—and with one of her boldest strokes, too— that should strike fear into the soul of even Joseph Putnam himself, and teach him that no one was too high to be above the reach of her indignation.

The woman was so fierce in this matter, that I sometimes have questioned, could she ever have loved and been scorned by Joseph Putnam?

CHAPTER XXI.

A Night Interview.

A few days passed and Master Raymond was back again; with a pleasant word and smile for all he met, as he rode through the village. Mistress Ann Putnam herself met him on the street and he pulled up his horse at the side-path as she stopped, and greeted her.

"So you have been to Boston?" she said.

"Yes, I thought I would take a little turn and hear what was going on up there."

"Who did you see—any of our people?"

"Oh, yes—the Nortons and the Mathers and the Higginsons and the Sewalls—I don't know all.

"Good day; remember me to my kind brother Joseph and his wife," said she, and Raymond rode on.

"What did that crafty creature wish to find out by stopping me?" he thought to himself.

"He did not mention Captain Alden. Yes, he went to consult him," thought Mistress Putnam.

Master Joseph Putnam was so anxious to meet his friend, that he was standing at the turning in the lane that led up to his house.

"Well, what did the Captain say?"

"He was astounded. Then he gave utterance to some emphatic expressions about hell-fire and damnation which he had probably heard in church."

"I know no more appropriate occasion to use them," commented young Master Joseph drily. "If it were not for certain portions of the psalms and the prophets, I could hardly get through the time comfortably nowadays."

"If we can get her safely to Boston, he will see that a fast vessel is ready to take us to New York; and he will further see that his own vessel—the Colony's rather, which he commands—never catches us."

"That looks well. I managed to see Dulcibel for a few minutes to-day, and"—

"How is she?" inquired Raymond eagerly. "Does she suffer much?"

"Not very much I think. No more than is necessary to save appearances. She told me that the jailer was devoted to her. He will meet you to-night after dark on the hill, to arrange matters."

"Say that we get from the prison by midnight. Then it will take at least three hours riding to reach Boston—though we shall not enter the town."

"Three hours! Yes, four," commented his friend; "or even five if the night be dark and stormy; and such a night has manifest advantages. Still, as I suppose you must wait for a northwest wind, that is pretty sure to be a clear one."

"Yes, the main thing is to get out into the open sea. Captain Alden plans to procure a Danish vessel, whose skipper once out of sight of land, will oppose any recapture by force."

"I suppose however you will sail for New York?"

"Yes, that is the nearest port and we shall be perfectly safe there. Still Jamestown would do. The Delaware is nearer than the James, but I am afraid the Quakers would not be able to protect us, as they are too good to oppose force by force."

"Too good! too cranky!" said Master Putnam. "A pretty world the rascals would make of it, if the honest men were too good to fight. It seems to me there is something absolutely wicked in their non-resistant notions."

"Yes, it is no worse to kill a two-legged tiger or wolf than a four-legged one; one has just as good a right to live as the other."

"A better, I think," replied Master Putnam. "The tiger or wolf is following out his proper nature; the human tiger or wolf is violating his."

"You know I rather like the Quakers," rejoined Master Raymond. "I like their general idea of considering the vital spirit of the Scripture more than the mere outward letter. But in this case, it seems to me, they are in bondage to the mere letter 'thou shalt not kill;' not seeing that to kill, in many cases, is really to save, not only life, but all that makes life valuable."

That evening just about dusk, the two young men mounted their horses, and rode down one of the roads that led to Salem town, leaving Salem village on the right—thinking best not to pass through the village. Within a mile or so of the town, Master Putnam said, "here is the place" and led the way into a bridle path that ran into the woods. In about five minutes he halted again, gave a low whistle, and a voice said, a short distance from them, "Who are you, strangers?"

"Friends in need," replied Master Putnam.

"Then ye are friends indeed," said the voice; and Robert Foster, the jailer, stepped from behind the trunk of a tree into the path.

"Well, Robie, how's the little girl?" said Master Joseph.

"Bonnie as could be expected," was the answer.

"She sends word to you, sir," addressing Master Raymond, "that you had better not come to see her. She knows well all you could say—just as well as if she heard it, the brave, bonnie lassie!"

"I know it," replied Master Raymond. "Tell her I think of her every moment—and that things look bright."

"Let us get out of this glooming, and where we can see a rod around us," suggested the jailer. "I like to see at least as far as my elbow, when I am talking confidentially."

"I will go—you stay here with the horses," said Raymond to Master Putnam. "I do not want you mixed up with this thing any more than is absolutely necessary."

"Oh, I do not care for the risk—I like it," replied his friend.

"Stay, nevertheless," insisted Master Raymond. And getting down from his horse, and handing the bridle rein to Master Putnam, he followed the jailer out into an open space, where the rocks coming to the surface, had prevented the growth of the forest. Here it was a little lighter than it had been in the wood-path; but, the clouds having gathered over the sky since they started, it was not possible to see very far around them.

"Hold up there!" cried Robie, catching Raymond by the arm—"why, man, do you mean to walk straight over the cliff?"

"I did not know any chasm was there," said Raymond. "I never saw this place before. Master Putnam said it was a spot where we should not be likely to be molested. And it does look desolate enough." He leaned back against one of two upright planks which seemed to have been placed there for some purpose, and looked at a little pile of dirt and stones not far from his feet.

"No," said the jailer. "I opine we shall not be disturbed here. I do not believe there is more than three persons in Salem that would be willing to come to this hill at this time of day,—and they are here already." And the jailer smiled audibly.

"Why, how is that?"

"Because they are all so damnably sooperstitious!" replied Robie, with an air of vast superiority.

"Ah! is this place then said to be haunted?"

"Yes,—poor Goodwife Bishop's speerit is said to haunt it. But as she never did anybody any harm while she was living, I see not why she should harm any one now that she is dead."

"And so brave Bridget was executed near this place? Where was the foul murder done?"

"You are leaning against the gallows," said Robie quietly. "And that pile of stones at your feet is over her grave."

Raymond was a brave man, physically and morally, and not at all superstitious; but he recoiled involuntarily from the plank against which he had been leaning, and no longer allowed his right foot to rest upon the top stones of the little heap that marked the grave.

"Oh, I thought you knew it," said the jailer calmly. "I say, let them fear goodwife Bishop's ghost who did her wrong. As for me, I favored her all I dared; and her last word to me was a blessing. But now for your honor's business, I have not long to stay."

"I have planned all but the getting out of jail. Can it be easily done?"

"As easy as walking out of a room."

"Will you not be suspected?"

"Not at all, I think—they are so mightily sooperstitious. I shall lock everything tight after her; and make up a good story about my wakening up in the middle of the night, just in time to see her flying out of the top o' the house, on her black mare, and thrashing the animal with a broom-handle. The bigger the lie the quicker they will believe it."

"If they should suspect you, let Master Putnam know, and he will get you off, if wit and money together can do it."

"Oh, I believe that," said the jailer. "Master Putnam is well known in all these parts, as a man that never deserts a friend; and I'll warrant you are one of the same grit."

"My hand on it, Robie!" and he shook the jailer's hand warmly. "I shall never forget this service."

"I am a rough, ignorant man," replied Robie quietly; "but I know gentle blood when I see it."

"What time of night will suit you best?"

"Just about twelve o'clock at night. That is the time all the ghosts and goblins and weetches choose; and when all honest people are in their beds, and in their first and soundest sleep."

"We shall not be able to give you much warning, for we must wait a favorable wind and tide."

"So you let me know by nightfall, it will do."

"And now for the last point—what do I pay you? I know we are asking you to run a great risk. The men that whip gentlewomen, at the cart's tail, and put little children into jail, and sell them as slaves, will not spare you, if they find out what you have done. Thank God, I am rich enough to pay you well for taking such a fearful risk and shall be only too glad to reward your unselfish deed."

"Not a shilling!" replied Robie proudly. "I am not doing this thing for pay. It is for the old Captain's little girl, that I have held in these arms many a day—and for the old Captain himself. While these bloody landsmen," continued the old sailor, "plague and persecute each other, Master Raymond, what is that to us, we men of the sea, who have a creed and a belief of our own, and who never even think of hurting a woman or a child? But as for these landsmen, sticking at home all the time, how can they be expected to know anything— compared to men that have doubled both Capes, and seen people living all sorts of ways, and believing all sorts of things? No, no," and Robie laughed disdainfully, "let these land-lubbers attend to their own affairs; but let them keep their hands off us seamen and our families."

"So be it then, Robie; I honor your feelings! But nevertheless I shall not forget you. And one of these days, if we get off safely, you shall hear from me again about this matter."

And then, their plans settled, Robie trudged down to the town; while the young men rode back the way they had come, to Master Putnam's.

CHAPTER XXII.

The Reverend Master Parris Exorcises "Little Witch."

It will be remembered that Squire Hathorne had directed that Dulcibel's little horse should be handed over to the Reverend Master Parris, in order that it might be brought into due subjection.

This had pleased Master Parris very much. In the first place he was of a decidedly acquisitive turn—as had been shown in his scheming to obtain a gift of the minister's house and orchard—and moreover, if he was able to cast out the devil that evidently possessed this horse, and make it a sober and docile riding animal, it would not only be the gain of a very pretty beast, but would prove that something of the power of casting out devils, which had been given to the disciples of old, had come down unto him. In such a case, his fame probably would equal, if not surpass, that of the great Boston ministers, Increase and Cotton Mather.

Goodman Buckley had brought down the little mare, the next morning after the examination. The mare would lead very well, if the person leading her was on horseback—very badly, if he were not, except under peculiar circumstances. She was safely housed in the minister's stable, and gazed at with mingled fear and admiration by the family and their immediate neighbors. Master Parris liked horses, had some knowledge of the right way to handle them, and showed more wisdom in his treatment of this rather perverse animal of Dulcibel's than he had ever manifested in his church difficulties.

He began by what he called a course of conciliation—to placate the devil, as it were. How he could bring his conscience to allow of this, I am not able to understand. But then the mare, if the devil were once cast out, would be, on account of her rare beauty, a very valuable animal. And so the minister, twice a day, made a point of going into the little passage, at the head of the stall, speaking kindly to the animal, and giving her a small lump of maple sugar.

Like most of her sex, Susannah—as Master Parris had renamed her, knowing the great importance of a good name—was very fond of sugar; and her first apparent aversion to the minister seemed gradually to change into a kind of tacit respect and toleration, under the influence of his daily medications. Finally, the wary animal would allow him to pat her neck without striking at him with one of her front feet, or trying to bite him; and even to stroke her glossy flanks without lunging at him with her hind heels, in an exceedingly dangerous fashion.

But spiritual means also were not neglected. The meeting-house was very near, and the mare was brought over regularly when there were religious services, and fastened in the near vicinity of the other more sober and orthodox horses, that she might learn how to behave and perhaps the evil spirit be thus induced to abandon one so constantly exposed to the doubtless unpleasant sounds (to it) of psalm and prayer and sermon.

A horse is an imitative animal, and very susceptible to impressions,—both of a material and a mental character—and I must confess that these proceedings of the minister's were very well adapted to the object he had in view.

The minister also had gone farther—but of this no one at the time knew but himself. He had gone into the stable on a certain evening, when his servant John Indian was off on an errand; and had pronounced a prayer over the possessed animal winding up with an exorcism which ought to have been sufficient to banish any reasonable devil, not only from the mare, but from the neighborhood. As he concluded, what seemed to be a huge creature, with outstretched wings, had buffeted him over the ears, and then disappeared through the open window of the stable. The creature was in the form of a big bat; but then it was well known that this was one of the forms which evil spirits were most fond of assuming.

The minister therefore had strong reasons for supposing that the good work was now accomplished; and that he should find the mare hereafter a Susannah not only in name but in nature—a black lily, as it were. But of course this could not be certainly told, unless some one should attempt to ride her; and he suggested it one day to John Indian. But John Indian—unknown to anybody but himself—had already tried the experiment; and after a fierce contest, was satisfied with his share of the glory. His answer was:—

"No, no, master—debbil hab no 'spect for Indian man. Master he good man! gospel man! debbil 'fraid of him—him too much for debbil!"

This seemed very reasonable for a poor, untutored Indian. Mistress Parris, too, said that she was certain he could succeed if any one could. The evil spirits would be careful how they conducted themselves towards such a highly respected and godly minister as her revered husband. Several of her acquaintances, pious and orthodox goodwives of the village, said the same thing. Master Parris thought he was a very good horseman besides; and began to take the same view. There was the horse, and he was the man!

So one afternoon John Indian saddled and bridled the mare, and brought her up to the horse-block. Susannah had allowed herself to be saddled without the slightest manifestation of ill-humor; probably the idea of stretching her limbs a little, was decidedly pleasant in view of the small amount of exercise she had taken lately.

But the wisest plan was not thought of. The minister's niece, Abigail Williams—one of the "afflicted"—had looked upon the black mare with longing eyes; and if she had made the experiment, it probably would have been successful. But they did not surmise that it might be the man's saddle and mode of riding, to which the animal was entirely unaccustomed, that were at the bottom of the difficulty. And, besides, Master Parris wanted the mare for his own riding, not for the women folks of his household.

Detained by various matters, it was not until quite late in the afternoon, that the minister found time to try the experiment of riding the now unbewitched animal. It was getting too near night to ride very far, but he could at least try a short ride of a mile or so; which perhaps would be better for the first attempt than a longer one. So he came out to the horse-block, attended by his wife and Abigail Williams, and a couple of parishioners who had been holding a consultation with him, but had stopped a moment to see him ride off upon the animal of which so many marvelous stories had been told.

"Yes," said the minister, as he came out to the horse-block, in answer to a remark made by one of his visitors, "I think I have been able with the Lord's help, to redeem this animal and make her a useful member of society. You will observe that she now manifests none of that viciousness for which formerly she was so noted."

The mare did stand as composedly and peacefully as the most dignified minister could desire.

"You will remember that she has never been ridden by any one, man or woman, save her witch mistress Dulcibel—Jezebel, I think would be a more fitting name for her, considering her wicked doings."

Here Master Parris took the bridle rein from John Indian and threw his right leg over the animal. As the foot and leg came down on that side, and the stirrup gave her a smart crack, the mare's ears, which had been pricked up, went backwards and she began to prance around, John Indian still holding her by the mouth.

"Let her go, John," said the minister; "she does not like to be held," and he tightened the rein.

John, by his master's orders, had put on a curbbit; in place of the easy snaffle to which the mare had always been accustomed. And now as the minister tightened the rein, and the chain of the curb began to press upon and pain the mouth of the sensitive creature, she began to back and rear in a most excited fashion.

"Loose de rein!" cried John Indian.

The minister did so. But the animal now was fully alarmed; and no loosening or tightening would avail much. She was her old self again—as bewitched as ever. She reared, she plunged, she kicked, she sidled, and went through all the motions, which, on previous occasions, she had always found eventually successful in ridding her back of its undesired burden.

"Oh, do get off of the wild beast," cried Mistress Parris, in great alarm.

"She is still bewitched," cried Abigail Williams. "I see a spectre now, tormenting her with a pitchfork."

"Oh, Samuel, you will be killed!—do get off that crazy beast!" again cried weeping Mistress Parris.

"'Get off!' yes!" thought the minister; "but how am I going to do it, with the beast plunging and tearing in this fashion?" The animal evidently wanted him off, and he was very anxious to get off; but she would not hold still long enough for him to dismount peaceably.

"Hold her while I dismount!" he cried to John Indian. But when John Indian came near to take hold of the rein by her mouth, the mare snapped at him viciously with her teeth; and then wheeled around and flung out her heels at his head, in the most embarrassing manner.

Finally, as with a new idea, the mare started down the lane at a quick gallop, turned to the left, where a rivulet had been damned up into a little pond not more than two feet deep, and plunged into the water, splashing it up around her like a many jetted fountain.

By this time, the minister, being only human, naturally was very angry; and commenced lashing her sides with his riding whip to get her into the lane again. This made the fiery little creature perfectly desperate, and she reared up and backwards, until she came down plump into the water; so that, if the saddle girth had not broken, and the saddle come off, and the minister with it, she might have tumbled upon him and perhaps seriously hurt him. But, as it was, no great damage was done; and the bridle also breaking, the mare spit the bit out of her mouth, and went down the lane in a run to the road, and thence on into the now fast-gathering night, no one could see whither.

Mistress Parris, John Indian and the rest were by this time at the side of the pond, and ready to receive the chapfallen minister as he emerged with the saddle and the broken bridle from the water.

"You are a sight, Samuel Parris!" said his wife, in that pleasant tone with which many wives are apt to receive their liege lords upon such unpleasant occasions. "Do get into the house at once. You will catch your death of cold, I know. And such a mess your clothes will be! But I only wonder you are not killed—trying to ride a mad witch's horse like that is."

The minister made no reply. The situation transcended words. And did not allow even of sympathy, as his visitors evidently thought— not at least until he got on some clean and dry clothes. So they simply shook their heads, and took their course homewards. While the bedraggled and dripping Master Parris made his way to the house wiping the water and mud from his face with his wife's handkerchief, and stopping to shake himself well, before he entered the door, lest, as his wife said, "he should spoil everything in his chamber."

Abigail Williams, when she went to see Mistress Ann Putnam that night, had a marvelous tale to tell; which in the course of the next day, went like wildfire through the village, growing still more and more marvelous as it went.

Abigail had seen, as I have already said, the spectre of a witch goading the furious animal with a pitchfork. When the horse tore down the lane, it came to the little brook and of course could not cross it—for a witch cannot cross running water. Therefore, in its new access of fury, it sprang into the pond—and threw off the minister. Abigail further declared that then, dashing down the lane it came to the gate which shut it off from the road, and took the gate in a flying leap. But the animal never came down again. It was getting quite dark then, but she could still plainly see that a witch was upon its back, belaboring it with a broomstick. And she knew very well who that witch was. It was the "spectre" of Dulcibel Burton—for it had a scarlet bodice on, just such as Dulcibel nearly always wore. They two—the mare and its rider—went off sailing up into the sky, and disappeared behind a black cloud. And Abigail was almost certain that just as they reached the cloud, there was a low rumbling like thunder.

It was noticeable that every time Abigail told this story, she remembered something that she had not before thought of; until in the course of a week or two, there were very few stories in the "Arabian Nights" that could surpass it in marvelousness.

As the mare had not returned to her old stable at Goodman Buckley's, and could not be heard of in any other direction, Abigail's story began to commend itself even to the older and cooler heads of the village. For if the elfish creature had not vanished in the black cloud, to the sound of thunder, where was she?

Joseph Putnam, and his household however held a different view of the subject, but they wisely kept their own counsel; though they had many a sly joke among themselves at the credulity of their neighbors. They knew that a little while after dark, a strange noise had been heard at the barn, and that one of the hired men going out, had found Dulcibel's horse, without saddle or bridle, pawing at the door of the stable for admission. As this was a place the animal had been in the habit of coming to, and where she was always well treated and even petted, it was very natural that she should fly here from her persecutors, as she doubtless considered them.

Upon being told of it, and not knowing what had occurred Master Joseph thought it most prudent not to put the animal into his stable, but ordered the man to get half-a-peck of oats, and some hay, and take the mare to a small cow-pen, in the woods in an out of the way place, where she might be for years, and no one outside his own people be any the wiser for it. The mare seemed quite docile, and was easily led, being in company with the oats, of which a handful occasionally was given to her; and so, being watered at a stream near by and fed daily, she was no doubt far more comfortable than she would have been in the black cloud that Abigail Williams was perfectly ready to swear she had seen her enter and where though there might be plenty of water, oats doubtless were not often meet with.

CHAPTER XXIII.

Master Raymond Also Complains of an "Evil Hand."

Master Raymond had everything now prepared upon his part, and was awaiting a message from Captain Alden, to the effect that he had made a positive engagement with the Danish captain.

He had caught a serious cold on his return from Boston and, turning the matter over in his mind—for it is a wise thing to try to get some good result out of even apparently evil occurrences—he had called in the village doctor.

But the good Doctor's medicine did not seem to work as it ought to—for one reason, Master Raymond regularly emptied the doses out of the window; thinking as he told Master Joseph, to put them where they would do the most good. And when the Doctor came, and found that neither purging nor vomiting had been produced, these with bleeding and sweating being the great panaceas of that day—as perhaps of this—he was naturally astonished. In a case where neither castor oil, senna and manna, nor large doses of Glauber's salts would work, a medical man was certainly justified in thinking that something must be wrong.

Master Raymond suggested whether "an evil hand" might not be upon him. This was the common explanation at that time in Salem and its neighborhood. The doctors and the druggists nowadays miss a great deal in not having such an excuse made ready to their hands—it would account alike for adulterated drugs and ill-judged remedies.

Master Raymond had the reputation of being rich, and the Doctor had been mortified by the bad behavior of his medicines—for if a patient be not cured, if he is at least vigorously handled, there seems to be something that can with propriety be heavily charged for. But if a doctor does nothing—neither cures, nor anything else—with what face can he bring in a weighty bill?

And so good Doctor Griggs readily acquiesced in his patient's supposition that "an evil hand," was at work, and even suggested that he should bring Abigail Williams or some other "afflicted" girl with him the next time he came, to see with her sharpened eyes who it was that was bewitching him.

But Master Raymond declined the offer—at least for the present. If the thing continued, and grew worse, he might be able himself to see who it was. Why should he not be as able to do it as Abigail Williams, or any other of the "afflicted" circle? Of course the doctor was not able to answer why; there seemed to be no good reason why one set of "afflicted" people should have a monopoly of the accusing business.

Of course this came very quickly from the Doctor to Mistress Ann Putnam—for he was a regular attendant of that lady, whose nervous system indeed was in a fearful state by this time. And she puzzled a good deal over it. Did Master Raymond intend to accuse anyone? Who was it? Or was it merely a hint thrown out, that it was a game that two parties could play at?

But then she smiled—she had the two ministers, and through them all the other ministers of the colony—the magistrates and judges—and the advantages of the original position. Imitators always failed. Still she rather liked the young man's craft and boldness—Joseph Putnam would never have thought of such a thing. But still let him beware how he attempted to thwart her plans. He would soon find that she was the stronger.

Joseph Putnam then began to answer inquiries as to the health of his guest,—that he was not much better, and thought somewhat of going up to Boston for further medical advice—as the medicines given him so far did not seem to work as well as they should do.

"Could he bear the ride?"

"Oh, very well indeed—his illness had not so far affected his strength much."

CHAPTER XXIV.

Master Raymond's Little Plan Blocked.

"Our game is blocked!" said Joseph Putnam to Master Raymond as he rode up one afternoon soon after, and dismounted at the garden gate, where his guest was awaiting him, impatient to hear if anything had yet come from Captain Alden.

"What do you mean?" said his guest.

"Mean? Why, that yon she-wolf is too much for us. Captain Alden is arrested!"

"What! Captain John Alden!"

"Yes, Captain John Alden!"

"On what charge?"

Master Joseph smiled grimly, "For witchcraft!"

"Nonsense!"

"Yes, devilish nonsense! but true as gospel, nevertheless."

"And he submits to it?"

"With all around him crazy, he cannot help it. Besides, as an officer of the government, he must submit to the laws."

"On whose complaint?"

"Oh, the she-wolf's of course—that delectable smooth-spoken wife of my brother Thomas. How any man can love a catty creature like that, beats me out."

"I suppose she found out that I went frequently to see the Captain, when in Boston?"

"I suppose so."

"Who could have informed her?"

"Her master, the devil, I suppose."

"Where is the Captain to be examined?"

"Oh, here in Salem, where his accusers are. It comes off tomorrow. They lose no time you see."

"Well, I would not have believed it possible. Whom will they attack next?"

"The Governor, I suppose," replied Master Joseph satirically.

"Or you?"

"If she does, I'll run my sword through her—not as being a woman, but as a foul fiend. I told her so. Let her dare to touch me, or any one under this roof!"

"What did she say when you threatened her?"

"She put on an injured expression; and said she could never believe anything wrong of her dear husband's family, if all the 'spectres' in the world told her so."

"Well, I hope you are safe, but as for me—"

"Oh, you are, too. You are within my gates. To touch you, is to touch me. She fully realizes that. Besides brother Thomas is her abject tool in most things; but some things even he would not allow."

Yes, Captain John Alden, son of that John Alden who was told by the pretty Puritan maiden, "Speak for yourself John," when he went pleading the love-suit of his friend Captain Miles Standish; John Alden, captain of the only vessel of war belonging to the colony, a man of large property, and occupying a place in the very front rank of Boston society, had been arrested for witchcraft! What a state of insanity the religious delusion had reached, can be seen by this high-handed proceeding.

Here again we come on to ground in which the details given in the old manuscript book, are fully confirmed, in every essential particular by existing public records. Mr. Upham, whose admirable account of "Salem Witchcraft" has been of great aid to me in the preparation of this volume, is evidently puzzled to account for Captain Alden's arrest. He is not able to see how the gallant Captain could have excited the ire of the "afflicted circle." He seems to have been entirely ignorant of this case of Dulcibel Burton—hers doubtless being one of the many cases in which the official records were purposely destroyed. If he had known of this case, he would have seen the connection between it and Captain Alden. It also might have explained the continual allusions to the "yellow bird" in so many of the trials—based possibly on Dulcibel's canary, which had been given to her by the Captain, and whose habit of kissing her lips with its little bill had appeared so mysterious and diabolical to the superstitious inhabitants of Salem village.

Master Raymond's health, as is not to be wondered at, had improved sufficiently by the next day, to allow of his accompanying Joseph Putnam to the village, to attend Captain Alden's examination. The meeting-house was even more crowded than usual, such was the absorbing interest taken in the case, owing to the Captain's high standing in the province.

The veteran Captain's own brief account of this matter, which has come down to us, does not go into many details, and is valuable mainly as showing that he regarded it very much in the same light that it is regarded now—owing probably to the fact that while a church member in good standing, he doubtless was a good deal better seaman than church member. For he says he was "sent for by the Magistrates of Salem, upon the accusation of a company of poor distracted or possessed creatures or witches." And he speaks further of them as "wenches who played their juggling tricks, falling down, crying out, and staring in people's faces."

The worthy Captain's account is however, as I have said, very brief—and has the tone of one who had been a participant, however unwillingly, in a grossly shameful affair, alike disgraceful to the colony and to everybody concerned in it. For some additional details, I am indebted to the manuscript volume.

Captain Alden had not been arrested in Boston. He says himself in his statement, that "he was sent to Salem by Mr. Stoughton"—the Deputy Governor, and Chief-Justice of the Special Court that had condemned and executed Bridget Bishop, and which was now about to meet again.

Before the meeting of the magistrates, Master Raymond had managed to have a few words with him in private, and found that no arrangements with any skipper had yet been made. The first negotiations had fallen through, and there was no other foreign vessel at that time in port whose master possessed what Captain Alden considered the requisite trustworthiness and daring. For he wanted a skipper that would show fight if he was pursued and overtaken; not that any actual fighting would probably be necessary, for a simple show of resistance would doubtless be all that was needed.

"When I get back to Boston, I think I shall be able to arrange matters in the course of a week or two."

"What—in Boston jail?" queried Master Raymond.

"You do not suppose the magistrates will commit me on such a trumped-up nonsensical charge as this?" said the stout old captain indignantly.

"Indeed I do," was the reply.

"Why, there is not a particle of truth in it. I never saw these girls. I never even heard of their being in existence."

"Oh, that makes no difference."

"The devil it doesn't!" said the old man, hotly. My readers must remember that he was a seaman.

Here the sheriff came up and told the Captain he was wanted.

CHAPTER XXV.

Captain Alden before the Magistrates.

There was an additional magistrate sitting on this occasion, Master Bartholomew Gedney—making three in all.

Mistress Ann Putnam, the she-wolf, as her young brother-in-law had called her, was not present among the accusers—leaving the part of the "afflicted" to be played by the other and younger members of the circle.

There was another Captain present, also a stranger, a Captain Hill; and he being also a tall man, perplexed some of the girls at first. One even pointed at him, until she was better informed in a whisper by a man who was holding her up. And then she cried out that it was "Alden! Alden!" who was afflicting her.

At length one of the magistrates ordering Captain Alden to stand upon a chair, there was no further trouble upon that point; and the usual demonstrations began. As the accused naturally looked upon the "afflicted" girls, they went off into spasms, shrieks and convulsions. This was nearly always the first proceeding, as it created a profound sympathy for them, and was almost sufficient of itself to condemn the accused.

"The tall man is pinching me!"

"Oh, he is choking me!"

"He is choking me! do hold his hands!"

"He stabs me with his sword—oh, take it away from him!"

Such were the exclamations that came from the writhing and convulsed girls.

"Turn away his head! and hold his hands!" cried Squire Hathorne. "Take away his sword!" said Squire Gedney while the old Captain grew red and wrathful at the babel around him, and at the indignities to which he was subject.

"Captain Alden, why do you torment these poor girls who never injured you?"

"Torment them!—you see I am not touching them. I do not even know them; I never saw them before in my life," growled the indignant old seaman.

"See! there is the little yellow bird kissing his lips!" cried Abigail Williams. "Now it is whispering into his ear. It is bringing him a message from the other witch Dulcibel Burton. See! see! there it goes back again to her—through the window!"

So well was this done, that probably half of the people present would have been willing to swear the next day, that they actually saw the yellow bird as she described it.

"Ask him if he did not give her the yellow bird," said Leah Herrick. "But probably he will lie about it."

"Did you not give the witch, Dulcibel Burton, a yellow bird, which is one of her familiars?" said Squire Hathorne sternly.

"I gave her a canary bird that I brought from the West Indies, if that is what you mean," replied the Captain. "But what harm was there in that?"

"I knew it! The yellow bird told me so, when it came to peck out my eyes," cried Mercy Lewis. "Oh! there it is again!" and she struck wildly into the air before her face. "Drive it away! Do drive it away, some one!"

Here a young man pulled out his rapier, and began thrusting at the invisible bird in a furious manner.

"Now it comes to me!" cried Sarah Churchill. And then the other girls also cried out, and began striking into the air before their faces, till there was anew a perfect babel of cries, shrieks and sympathizing voices.

Master Raymond, amid all his indignation at such barefaced and wicked and yet successful imposture, could hardly avoid smiling at the expression of the old seaman's face as he stood on the chair, and fronted all this tempest of absurd and villainous accusation. At first there had been a deep crimson glow of the hottest wrath upon the old man's cheeks and brow; but now he seemed to have been shocked into a kind of stupor, so unexpected and weighty were the charges against him, and made with such vindictive fierceness; and yet so utterly absurd, while at the same time, so impossible of being refuted.

"He bought the yellow bird from Tituba's mother—her spectre told me so!" cried Abigail Williams.

"What do you say to that, Master Alden?" said Squire Gedney. "That is a serious charge."

"I never saw any Tituba or her mother," exclaimed the Captain, again growing indignant.

"Who then did you buy the witch's familiar of?" asked Squire Hathorne.

"I do not know—some old negro wench!"

Here the magistrates looked at each other sagely, and nodded their wooden heads. It was a fatal admission. "You had better confess all, and give glory to God!" said Squire Gedney solemnly.

"I trust I shall always be ready to give glory to God," answered the old man stoutly; "but I do not see that it would glorify Him to confess to a pack of lies. You have known me for many years, Master Gedney, but did you ever know me to speak an untruth, or seek to injure any innocent persons, much less women and children?"

Squire Gedney said that he had known the accused many years, and had even been at sea with him, and had always supposed him to be an honest man; but now he saw good cause to alter that judgment.

"Turn and look now again upon those afflicted persons," concluded Squire Gedney.

As the accused turned and again looked upon them, all of the "afflicted" fell down on the floor as if he had struck them a heavy blow—moaning and crying out against him.

"I judge you by your works; and believe you now to be a wicked man and a witch," said Squire Gedney in a very severe tone.

Captain Alden turned then and looked directly at the magistrate for several moments. "Why does not my look knock you down too?" he said indignantly. "If it hurts them so much, would it not hurt you a little?"

"He wills it not to hurt you," cried Leah Herrick. "He is looking at you, but his spectre has its back towards you."

There was quite a roar of applause through the crowded house at such an exposure of the old Captain's trickery. He was very cunning to be sure; but the "afflicted" girls could see through his knavery.

"Make him touch the poor girls," said the Reverend Master Noyes. For it was the accepted theory that by doing this, the witch, in spite of himself, reabsorbed into his own body the devilish energy that had gone out of him, and the afflicted were healed. This was repeatedly done through the progress of these examinations and the after trials; and was always found to be successful, both as a cure of the sufferers, and an undeniable proof that the person accused was really a witch.

In this case the "afflicted" girls were brought up to Captain Alden, one after the other and upon his being made to touch them with his hand, they invariably drew a deep breath of relief, and said they felt entirely well again.

"You see Captain Alden," said Squire Gedney solemnly, "none of the tests fail in your case. If there were only one proof, we might doubt; but as the Scripture says, by the mouths of two or three witnesses shall the truth be established. If you were innocent a just God would not allow you to be overcome in this manner."

"I know that there is a just God, and I know that I am entirely innocent" replied the noble old seaman in a firm voice. "But it is not for an uninspired man like me, to attempt to reconcile the mysteries of His providence. Far better men than I am, even prophets and apostles, have been brought before magistrates and judges, and their good names lied away, and they condemned to the prison and the scaffold and the cross. Why then, should I expect to fare better than they did? All I can do, like Job of old, is to maintain my integrity—even though Satan and all his imps be let loose for a time against me."

Here the Reverend Master Noyes rose excitedly, and said that the decisions of heathen courts and judges were one thing; and the decisions of godly magistrates, who were all members of the church of the true God, and therefore inspired by his spirit, was a very different thing. He said it was simply but another proof of the guilt of the accused, that he should compare himself with the apostles and the martyrs; and these worshipful Christian magistrates with heathen magistrates and judges. Hearing him talk in this ribald way, he could no longer doubt the accusation brought against him; for there was no surer proof of a man or woman having dealings with Satan, than to defame and calumniate God's chosen people.

As Mr. Noyes took his seat, the magistrates said they had heard sufficient, and ordered the committal of the accused to Boston prison to await trial.

"I will give bail for Captain Alden's appearance, to the whole amount of my estate," said Joseph Putnam coming forward. "A man of his age, who has served the colony in so many important positions, should be treated with some leniency."

"We are very sorry for the Captain," answered Squire Gedney, "but as this is a capital offence, no bail can be taken."

"Thank you, Master Putnam, but I want no bail," said the old seaman proudly. "If the colony of Massachusetts Bay, which my father helped to build up, and for which I have labored so long and faithfully, chooses to requite my services in this ungrateful fashion, let it be so. The shame is on Massachusetts not on me!"

CHAPTER XXVI.

Considering New Plans.

"Well, what now?" said Master Joseph Putnam to his guest, as they rode homeward. "You might give up the sea-route and try a push through the wilderness to the Hudson River."

"Rather dangerous that."

"Yes, unless you could secure the services of some heathen savages to pilot you through."

"Could we trust them?"

"Twenty years ago, according to my father's old stories, we could; but they are very bitter now—they do not keep much faith with white men.

"Perhaps the white men have not kept much faith with them."

"Of course not. You know they are the heathen; and we have a Bible communion to exterminate them, and drive them out of our promised land."

"Do you believe that?"

"Well, not exactly," and Master Joseph laughed. "Besides, I think the Quaker plan both cheaper in the end and a great deal safer. Not that I believe they have any more right to the land than we have."

"Penn and the Quakers think differently."

"I know they do—but they are a set of crazy enthusiasts."

"What is your view? That of your ministers? The earth is the Lord's. He has given it to His saints. We are the saints."

Master Joseph laughed again. "Well, something like that. The earth is the Lord's. He has intended it for the use of His children. We are His children quite as much as the savages. Therefore we have as much right to it as they have."

"Only they happen to be in possession," replied Master Raymond, drily.

"Are they in possession? So far as they are actually in possession, I admit their right. But do you seriously mean that a few hundred or thousand of wild heathen, have a right to prior occupancy to the whole North American continent? It seems to me absurd?"

"A relative of mine has ten square miles in Scotland that he never occupies, in your sense of the word any more than your red-men do; and yet he is held to have a valid right to it, against the hundreds of peasants who would like to enter in and take possession."

"Oh, plenty of things are done wrong in the old world," replied Master Putnam; "that is why we Puritans are over here. But still the fact remains that the earth is the Lord's and that He intended it for His children's use; and no merely legal or personal right can be above that. If ever the time comes that your relative's land is really needed by the people at large, why then some way will have to be contrived to get hold of it for them."

"The Putnam family have a good many broad acres too," said Master Raymond, with a smile, looking around him.

"Oh, you cannot scare me," replied his friend, also smiling. "What is sauce for the Campbell goose is sauce for the Putnam gander. If the time ever comes when the public good requires that the broad lands of the Putnams—if there be any Putnams at that time—have to be appropriated to meet the wants of their fellow men, then the broad Putnam lands will have to go like the rest, I imagine. We have taken them from the Indians, just as the Normans took them from the Saxons—and as the Saxons took them from the Danes and the ancient inhabitants—by the strong hand. But the sword can give no right—save as the claim of the public good is behind it. Show me that the public good requires it, and I am willing that the title-deeds for my own share of the broad Putnam lands shall be burnt up tomorrow."

"I believe you, my dear friend," said Master Raymond, gazing with admiration upon the manly, glowing face of this nature's nobleman. "And I am inclined to think that your whole view of the matter is correct. But, coming back to our first point, do you know of any savage that we could trust to guide us safely to the settlements on the Hudson?"

"If old king Philip, whose head has been savagely exposed to all weathers on the gibbet at Plymouth for the last sixteen years, were alive, something perhaps might be done. His safeguard would have carried you through."

"Is there not another chief, called Nucas?"

"Oh, old Nucas, of the Mohegans. He was a character! But he died ten years ago. Lassacus, too, was killed. There are a couple of Pequod settlements down near New Haven I believe; but they are too far off."

"And then you could not tell me where to put my hand on some dozen or so of the Indians, whom I might engage as a convoy."

"Not now. A roving party may pass in the woods at any time. But they would not be very reliable. If they could make more by selling your scalps than by keeping them safely on your heads, they would be pretty sure to sell them."

"Then I see nothing to do, but to go again to Boston, and arrange another scheme on the old plan."

"You ought not to travel long in Dulcibel's company without being married," said Master Putnam bluntly.

"Very true—but we can not well be married without giving our names to the minister; and to do that, would be to deliver ourselves up to the authorities."

"Mistress Putnam and myself might accompany you to New York— we should not mind a little trip."

"And thus make yourselves parties to Dulcibel's escape? No, no, my good friend—that would be to put you both in prison in her place."

"It is not likely there would be any other woman on board the vessel—that is of any reputation. You must try to get some one to go with you."

"And incur the certainty of punishment when she returns?"

"Perhaps you could find some one who would like to settle permanently in New York. I should like to go myself if I could, and get out of this den of wild beasts."

"Yes, I may be able to do that—though I shall not dare to try that until the last day almost—for the women always have some man to consult, and thus our secret plan would get blown about, to our great peril."

"I have a scheme!" cried Master Joseph in exultation. "It is the very thing," and he burst out laughing. "Kidnap Cotton Mather, or one of the other Boston ministers, and take him with you."

"That would be a bold stroke," replied Master Raymond, also laughing heartily. "But, like belling the cat, it is easier said than done. Ministers are apt to be cautious and wary. They are timid folk."

"Not when a wedding is to be solemnized, and a purse of gold-pieces is shaken before them," returned Master Putnam. "Have everything ready to sail. Then decoy the minister on board, to marry a wealthy foreign gentleman, a friend of the skipper's—and do not let him go again. Pay him enough and the skipper will think it a first rate joke."

"But he might be so angry that he would refuse to marry us after all our trouble."

"Oh, do not you believe that—if you make the fee large enough. Treat him kindly, represent to him the absolute necessity of the case, say that you never would have thought of such a thing if it could in any way have been avoided, and I'll warrant he will do the job before you reach New York."

"I wish I felt as certain as you do."

"Well, suppose he will not be mollified. What then? Your end is attained. He has acted as chaperon, and involuntary master of propriety whether he would or not. A minister is just as good as a matron to chaperon the maiden. Of course he will have his action for damages against you, and you will be willing to pay him fairly, but if he brings you before a jury of New Yorkers, and you simply relate the facts, and the necessity of the case, little will he get of damages beyond a plentiful supply of jokes and laughter. You know there is very little love lost between the people of the two colonies; and that the Manhattan people have no more respect for all the witchcraft business, than you and I have."

Master Raymond made no reply. He did not want to kidnap a minister, if it could be in any way avoided. With Master Putnam, however, that seemed to be one of the most desirable features of the proposed plan, only he was tenfold more sorry now than ever, that such weighty prudential reasons prevented his taking any active share in the enterprise. To kidnap a minister—especially if it could be the Reverend Cotton Mather—seemed to him something which was worth almost the risking of his liberty and property in which to take a hand.

CHAPTER XXVII.

The Dissimulation of Master Raymond.

About this time the gossips of Salem village began to remark upon the attentions that were being paid by the wealthy young Englishman, Master Ellis Raymond, to various members of the "afflicted circle." He petted those bright and terribly precocious children of twelve, Ann Putnam and Abigail Williams; he almost courted the older girls, Mary Walcot, Mercy Lewis and Leah Herrick and had a kindly word for Mary Warren, Sarah Churchill and others, whenever he saw them. As for Mistress Ann Putnam, the mother, he always had been very respectful to her. While in Boston he had purchased quite an assortment of those little articles which the Puritan elders usually denominated "gew-gaws" and "vain adornments" and it was observed that Abigail Williams especially had been given a number of these, while the other girls had one or more of them, which they were very careful in not displaying except at those times when no grave elder or deacon was present to be shocked by them.

I will acknowledge that there was some dissimulation in this conduct of Master Raymond's, and Joseph Putnam by no means approved of it.

"How you can go smiling around that den of big and little she-wolves, patting the head of one, and playing with the paw of another, I cannot understand, friend Raymond. I would not do it to save my life."

"Nor I," answered Master Raymond gravely. "But I would do it to save your life, friend Joseph, or that of your sweet young wife there—or that of the baby which she holds upon her knee."

"Or that of Mistress Dulcibel Burton!" added sweet Mistress Putnam kindly.

"Yes, or that of Dulcibel Burton."

"You know, my dear friends, the plan I have in view may fail. If that should fail, I am laying the foundation of another—so that if Dulcibel should be brought to trial, the witnesses that are relied upon may fail to testify so wantonly against her. Even little Abigail Williams has the assurance and ingenuity to save her, if she will."

"Yes, that precocious child is a very imp of Satan," said Joseph Putnam. "What a terrible woman she will make."

"Oh, no, she may sink down into a very tame and commonplace woman, after this tremendous excitement is over," rejoined his friend. "I think at times I see symptoms of it now. The strain is too great for her childish brain."

"Well, I suppose your dissimulation is allowable if it is to save the life of your betrothed," said Master Putnam, "but I would not do it if I could and I could not if I would."

"Do you remember Junius Brutus playing idiot—and King David playing imbecile?"

"Oh, I know you have plenty of authority for your dissimulation."

"It seems to me," joined in young Mistress Putnam, "that the difference between you is simply this. Joseph could not conscientiously do it; and you can."

"Yes, that is about the gist of it," said her young husband. "And now that I have relieved my conscience by protesting against your course, I am satisfied you should go on in your own way just the same."

"And yet you feel no conscientious scruples against abducting the minister," rejoined Raymond laughing; "a thing which I am rather loath to do."

"I see," replied Joseph, also laughing. "I scruple at taking mustard, and you at cayenne pepper. It is a matter of mental organization probably."

"Yes—and if a few or many doses of mustard will prevent my being arrested as a witch, which would put it entirely out of my power to aid Dulcibel in her affliction—and perhaps turn some of the "afflicted" girls over to her side, in case she has to stand a trial for her life—I shall certainly swallow them with as much grace as if they were so many spoonfuls of honey. There is a time to be over-scrupulous, friend Joseph, but not when my beloved one is in the cage of the tigers. Yes, I shall not hesitate to meet craft with craft."

And Mistress Putnam, sweet, good woman as she was, nodded her head, woman-like, approvingly, carried away perhaps by the young man's earnestness, and by the strength of his love.

CHAPTER XXVIII.

The Cruel Doings of the Special Court.

Meanwhile the Special Court of seven Judges—a majority of whom were from Boston, with the Deputy Governor of the Colony, William Stoughten, as Chief-Justice—was by no means indolent. Of the proceedings of this court, which embodied apparently the best legal intellect of the colony, no official record is in existence. Its shameful pages, smeared all over with bigotry and blood, no doubt were purposely destroyed. So far as we are acquainted with the evidence given before it, it was substantially the same as had been given at the previous examinations before the committing magistrates.

That nothing was too extravagant and absurd to be received as evidence by this learned court, is proven by the statement of the Reverend Cotton Mather, already alluded to, relative to a demon entering the meeting-house and tearing down a part of it, in obedience to a look from Mistress Bridget Bishop—of which diabolical outrage the Court was duly informed. Besides, there could have been no other kind of evidence forthcoming, that would apply to the crime of which all the accused were charged, Witchcraft. Many of the prisoners indeed were accused of murdering children and others, whose illness had been beyond the physician's power to cure; but the murders were all committed, it was alleged, by the use of "spectres," "familiars," "puppets," and other supernatural means. Against such accusations it was impossible for men and women of the highest character and reputation to make any effectual defence, before a court and jury given over so completely to religious fanaticism and superstitious fancies. To be accused was therefore to be condemned.

Yes, this Special Court, having had all its misgivings, if it ever really had any, quieted by the answer of the council of ministers, was doing quick and fearful work.

Meeting again in the latter part of June, it speedily tried, convicted and sentenced to death five persons:—Sarah Good, Sarah Wildes, Elizabeth How, Susanna Martin and Rebecca Nurse.

Then, adjourning till August 5th, it tried and convicted George Burroughs, John Procter, Elizabeth Procter, George Jacobs, John Willard and Martha Carrier.

Then meeting on September 9th, it tried and condemned Martha Corey, Mary Easty, Alice Parker and Ann Pudeator; and on September 17th, Margaret Scott, Wilmot Reed, Samuel Wardwell and Mary Parker.

It will be noticed that of the above nineteen persons, only five were men. As the greater number of the accusers were also of the female sex, it was natural, I suppose, that this should be so. And thus we find that the word witch is applied indifferently in the old records, to men and women; the masculine term wizard being seldom used.

That the learned Judges were fully as superstitious as the people at large, is conclusively proved by certain facts that have come down to us. In the case of that lovely and venerable matron, Rebecca Nurse, the jury at first brought in the verdict "Not guilty."

But immediately all the accusers in the Court, and all the "afflicted" out of it, made a hideous outcry. Two of the Judges said they were not satisfied. The Chief-Justice intimated that there was one admission of the prisoner that the jury had not properly considered. These things induced the jurors to go out again, and come back with a verdict of "Guilty."

One of the charges against Rebecca Nurse, testified to by Edward Putnam, was that, after the said Rebecca Nurse had been committed to jail, and was thus several miles distant in the town of Salem, "she, the said Nurse, struck Mistress Ann Putnam with her spectral chain, leaving a mark, being a kind of round ring, and three streaks across the ring. She had six blows with a chain in the space of half-an-hour; and she had one remarkable one, with six streaks across her arm. Ann Putnam, Jr., also was bitten by the spectre of the said Rebecca

Nurse about two o'clock of the day. I, Edward Putnam, saw the marks, both of bite and chains."

It was a great hardship in all these trials, that the prisoners were not allowed any counsel; while on the other hand, the members of the Court seemed to take it for granted from the first, that they were guilty. The only favor allowed them was the right of objecting to a certain extent to those jurors whose fairness they mistrusted.

One of the accused, a reputable and aged farmer named Giles Corey, refused to plead. His wife, Martha Corey, was among the convicted. At her examination, some time previous, he had allowed himself to testify in certain respects against her; involved as he was for a time in the prevailing delusion. But he was a man of strong mind and character; and though not entirely able to throw off the chains which superstition had woven around him, he repented very sorely the part he had taken against his wife. This was enough to procure his own accusation. The "afflicted girls" brought their usual complaints that his spectre tormented them. They fell down and shrieked so wildly at his examination, that Squire Hathorne asked him with great indignation, "Is it not enough that you should afflict these girls at other times without doing it now in our presence?"

The honest and sturdy man was visibly affected. He knew he was not consciously doing anything; but what could it all mean? If he turned his head, the girls said he was hurting them and turned their heads the same way. The Court ordered his hands tied—and then the girls said they were easier. But he drew in his cheeks, after a habit he had, and the cheeks of the girls were sucked in also, giving them great pain. The old man was fairly dumfounded. When however one of the girls testified that Goodman Corey had told her that he saw the devil in the shape of a black hog in the cow-house, and was very much frightened by it, the spirited old man said that he never was frightened by man or devil in his life.

But he had a fair property, and two sons-in-law to whom he wished to leave it. He knew well that if he were tried he would be convicted, and that would carry with it the confiscation of his property. So, as other noble-hearted men had done in that and the previous age, he refused when brought before the Special Court, to plead either "guilty" or "not guilty." In these later times the presiding Judge would simply order a plea of "not guilty" to be entered, and the trial would proceed. But then it was otherwise—the accused himself must plead, or the trial could not go on. Therefore he must be made to plead—by placing heavy weights upon his breast, and adding to them until the accused either agreed to plead, or died under the torture. In which last case, the prisoner lost his life as contumacious; but gained his point of preserving his estate, and title of nobility if he had any, to his family.

So, manly old Giles Corey, remorseful for the fate he had helped to bring upon his wife, and determined that his children should inherit the property he had acquired, maintained a determined silence when brought before the Special Court. Being warned, again and again, he simply smiled. He could bear all that they in their cruel mockery of justice could inflict upon him.

Joseph Putnam and Master Raymond rode down to Salem that day—to the orchard where the brave old man was led out of jail to meet his doom. They saw him, tied hand and foot, and heavy flat stones and iron weights laid one by one upon him.

"More! More!" pleaded the old man at last. "I shall never yield. But, if ye be men, make the time short!"

"I cannot stand this," said Master Raymond.

"We are powerless to help him—let us go."

"To torture an old man of eighty years in this way! What a sight for this new world!" exclaimed Master Putnam, as they turned their horses' heads and rode off.

His executioners took Giles Corey at his word. They knew the old man would never yield. So they mercifully heaped the heavy weights upon him until they had crushed out his life.

CHAPTER XXIX.

Dulcibel's Life in Prison.

Dulcibel's life in prison was of course a very monotonous one. She did not suffer however as did many other women of equally gentle nature. In the jails of Ipswich, Boston and Cambridge, there were keepers who conformed in most cases strictly to the law. In many instances delicate and weakly women, often of advanced years, were chained, hands and feet, with heavy irons, night and day.

But Robert Foster and his son, who assisted him as under-keeper, while indulging before the marshal and the constables in the utmost violence and severity of language, and who were supposed to be strict enforcers of all the instructions received from the magistrates, were as we have seen, at heart, very liberal and kind-hearted men. And the only fear the prisoners had, was that they would throw up their positions some day in disgust. Uncle Robie often declared to Dulcibel that he would, when she was once fairly out of the clutches of her enemies.

Every now and then instructions would come to jailer Foster from one of the magistrates—generally Squire Hathorne—to put heavier irons on some one of the prisoners, whose spectre was still tormenting the "afflicted girls." It being generally held that the more heavily you chained a witch, the less able she was to afflict her victims. And at these times Master Foster would get out his heaviest irons, parade them before the eyes of the constables, declare in a fierce tone what he was about to do, get the constable off on one pretext or another—and do nothing.

It was thought best and wisest for neither Master Joseph Putnam nor Master Raymond to seek many interviews with Dulcibel; the means of intercourse between the two lovers being restricted to little notes, which goodwife Buckley, who frequently visited the maiden, transmitted from one to the other through the agency of either her husband or of Joseph Putnam. This kept them both in heart; and Dulcibel being sustained by the frequent assurances of her lover's devotion, and by the hope of escape, kept the roses of her cheeks in marvelous bloom during her close confinement.

One of the constables, who managed to get sight of her one day through the half-opened door of her cell, expressed surprise to the jailer that she should still look so blooming, considering the weight of the heavy chains to which she was continually subjected.

"And why should not the young witch look so?" replied the jailer. "Is not her spectre riding around on that devil's mare half the night, and having a good time of it?"

The constable assented to this view of the case; and his suspicions, if he had any, were quieted. In fact even Squire Hathorne himself probably would have been perfectly satisfied with an explanation of so undeniable a character.

Of course it was not considered prudent by Uncle Robie, that the furniture or general appearance of Dulcibel's cell should be changed in the least for the better. Not even a bunch of flowers that Goodwife Buckley once brought to Dulcibel, could be allowed to remain there. While in a corner of the cell, lay the heavy chains which, if the marshal or one of the magistrates, should insist upon seeing the prisoner, could be slipped on her wrists and ankles in a few minutes. Fortunately, however, for Dulcibel, the interest of all these was now centered upon the trials that were in progress, the contumacious obstinacy of Giles Corey, the host of new accusations at Ipswich and other neighboring places, and the preparations for the execution of those already condemned to death.

If they had a passing thought of the young witch Dulcibel Burton, it was that her time would come rapidly around in its turn, when speedy justice no doubt would be done to her.

As to Antipas, her faithful servitor, he had relapsed again into his old staidness and sobriety in the comparative quietude of the prison. Only on the day of Giles Corey's execution had the prevailing excitement attending that event, and which naturally affected the constables and jailers, made him raging. To pass the constable's inspection, as well as for his own safety, the jailer had chained him;

but his voice could be heard ringing through the closed door of his cell at intervals from morning till evening.

The burden of his thoughts seemed to be a blending of denunciation and exultation. The predictions of the four Quakers executed many years before on Boston common, and those of men and women who had been whipped at the cart's tail through the towns of the colony, evidently seemed to him in progress of fulfillment: —

"They have torn the righteous to pieces; now the judgment is upon them, and they are tearing each other! Woe to the bloody towns of Boston and Salem and Ipswich! Satan is let loose by the Lord upon them! They have slain the saints, they have supped full of innocent blood; now the blood of their own sons, their own daughters, is filling the cup of God's vengeance! They have tortured the innocent women, the innocent children—and banished them and sold them to the Philistines as slaves. But the Lord will avenge His own elect! They are given up to believe a lie! The persecutors are persecuting each other! They are pressing each other to death beneath heavy stones! They are hanging each other on the gallows of Haman! Where they hung the innocent, they are hanging themselves! Oh, God! avenge now the blood of thy Saints! As they have done, let it be done unto them! Whip and kill! Whip and kill! Ha! ha! ha!"—and with a blood-curdling laugh that rang through the narrow passages of the prison, the insane old man would fall down for a time on his bed exhausted.

That was an awful day, both outside and inside the prison—for all the prisoners knew what a savage death old Giles Corey was meeting. It seemed to Dulcibel afterwards, that if she had not been sustained by the power of love, and a hopeful looking forward to other scenes, she must have herself gone crazy during that and the other evil days that were upon them. To some of the prisoners, the most fragile and sensitive ones, even the hour of their execution seemed to come as a relief. Anything, to get outside of those close dark cells—and to make an end of it!

126

CHAPTER XXX.

Eight Legal Murders on Witch Hill.

A mile or so outside of the town of Salem, the ground rises into a rocky ledge, from the top of which, to the south and the east and the west, a vast expanse of land and sea is visible. You overlook the town; the two rivers, or branches of the sea, between which the town lies; the thickly wooded country, as it was then, to the south and west; and the wide, open sea to the eastward.

Such a magnificent prospect of widespread land and water is seldom seen away from the mountain regions; and, as one stands on the naked brow of the hill, on a clear summer day, as the sunset begins to dye the west, and gazes on the scene before and around him, he feels that the heavens are not so very far distant, and as if he could almost touch with these mortal hands the radiance and the glory.

The natural sublimity of this spot seems to have struck the Puritan fathers of Salem, and looking around on its capabilities, they appear to have come to the conclusion that of all places it was the one expressly designed by the loving Father of mankind for—a gallows!

"Yes, the very spot for a gallows!" said the first settlers. "The very spot!" echoed their descendants. "See, the wild "Heathen Salvages" can behold it from far and near; the free spoken, law-abiding sailors can descry it, far out at sea; and both know by this sign that they are approaching a land of Christian civilization and of godly law!"

I think if I were puzzled for an emblem to denote the harsher and more uncharitable side of the Puritan character, I should pick out this gallows on Witch Hill near Salem, as being a most befitting one.

This was the spot where, as we have already related, approaching it from the north, Master Raymond had his interview with jailer Foster. But that was night, and it was so dark that Master Raymond had no idea of its commanding so fine a view of both land and water. He had been in Boston during the execution of poor Bridget Bishop; and though he had often seen the gallows from below, and wondered at the grim taste which had reared it in such a conspicuous spot, he had never felt the least desire, but rather a natural aversion, to approach the place where such an unrighteous deed had been enacted.

But now the carpenters had been again at work and supplanted the old scaffolding by another and larger one. Now the uprights had been added too—and on the beam which they supported there was room for at least ten persons. This seemed to be enough space to Marshall Herrick and Squire Hathorne; though at the rate the arrests and convictions were going on, it might be that one-half of the people in the two Salems and in Ipswich, would be hung in the course of a year or so by the other half.

But for this special hanging, only eight ropes and nooses were prepared. The workmen had been employed the preceding afternoon; and now in the fresh morning light, everything was ready; and eight of those who had been condemned were to be executed.

The town, and village, and country around turned out, as was natural, in a mass, to see the terrible sight. And yet the crowd was comparatively a small one, the colony then being so thinly settled. But this, to Master Raymond's eyes, gave a new horror to the scene. If there had been a crowd like that when London brought together its thousands at Tyburn, it would have seemed less appalling. But here were a few people—not alienated from each other by ancestral differences in creed or politics, and who had never seen each other's faces before—but members of the same little band which had fled together from their old home, holding the same political views, the same religious faith; who had sat on the same benches at church, eaten at the same table of the Lord's supper, near neighbors on their farms, or in the town and village streets; now hunting each other down like wolves, and hanging each other up in cold blood! This it was that set apart the Salem persecution from all other persecutions of those old days against witches and heretics; and which has given it a painful pre-eminence in horror. It was neighbor hanging neighbor; and brother and sister persecuting to death with the foulest lies and juggling tricks their spiritual brothers and sisters. And the plea of "delusion" will not excuse it, except to those who have not investigated its studied cruelty and malice. Sheer, unadulterated wickedness had its full share in the persecution; and that wickedness can only be partly extenuated by the plea of possible insanity or of demoniacal possession.

Marched from jail for the last time

The route to the gallows hill was a rough and difficult one; but the condemned were marched from the jail for the last time, one by one, and compelled to walk attended by a small guard and a rude and jeering company. There was Rebecca Nurse, infirm but venerable and lovely, the beloved mother of a large family; there was the Reverend George Burroughs, a small dark man, whose great physical strength was enough, as the Reverend Increase Mather, then President of Harvard College, said, to prove he was a witch; but who did not believe in infant baptism, and probably was not up to the orthodox standard of the day in other respects, though in conduct a very correct and exemplary man; there was old John Procter, with his two staffs, and long thin white hair; there was John Willard, a good, innocent young man, lied to death by Susanna Sheldon, aged eighteen; there was unhappy Martha Carrier four of whose children, one a girl of eight, had been frightened into testifying before the Special Court against her; saying that their mother had taken them to a witch meeting, and that the Devil had promised her that she should be queen of hell; there was gentle, patient and saintlike Elizabeth How, with "Father, forgive them!" on her mild lips; and two others of whom we now know little, save that they were most falsely and wickedly accused.

There also were the circle of the "afflicted," gazing with hard dry eyes on the murder they had done and with jeers and scoffs on their thin and cruel lips.

There, too, were the reverend ministers, Master Parris of Salem village, and Master Noyes of Salem town, and Master Cotton Mather, who had come down from Boston in his black clothes, like a buzzard that scents death and blood a long way off, to lend his spiritual countenance to the terrible occasion.

Master Noyes, however, the most of the time, seemed rather quiet and subdued. He was thinking perhaps of Sarah Good's fierce prediction, when he urged her, as she came up to the gallows to confess, saying to her that, "she was a witch, and she knew it!" Outraged beyond all endurance at this last insult at such a moment, Sarah Good cried out: "It is a lie! I am no more a witch than you are. God will yet give you blood to drink for this day's cruel work!" Which prediction it is said in Salem, came true—Master Noyes dying of an internal hemorrhage bleeding profusely at the mouth.

It was not a scene that men of sound and kindly hearts would wish to witness; and yet Joseph Putnam and Ellis Raymond felt drawn to it by an irresistible sense of duty. Hard, indeed, it was for Master Raymond; for the necessity of the case compelled him to suppress all show of sympathy with the sufferer, in order that he might more effectually carry out his plans for Dulcibel's escape from the similar penalty that menaced her. And he, therefore, could not even ride around like Master Putnam, with a frowning face, uttering occasional emphatic expressions of his indignation and horror, that the crowd would probably not have endured from any one else.

There were some incidents that were especially noticeable. Samuel Wardwell had "confessed" in his fear, but subsequently taken back his false confession, and met his death. While he was speaking at the foot of the gallows declaring his innocence, the tobacco smoke from the pipe of the executioner, blew into his face and interrupted him.

Then one of the accusing girls laughed out, and said that "the Devil did hinder him," but Joseph Putnam cried, "If the Devil does hinder him, then it is good proof that he is not one of his." At which some few of the crowd applauded; while others said that Master Putnam himself was no better than he ought to be.

The Reverend Master Burroughs, when upon the ladder, addressing the crowd, asserted earnestly his entire innocence. Such was the effect of his words that Master Raymond even hoped that an effort would be made to rescue him. But one of the "afflicted girls" cried out, "See! there stands the black man in the air at his side."

Then another said, "The black man is telling him what to say."

But Master Burroughs answered: "Then I will repeat the Lord's prayer. Would the Devil tell me to say that?"

But when he had ended, Master Cotton Mather, who was riding around on his horse, said to the people that "the Devil often transformed himself into an angel of light; and that Master Burroughs was not a rightly ordained minister;" and the executioner at a sign from the official, cut the matter short by turning off the condemned man.

Rebecca Nurse and the other women, with the exception of their last short prayers, said nothing—submitting quietly and composedly to their legal murder. And before the close of one short hour eight lifeless bodies hung dangling beneath the summer sun.

Joseph Putnam and Master Raymond, and a few others upon whom the solemn words of the condemned had made an evident impression, turned away from the sad sight, and wiped their tearful eyes. But Master Parris and Master Noyes, and Master Cotton Mather seemed rather exultant than otherwise; though Master Noyes did say; "What a sad thing it is to see eight firebrands of hell hanging there!" But, as Master Cotton Mather more consistently answered: "Why should godly ministers be sad to see the firebrands of hell in the burning."

Then, as the hours went on, the bodies were cut down, and stuck into short and shallow graves, dug out with difficulty between the rocks—in some instances, the ground not covering them entirely. There some remained without further attention; but, in the case of others, whose relatives were still true to them, there came loving hands by night, and bore the remains away to find a secret sepulcher, where none could molest them.

But the gallows remained on the Hill, where it could be seen from a great distance; causing a thrill of wonder in the bosom of the wandering savage, as of the wandering sailor, gazing at its skeleton outline against the sunset sky from far out at sea—waiting for ten more victims!

CHAPTER XXXI.

A New Plan of Escape.

About this time a new plan of escape was suggested to Master Raymond; coming to him in a note from Dulcibel.

Master Philip English, one of the wealthiest inhabitants of Salem town, and his wife Mary, had been arrested—the latter a short time previous to her husband. He was a merchant managing a large business, owning fourteen houses in the town, a wharf, and twenty-one vessels. He had one of the best dwellings in Salem—situated at its eastern end, and having a fine outlook over the adjacent seas. He had probably offended some one in his business transactions; or, supposing that he was safely entrenched in his wealth and high social position, he might have expressed some decided opinions, relative to Mistress Ann Putnam and the "afflicted children."

As for his wife, she was a lady of exalted character who had been an only child and had inherited a large property from her father. The deputy-marshall, Manning, came to arrest her in the night time, during her husband's absence. She had retired to her bed; but he was admitted to her chamber, where he read the warrant for her apprehension. He allowed her till morning, however, placing guards around the house that she might not escape. Knowing that such an accusation generally meant conviction and death, "she arose calmly in the morning, attended the family prayers, spoke to a near relative of the best plan for the education of her children, kissed them with great composure, amid their agony of cries and tears, and then told the officer that she was ready to die."

On her examination the usual scene ensued, and the usual falsehoods were told. Perhaps the "afflicted girls" were a little more bitter than they would have been, had she not laughed outright at a portion of their testimony. She was a very nice person in her habits, and it was testified against her, that being out one day in the streets of Salem walking around on visits to her friends during a whole morning, notwithstanding the streets were exceedingly sloppy and muddy, it could not be perceived that her shoes and white stockings were soiled in the least. As we have said, at this singular proof of her being a witch, the intelligent lady had laughed outright. And this of course brought out the additional statement, that she had been carried along on the back of an invisible "familiar"—a spectral blue boar—the whole way. Of course this was sufficient, and she was committed for trial.

And now wealthy Master Philip English and his wife were both in prison; and he daily concocting plans by which he might find himself on the deck of the fastest sailer of all those twenty-one vessels of his.

Uncle Robie had thought this might be also a good opportunity for Dulcibel. And it struck Master Raymond the same way; while Master English had no objection, especially as it was mainly for Dulcibel that the jailer would open the prison doors. And this was better than the violence he had at first contemplated; for, as his vessels gradually began to accumulate in port, owing to the interruption to his business caused by his arrest, he had only to give the word, and a party of his sailors would have broken open the prison some dark night, and released him from captivity.

The "Albatross," Master English's fastest sailer at length came into port; and the arrangements were speedily made. The first north-westerly wind, whether the night were clear or stormy—though of course with such a wind it would probably be clear—the attempt was to be made, immediately after midnight. Uncle Robie was to unlock the jail-doors, let them out, lock the doors again behind them, and have a plentiful supply of witch stories to account for the escape. And Master Raymond had some hopes also, that Abigail Williams would come to the jailer's support in anything that seemed to compromise him in the least; for he had promised to send her a beautiful gift from England, when he returned home again. And with such a sharpener to the vision, the precocious child would be able to see even more wonderful things than any she had already testified to.

The favorable wind came at length, and with it an exceedingly propitious night; there being a moon just large enough to enable them to see their way, with not enough light to disclose anything sharply. Master Raymond had planned all along to take Dulcibel's horse also with them; and if he could ride the animal, it would obviate the necessity of taking another horse also, and being plagued what to do with it when they arrived at the prison. For he was very desirous that Master Putnam should not be in the least involved in the matter.

Master Raymond therefore had been practising up in the woods for about a week, at what the minister had failed so deplorably in, the riding of the little black mare. At first he could absolutely do nothing with her; she would not be ridden by any male biped. But finally he adopted a suggestion of quick-witted Mistress Putnam. He put on a side saddle and a skirt, and rode the animal woman fashion—and all without the least difficulty. The little mare seeming to say by her behavior, "Ah, now, that is sensible. Why did you not do it before?"

So, late on the evening appointed for the attempted escape, after taking an affectionate leave of his host and hostess, and putting a few necessary articles of apparel into a portmanteau strapped behind the saddle, Master Raymond started for Salem town.

Leaving the village to the right, he made good time to the town, meeting no one at that late hour. He had covered the mare with a large horse-blanket, so that she should not easily be recognized by any one who might happen to meet them. There was a night watchman in Salem town; but a party of sailors had undertaken to get him off the principal street at the appointed hour, by the offer of refreshments at one of their haunts; and by this time he was too full of Jamaica spirits to walk very steadily or see very clearly.

Arrived at the prison, Master Raymond found the Captain and mate of the "Albatross" impatiently awaiting him. It was not full time yet, but they concluded to give the signal, three hoots of an owl; which the mate gave with great force and precision. Still all seemed dark and quiet as before.

Then they waited, walking up and down to keep the blood in their veins in motion, as the nights were a little cool.

"It is full time now," said the Captain, "give the signal again, Brady."

Brady gave it—if anything with greater force and precision than before.

But not a sign from within.

Had the jailer's courage given away at the last moment? Or could he have betrayed them? They paced up and down for an hour longer. It was evident that, for some reason or other, the plan had miscarried.

"Well, there is no use awaiting here," exclaimed the Captain of the "Albatross" with an oath; "I am going back to the ship."

Master Raymond acquiesced. There was no use in waiting longer. And so he re-donned his petticoat—much to the amusement of the seamen and started back to Master Putnam's arriving there in the darkest hours of the night, just before the breaking of the day.

CHAPTER XXXII.

Why the Plan Failed.

The reason of the failure of the plan of escape may be gathered from a little conversation that took place between Squire Hathorne and Thomas Putnam the morning of the day fixed upon by Master Philip English.

Thomas Putnam had called to see the magistrate at the suggestion of that not very admirable but certainly very sharp-witted wife of his. I do not suppose that Thomas Putnam was at all a bad man, but it is a lamentable sight to see, as we so often do, a good kind honest-hearted man made a mere tool of by some keen-witted and unscrupulous woman; in whose goodness he believes, in a kind of small-minded and yet not altogether ignoble spirit of devotion, mainly because she is a woman. Being a woman, she cannot be, as he foolishly supposes, the shallow-hearted, mischievous being that she really is.

"Do you know, Squire, how Master English's sailors are talking around the wharves?"

"No! What are the rascals saying?"

"Well, Mistress Putnam has been told by a friend of hers in the town, that he heard a half-drunken sailor, belonging to one of Master English's vessels, say that they meant to tear down the jail some night, hang the jailers, and carry off their Master and Mistress."

"Ah," said the Squire, "this must be looked into."

"Another of the sailors is reported to have said, that if the magistrates attempted to hang Mistress English they would hang Squire Hathorne, and Squire Gedney, if they could catch him, by the side of her."

"The impudent varlets!" exclaimed Squire Hathorne, his wine-red face growing redder. "Master English shall sweat for this. How many of his sailors are in port now?"

"Oh, I suppose there are fifty of them; and all reckless, unprincipled men. To my certain knowledge, there is not a member of church among them."

"The godless knaves!" cried the magistrate. "I should like to set the whole lot of them in the stocks, and then whip them out of the town at the cart's tail."

"Yes, that is what they deserve, but then we cannot forget that they are necessary to the interests of the town—unless Salem is to give up all her shipping business—and these sailors are so clannish that if you strike one of them, you strike all. No, it seems to me, Squire, we had better take no public notice of their vaporing; but simply adopt means to counteract any plans they may be laying."

"Well, what would you suggest, Master Putnam? Has Mistress Putnam any ideas upon the subject? I have always found her a very sensible woman."

"Yes, my wife is a very remarkable woman if I do say it," replied Master Putnam. "Her plan is to send Master English and his wife off at once to Boston—that will save us all further trouble with them and their sailors."

"A capital idea! It shall be carried out this very day," said the magistrate.

"And she also suggests that the young witch woman, Dulcibel Burton, should be sent with them. That friend of my brother Joseph, is still staying around here; and Mistress Putnam does not exactly comprehend his motives for so long a visit."

"Ah, indeed—what motive has he?" And Squire Hathorne rubbed his broad forehead.

"There was some talk at one time of his keeping company with Mistress Burton."

"What, the witch! that is too bad. For he seems like a rather pleasant young gentleman; and I hear he is the heir of a large estate in the old country."

"Of course there may be nothing in it—but Mistress Putnam also heard from one of her female cronies the other day, that jailer Foster was at one time a mate on board Captain Burton's vessel."

"Ah!"

"And you know how very handsome that Mistress Dulcibel is; and, being besides a witch of great power, it seems to Mistress Putnam that it is exposing jailer Foster to very great temptation."

"Mistress Putnam is quite correct," said Squire Hathorne. "Mistress Dulcibel had better be transferred to Boston also. There the worshipful Master Haughton has the power and the will to see that all these imps of Satan are kept safely."

"As the seamen may be lying around and make a disturbance if the removal comes to their knowledge, Mistress Putnam suggested that it had better not be done until evening. It would be a night ride; but then, as Mistress Putnam said, witches rather preferred to make their journeys in the night time—so that it would be a positive kindness to the prisoners."

"Very true! very well thought of!" replied Squire Hathorne, with a grim smile. "And no doubt they will be very thankful that we furnish them with horses instead of broomsticks. Though as for Mistress Dulcibel, I suppose she would prefer her familiar, the black mare, to any other animal."

"That was very marvelous. Abigail Williams says that she is certain that the mare, after jumping the gate, never came down to earth again, but flew straight on up into the thundercloud."

"And it thundered when the black beast entered the cloud, did it not?" said the magistrate in a sobered tone. He evidently saw nothing unreasonable in the story.

"Yes—it thundered—but not the common kind of thunder—it was enough to make your flesh creep. The minister says he is only too thankful that the Satanic beast did throw him off. He might have been carried off to hell with her."

"Yes, it was a very foolish thing to get on the back of a witch's familiar," said the magistrate. "It was tempting Providence. And Master Parris has cause for thankfulness that only such a mild reproof as a slight wetting, was allowed to be inflicted upon him. These are perilous times, Master Putnam. Satan is truly going about like a roaring lion, seeking what he may devour. Against this chosen seed,—this little remnant of God's people left upon the whole earth—no wonder that he is tearing and raging."

"Ah me, my Christian friend, it is too true! And no wonder that he is so bold, and full of joyful subtlety. For is he not prevailing, in spite of all our efforts? You know there are at least four hundred members of what rightly calls itself the Church of England—for certainly it is not the church of Christ—in Boston alone! When the royal Governor made the town authorities give up the South Church—even our own Church, built with our own money—to their so-called Rector to hold their idolatrous services in, we might have known that Satan was at our doors!"

"Oh, that such horrible things should happen in the godly town of Boston!" responded Squire Hathorne. "But when the King interfered between Justice and the Quakers, and forbade the righteous discipline we were exercising upon them, of course a door was opened for all other latitudinarianism and false doctrine. Why, I am told that there are now quite a number of Quakers in Boston; and that they even had the assurance to apply to the magistrates the other day, for permission to erect a meeting-house!"

"Impossible!" exclaimed Master Putnam. "They ought to have been whipped out of their presence."

"Yes," continued the worthy Magistrate irefully; "but when the King ordered that the right of voting for our rulers should no longer be restricted to church-members; but that every man of fair estate and good moral character, as he phrases it, should be allowed to vote, even if he is not a member at all, he aimed a blow at the very Magistracy itself."

"Yes, that is worse than heresy! And how can a man possess a good moral character, without being a member of the true church?"

"Of course—that is self-evident. But it shows how the righteous seed is being over-flooded with iniquity, even in its last chosen house; how our Canaan is being given up to the Philistines. And therefore it is, doubtless, that Satan, in the pride of his success, is introducing his emissaries into the very house of the Lord itself; and promising great rewards to them who will bow down and sign their names in his red book, and worship him. Ah! we have fallen on evil times, Master Putnam."

And so the two worthy Puritans condoled with each other, until, Master Putnam, bethinking himself that he had some worldly business to attend to, Squire Hathorne proceeded to give the necessary directions for the removal of the three prisoners from Salem to Boston jail.

This was accomplished that very night, as Mistress Putnam had suggested; Deputy Marshall Herrick and a constable guarding the party. Dulcibel occupied a pillion behind jailer Foster; Master English and his wife rode together; while Master Herrick and the constable each had a horse to himself.

The original plan was for Dulcibel to ride behind Master Herrick; but upon jailer Foster representing that there might be some danger of a rescue, and offering to join the party, it was arranged that he should have special charge of Mistress Dulcibel, whom he represented to Herrick as being in his opinion a most marvelous witch.

Uncle Robie's true reason for going, however, was that the jailer in Boston was an old friend of his, and he wished to speak a secret word to him that might insure Dulcibel kinder treatment than was usually given in Boston jail to any alleged transgressor.

CHAPTER XXXIII.

Mistress Ann Putnam's Fair Warning.

In the course of the next day the removal of the three prisoners became known to everybody. Master Raymond wondered when he heard it, whether it was a check-mate to the plan of escape, with which the magistrates, in some way had become acquainted; or whether it was a mere chance coincidence. Finally he satisfied himself that it was the latter—though no doubt suggested by the rather loose threats of Master English's many sailors.

When jailer Foster returned, he found means to inform Master Raymond that it had been entirely impossible—so suddenly was the whole thing sprung upon him—to let anyone in their secret know of what was going on. He had not even taken the assistant jailer, his own son, into his confidence, because he did not wish to expose him to needless danger. His son was not required to afford any help, and therefore it would be unwise to incur any risk of punishment. Besides, while Uncle Robie had made up his mind to do some tall lying of his own for the sake of saving innocent lives, he saw no reason why his son, should be placed under a similar necessity. Lying seemed to be absolutely needful in the case; but it was well to do as little of it as possible.

From his conversation with Master Herrick, Uncle Robie concluded that nothing had been divulged; and that the magistrates had acted only on the supposition that trouble of some kind might result from the sailors. And, looked at from that point of view, it was quite sufficient to account for the removal of two of the prisoners. As to why Dulcibel also should be sent to Boston, he could get no satisfactory explanation. It seemed in fact to be a matter of mere caprice, so far as uncle Robie could find out.

They had pushed on through the night to Boston—about a four hours' slow ride—and delivered the three prisoners safely to the keeper of Boston jail. Uncle Robie adding the assurance to Goodwife Buckley—who acted as Master Raymond's confidential agent in the matter—that he had spoken a word to his old crony who believed no more in witches than he did, which would insure to her as kind treatment as possible. And Robie further said that he had been assured by the Boston jailer, that Mistress Phips, the wife of the Governor, had no sympathy whatever with the witchcraft prosecutions, but a great deal of sympathy for the victims of it.

The game was therefore played out at Salem, now that Dulcibel had been transferred to Boston; and Master Raymond began to make arrangements at once to leave the place. In some respects the change of scene was for the worse; for he had no hold upon the Boston jailer, and had no friend there like Joseph Putnam, prepared to go to any length on his behalf. But, on the other hand, in Boston they seemed outside of the circle of Mistress Ann Putnam's powerful and malign influence. This of itself was no small gain; and, thinking over the whole matter, Master Raymond came to the conclusion that perhaps the chances of escape would be even greater in Boston than in Salem.

So, in the course of the ensuing week, Master Raymond took an affectionate leave of his kind young host and hostess, and departed for Boston town, avowedly on his way back to his English home. This last was of course brought out prominently in all his leave-takings—he was, after a short stay in Boston, to embark for England. "What shall I send you from England?" was among his last questions to the various members of the "afflicted circle." And one said laughingly one thing, and one another; the young man taking it gravely, and making a note in his little notebook of each request. If things should come to the worst, he was putting himself in a good position to influence the character of the testimony. A hundred pounds in this way would be money well employed.

Even to Mistress Ann Putnam he did not hesitate to put the same question, after a friendly leave-taking. Mistress Putnam rather liked the young Englishman; it was mainly against Dulcibel as the friend of her brother-in-law that she had warred; and if Master Raymond had not also been the warm friend and guest of Joseph Putnam, she might have relented in her persecution of Dulcibel for his sake. But her desire to pain and punish Master Joseph,—who had said so many things against her in the Putnam family—overpowered all such sentimental considerations. Besides, what Dulcibel had said of her when before the magistrates, had greatly incensed her.

"What shall you send me from England? And are you really going back there?" And she fixed her cold green eyes upon the young man's face.

"Oh, yes, I am going back again, like the bad penny," replied Master Raymond smiling.

"How soon?"

"Oh, I cannot say exactly. Perhaps the Boston gentlemen may be so fascinating that they will detain me longer than I have planned."

"Is it because the Salem gentlewomen are so fascinating that you have remained here? We feel quite complimented in the village by the length of your visit."

"Yes, I have found the Salem gentlewomen among the most charming of their sex. But you have not told me what I shall send you from London when I return?"

"Oh, I leave that entirely with you, and to your own good taste. Perhaps by the time you get back to London, you will not wish to send me anything."

"I cannot imagine such a case. But I shall endeavor, as you leave it all to me, to find something pretty and appropriate; something suited to the most gifted person, among men and women, that I have found in the New World."

Mistress Putnam's face colored with evident pleasure—even she was not averse to a compliment of this kind; knowing, as she did, that she had a wonderful intellectual capacity for planning and scheming. In fact if she had possessed as large a heart as brain, she would have been a very noble and even wonderful woman. Master Raymond thought he had told no falsehood in calling her the "most gifted"— he considered her so in certain directions.

And so they parted—the last words of Mistress Putnam being, the young man thought, very significant ones.

"I would not," she said in a light, but still impressive manner, "if I were you, stay a very long time in Boston. There is, I think, something dangerous to the health of strangers in the air of that town, of late. It would be a very great pity for you to catch one of our deadly fevers, and never be able to return to your home and friends. Take my advice now—it is honest and well meant—and do not linger long in the dangerous air of Boston."

Thanking her for her solicitude as to his health, Master Raymond shook her thin hand and departed. But all the ride back to Joseph Putnam's, he was thinking over those last words.

What was their real meaning? What could they mean but this? "You are going to Boston to try to save Dulcibel Burton. I do not want to hurt you; but I may be compelled to do it. Leave Boston as soon as you can, and spare me the necessity that may arise of denouncing you also. Joseph Putnam, whom I hate, but whose person and household I am for family reasons compelled to respect, when you are in Boston is no longer your protector. I can just as easily, and even far more easily, reach you than I could reach Captain Alden. Beware how you interfere with my plans. Even while I pity you, I shall not spare you!"

CHAPTER XXXIV.

Master Raymond Goes Again to Boston.

Master Raymond had agreed to keep his friend Joseph Putnam informed by letter of his movements—for there had been a postal system established a number of years before through the Massachusetts colony—but of course he had to be very careful as to what he put upon paper; the Puritan official mind not being over-scrupulous as to the means it took of attaining its ends.

He had brought excellent letters to persons of the highest character in Boston, and had received invitations from many of them to make his home in their houses—for the Boston people of all classes, and especially the wealthy, obeyed the Scriptural injunction, and were "given to hospitality;" which I believe is true to the present day. But Master Raymond, considering the errand he was on, thought it wisest to take up his abode at an Inn—lest he might involve his entertainers in the peril attending his unlawful but righteous designs. So he took a cheery room at the Red Lion, in the northern part of the town, which was quite a reputable house, and convenient for many purposes not the least being its proximity to the harbor, which made it a favorite resort for the better class of sea-captains.

Calling around upon the families to which he had presented letters on his first visit, immediately after his arrival in the colony, he speedily established very pleasant social relations with a good many very different circles. And he soon was able to sum up the condition of affairs in the town as follows:

First, there was by far the most numerous and the ruling sect, the Puritans. The previous Governor, shut out by King James, Sir Edmund Andros, had been an Episcopalian; but the present one sent out on the accession of William and Mary, Sir William Phips, was himself a Puritan, sitting under the weekly teachings of the Reverend Master Cotton Mather at the North church.

Then there was an Episcopal circle, composed of about four hundred people in all, meeting at King's Chapel, built about three years before, with the Reverend Master Robert Ratcliffe as Rector.

Besides these, there was a small number of Quakers, now dwelling in peace, so far as personal manifestations were concerned, being protected by the King's mandate. These had even grown so bold of late, as to be seeking permission to erect a meeting-house; which almost moved the Puritan divines to prophesy famine, earthquakes and pestilence as the results of such an ungodly toleration of heresy.

Then there were a number of Baptists, who also now dwelt in peace, under the King's protection.

Adding to the foregoing the people without any religion to speak of, who principally belonged to or were connected with the seafaring class, and Master Raymond found that he had a pretty clear idea of the inhabitants of Boston.

In relation to the Witchcraft prosecutions, the young Englishman ascertained that the above classes seemed to favor the prosecutions just in proportion to the extent of their Puritan orthodoxy. The great majority of the Puritans believed devoutly in witches, and in the duty of obeying the command, "Thou shalt not suffer a witch to live." And generally in proportion to a Puritan church-member's orthodoxy, was the extent of his belief in witchcraft, and the fierceness of his exterminating zeal.

The Episcopalians and the Baptists were either very lukewarm, or else in decided opposition to the prosecutions looking upon them as simply additional proofs of Puritan narrowness, intolerance and bigotry.

The Quakers held to the latter opinion even more firmly than the liberal Episcopalians and Baptists: adding to it the belief that it was a judgment allowed to come upon the Puritans, to punish them for their cruelty to God's chosen messengers.

As for the seafaring class, they looked upon the whole affair as a piece of madness, which could only overtake people whose contracted notions were a result of perpetually living in one place, and that on the land. And since the arrest of a man so well thought of, and of their own class as Captain Alden, the vocabulary allowed by the law in Boston was entirely too limited to embrace adequately a seaman's emphatic sense of the iniquitous proceedings. As one of them forcibly expressed himself to Master Raymond:—"He would be *condemned*, if he wouldn't like to see the *condemned* town of Boston, and all its *condemned* preachers, buried like Port Royal, ten *condemned* fathoms deep, under the *condemned* soil upon which it was built!" He used another emphatic word of course, in the place of the word *condemned*; but that doubtless was because at that time they had not our "revised version" of the New Testament.

The sea-captain who expressed himself in this emphatic way to Master Raymond, was the captain in whose vessel he had come over from England, and who had made another voyage back and forth since that time. The young man was strolling around the wharves, gazing at the vessels when he had been accosted by the aforesaid captain. At that particular moment however, he had come to a stand, earnestly regarding, as he had several times before, a vessel that was lying anchored out in the stream.

After passing some additional words with the captain upon various matters, and especially upon the witches, a subject that every conversation at that time was apt to be very full of, he turned towards the water and said:—

"That seems to be a good craft out there."

It was a vessel of two masts, slender and raking, and with a long, low hull—something of the model which a good many years later, went by the name of the Baltimore clipper.

"Yes, she is a beauty!" replied the captain.

"She looks as if she might be a good sailer."

"Good! I reckon she is. The Storm King can show her heels to any vessel that goes out of this port—or out of London either, for that matter."

"What is she engaged in?"

Here the captain gave a low whistle, and followed it up with a wink.

"Buccaneers occasionally, I suppose?"

"Oh, Captain Tolley is not so very *condemned* particular what he does—so that of course it is entirely lawful," and the captain winked again. "He owns his vessel, you see—carries her in his pocket—and has no *condemned* lot of land-lubber owners on shore who cannot get away if there is any trouble, from the *condemned* magistrates and constables."

"That is an advantage sometimes," said the young man. He was thinking of his own case probably.

"Of course it is. Law is a very good thing—in its place. But if I buy a bag of coffee in the East Indies or in South America, why should I have to pay a lot of money on it, before I am allowed to sell it to the people that like coffee in some other country? *Condemn* it! There's no justice in it."

Master Raymond was in no mood just then to argue great moral questions. So he answered by asking:—

"Captain Tolley does not make too many inquiries then when a good offer is made him?"

"Do not misunderstand me, young man," replied the captain gravely. "My friend, Captain Tolley, would be the last man to commit piracy, or anything of that kind. But just look at the case. Here Captain Tolley is, off at sea, attending to his proper business. Well, he comes into some *condemned* port, just to get a little water perhaps, and some fresh provisions; and hears that while he has been away, these *condemned* land-lubbers have been making some new rules and regulations, without even asking any of us seafaring men anything about it. Then, if we do not obey their foolish rules, they nab us when we come into port again, and fine us—perhaps put us in the bilboes. Now, as a fair man, do you call that justice?"

Master Raymond laughed good-humoredly. "I see it has its unfair side," said he. "By the way, I should like to look over that vessel of his. Could you give me a line of introduction to him?"

"Of course I can—nothing pleases Tolley more than to have people admire his vessel—even though a landsman's admiration, you know, really cannot seem of much account to a sailor. But I cannot write here; let us adjourn to the Lion."

CHAPTER XXXV.

Captain Tolley and the Storm King.

The next day furnished with a brief note of introduction, Master Raymond, with the aid of a skiff, put himself on the deck of the Storm King. Captain Tolley received him with due courtesy, wondering who the stranger was. The Captain was a well-built, athletic, though not very large man, with a face naturally dark in hue, and bronzed by exposure to the southern sun. As Master Raymond ascertained afterwards, he was the son of an English father and a Spanish mother; and he could speak English, French and Spanish with equal facility. While he considered himself an Englishman of birth, his nationality sat very loosely upon him; and, if need be, he was just as willing to run up the French or Spanish colors on the Storm King, as the red cross of St. George.

After reading the note of introduction, Captain Tolley gave a keen look at his visitor. "Yes, the Storm King is a bird and a beauty," said he proudly. "Look at her! See what great wings she has! And what a hull, to cut the seas! She was built after my own plans. Give me plenty of sea-room, and a fair start, and I will laugh at all the gun frigates of the royal navy."

"She looks to be all you say," said his visitor admiringly—but rather surprised that not an oath had yet fallen from the lips of the Captain. He had not learned that Captain Tolley, to use his own language, "never washed his ammunition in port or in mild weather." When aroused by a severe storm or other peril, the Captain was transformed into a different man. Then, in the war of the elements, or of man's angry passions, he also lightened and thundered, and swore big guns.

"Let us go down into the cabin," said the Captain. Reaching there, he filled a couple of glasses with wine and putting the decanter on the table, invited his visitor to be seated. Then, closing the door, he said with a smile, "nothing that is said inside this cabin ever is told anywhere else."

There was that in the speech, bearing and looks of Captain Tolley which inspired Master Raymond with great confidence in him. "I feel that I may trust you, Captain," he said earnestly.

"I have done business for a great many gentlemen, and no one ever found me untrue to him," replied Captain Tolley, proudly. "Some things I will not do for anybody, or for any price; but that ends it. I never betray confidence."

"Do you believe in witches, Captain?"

"Indeed I do."

"Well I suppose that settles it," replied the young man in a disappointed tone, rising to his feet.

"I know a little witch down in Jamaica, that has been tormenting me almost to death for the last three years. But I tell you she is a beauty—as pretty as, as—the Storm King! She doesn't carry quite as many petticoats though," added the Captain laughing.

"Oh! That is the kind of witch you mean!" and Master Raymond sat down again.

"It is the only kind that I ever came across—and they are bad enough for me," responded the Captain drily.

"I know a little witch of that kind," said Master Raymond, humoring the Captain's fancy; "but she is now in Boston prison, and in danger of her life."

"Ah! I think I have heard something of her—very beautiful, is she not? I caught a glimpse of her when I went up to see Captain Alden, who the bigoted fools have got in limbo there. I could not help laughing at Alden—the idea of calling him a witch. Alden is a religious man, you know!"

"But it may cost him his life!"

"That is what I went to see him about. I offered to come up with a party some night, break open the jail, and carry him off to New York in the Storm King."

"Well?"

"Oh, you know the better people are not in the jail, but in the jailer's house—having given their promise to Keeper Arnold that they will not try to escape, if thus kindly treated. And besides, if he runs off, they will confiscate his property; of which Alden foolishly has a good deal in houses and lands. So he thinks it the best policy to hold on to his anchor, and see if the storm will not blow itself out."

"And so you have no conscientious scruples against breaking the law, by carrying off any of these imprisoned persons?"

"Conscientious scruples and the Puritan laws be d——!" exclaimed the Captain; thinking perhaps that this was an occasion when he might with propriety break his rule as to swearing while in port.

"Your language expresses my sentiments exactly!" responded the young Englishman, who had never uttered an oath in his life. "Captain, I am betrothed to that young lady you saw when you went to see Captain Alden. If she is ever brought to trial, those Salem hell-hounds will swear away her life. I mean to rescue her—or die with her. I am able and willing to pay you any reasonable price for your aid and assistance, Will you help me?"

The Captain sprang to his feet. "Will I help you? The great God dash the Storm King to pieces on her next voyage if I fail you! See here," taking a letter out of a drawer, "it is a profitable offer just made me. But it is a mere matter of merchandise; and this is a matter of a woman's life! You shall pay me what you can afford to, and what you think right; but, money or no money, I and the Storm King, and her brave crew, who will follow wherever I lead, are at your service!"

As Captain Tolley uttered these words, in an impassioned, though low voice, and with a glowing face and sparkling blue eyes, Master Raymond thought he had never seen a handsomer man. He grasped the Captain's extended hand, and shook it warmly. "I shall never forget this noble offer," he exclaimed. And he never did forget it; for from that moment the two were life-long friends.

"What is your plan?" said the Captain.

"A peaceable escape if possible. If not, what you propose to Captain Alden."

"I should like the last the best," said the Captain.

"Why, it would expose you to penalties—and keep your vessel hereafter out of Boston harbor."

"You see that I have an old grudge of my own," replied the Captain. "These Puritan rascals once arrested me for bringing some Quakers from Barbados—good, honest, innocent people, a little touched here, you know,"—and the Captain tapped his broad, brown brow with his finger. "They caught me on shore, fined me, and would have put me in the stocks; but my mate got word of it, we were lying out in the storm, trained two big guns to bear upon the town, and gave them just fifteen minutes to send me on board again. That was twenty years ago, and I have not been here since."

"They sent you on board, I suppose?"

"Oh, the Saints are not fools," replied the Captain, laughing. "As for being shut out of Boston harbor hereafter, I do not fear that much. The reign of the Saints is nearly over. Do you not see that the Quakers are back, and the Baptists, and the prayer-book men, as they call the Episcopalians!—and they do not touch them, though they would whip the whole of them out of the Province, at the cart's tail, if they dared. But there are Kings in Israel again!" and the Captain laughed heartily. "And the Kings are always better shepherds to the flock than the Priests."

"You may have to lie here idle for a while; but I will bear the expense of it," said Master Raymond. "Have the proper papers drawn up, and I will sign them."

"No, there shall be no papers between you and me," rejoined the Captain stoutly. "I hate these lawyers' pledges. I never deal with a man, if I can help it, who needs a signed and sealed paper to keep him to his word. I know what you are, and you ought to be able to see by this time what I am. The Storm King shall lie here three months, if need be—and you shall pay me monthly my reasonable charges. But I will make out no bill, and you shall have no receipt, to cause any trouble to anybody, hereafter."

"That will suit me," replied Master Raymond, "I shall be in the bar-room of the Red Lion every morning at ten. You must be there too. But we will only nod to each other, unless I have something to tell you. Then I will slip a note into your hand, making an appointment for an interview. I fear there may be spies upon my movements."

Captain Tolley assenting to these arrangements, Master Raymond and he again shook hands, and the latter was put ashore in one of the Storm King's boats. It was a little curious that as the young man reached the wharf, ascending a few wooden steps from the boat, whom should he see at a little distance, walking briskly into the town, but one who he thought was Master Thomas Putnam. He could not see the man's face, for his back was toward him; but he felt certain that it was the loving and obedient husband of Mistress Ann Putnam.

CHAPTER XXXVI.

Sir William Phips and Lady Mary.

When Mistress Dulcibel Burton, in company with Master Philip English and his wife, arrived at Boston jail, and were delivered into the care of Keeper Arnold, they received far better treatment than they had expected.

The prison itself, situated in a portion of Boston which is now considered the centre of fashion and elegance, was one of those cruel Bridewells, which were a befitting illustration of what some suppose to have been the superior manners and customs of the "good old times." It was built of stone, its walls being three feet thick. Its windows were barred with iron to prevent escape; but being without glazed sashes, the wind and rain and snow and cold of winter found ready access to the cells within. The doors were covered with the large heads of iron spikes—the cells being formed by partitions of heavy plank. And the passage ways of the prison were described by one who had been confined in this Boston Bridewell, as being "like the dark valley of the shadow of death."

But the jailers seem to have been more humane than the builders of the prison; and those awaiting trial, especially, were frequently allowed rooms in the Keeper's house—probably always paying well, however, for the privilege.

Thus, as Captain Tolley had said, Captain Alden was confined in Keeper Arnold's house; and, when the party in which the readers of this story are especially interested, arrived late at night from Salem, they were taken to comparatively comfortable apartments. The jailer knew that Master Philip English was a very wealthy man; and, as for Dulcibel, Uncle Robie did not forget to say to his old crony Arnold, among other favorable things, that she not only had warm friends, among the best people of Salem, but that in her own right, she possessed a very pretty little fortune, and was fully able to pay a good price for any favors extended to her.

The magistrates in Salem had refused to take bail for Captain Alden; but Master English was soon able to make an arrangement, by which he and his wife were allowed the freedom of the town in the daytime; it being understood that they should return regularly, and pass the night in the jail—or, speaking strictly, in the Keeper's house.

For things in Boston were different from what they were at Salem. In Salem the Puritan spirit reigned supreme in magistrates and in ministers. But in Boston, there was, as we have said, a strong anti-Puritan influence. The officials sent over from England were generally Episcopalians—the officers of the English men-of-war frequently in port, also were generally Episcopalians. And though the present Governor, Sir William Phips, was a member of the North Church, the Reverend Cotton Mather taking the place of his father, the Reverend Increase Mather—and though the Governor was greatly under the influence of that dogmatic and superstitious divine—his wife, Lady Mary, was utterly opposed to the whole witchcraft delusion and persecution.

Sir William himself had quite a romantic career. Starting in life as one of the later offspring of a father and mother who had twenty-six children, and had come as poor emigrants to Maine, he was a simple and ignorant caretaker of sheep until eighteen years of age. Then he became a ship carpenter; and at the age of twenty-two went to Boston, working at his trade in the day time, and learning how to read and write at night. In Boston he had the good fortune to capture the heart of a fair widow by the name of Mistress Hull, who was a daughter of Captain Robert Spencer. With her hand he received a fair estate; which was the beginning of a large fortune. For, it enabled him to set up a ship-yard of his own; and by ventures to recover lost treasure, sunk in shipwrecked Spanish galleons, under the patronage of the Duke of Albemarle, he took back to England at one time the large amount of £300,000 in gold, silver and precious stones, of which his share was £16,000—and in addition a gold cup, valued at £1,000 presented to his wife Mary. And such was the able conduct and the strict integrity he had shown in the face of many difficulties and temptations, that King James knighted him, making him Sir William.

Now, through his own deserts, and the influence of the Reverend Increase Mather, agent in England of the colony, he was Governor-in-Chief of the Province of Massachusetts Bay, and Captain General (for military purposes) of all New England. And he was living in that "fair brick house in Green lane," which, years before, he had promised his wife that he would some day build for her to live in.

Lady Mary was a very sweet, nice woman; but she had a will of her own, and never could be persuaded that Sir William's rise in the world was not owing entirely to her having taken pity on him, and married below her station. And really there was considerable truth in this view of the matter, which she was not inclined to have him forget; and Sir William, being a manly and generous, though at times rather choleric gentleman, generally admitted the truth of her assertion that "she had made him," rather than have any controversy with her about it. One of the first acts of Sir William on arriving to fill his position as Governor, was to order chains put upon all the alleged witches in the prisons. In this order might be very plainly traced the hand of his pastor, the Reverend Cotton Mather. Lady Mary was outraged by such a command. One of her first visits had been to the jail, to see Captain Alden, whom she knew well. Keeper Arnold had shown her the order. "Put on the irons," said Lady Mary. The jailer did so. "Now that you have obeyed Sir William, take them off again." The jailer smiled, but hesitated. "Do as I command you, and I will be accountable to Sir William." Very gladly did Keeper Arnold obey—he had no faith in such accusations, brought against some of the best behaved people he ever had in his charge.

"Now, do the same to all the other prisoners!" commanded the spirited lady.

"I may as well be hung for a cow as a calf," said the jailer laughing— and he went gravely with one pair of fetters all through the cells, complying literally with the new Governor's orders.

Of course this soon got to the ears of the Rev. Cotton Mather, who went in high indignation to the Governor. But the latter seemed to be very much amused, and could not be brought to manifest any great amount of indignation. "You know that Lady Mary has a will of her own," said he to his pastor. "If you choose to go and talk to her, I will take you to her boudoir; but I am not anxious to get into hot water for the sake of a few witches." The minister thought of it a moment; but then concluded wisely not to go. For, as Lady Mary said to her husband afterwards, "I wish that you had brought him to me. I would have told him just what I think of him, and his superstitious, hard-hearted doings. For me, I never mean to enter North Church more. I shall go hereafter to South Church; Masters Willard and Moody have some Christian charity left in them."

"I think you are too hard on Master Cotton Mather, my dear," replied Sir William mildly.

"Too hard, am I? What would you say if those girl imps at Salem should accuse me next! Your own loving wife,—to the world."

"Oh, my dear wife, that is too monstrous even to think of!"

"No more monstrous than their accusation of Mistress English of Salem, and her husband. You know them—what do you think of that?"

"Certainly, that is very singular and impossible; but Master Mather says—"

"Master Mather ought to be hung himself," said the indignant lady; "for he has helped to murder better people than he is, a great deal."

"My dear, I must remonstrate—"

"And there is Captain Alden—he is a witch, too, it seems!" And Lady Mary laughed scornfully. "Why not you too? You are no better a man than Captain Alden."

"Oh, the Captain shall not be hurt."

"It will not be through any mercy of his judges then. But, answer my question: what will you do, if they dare to accuse me? Answer me that!"

"You certainly are not serious, Lady Mary?"

"I am perfectly serious. I have heard already a whisper from Salem that they are thinking of it. They even have wished me warned against the consequences of my high-handed proceedings. Now if they cry out against me, what will you do?"

We have said that Sir William was naturally choleric—though he always put a strong constraint upon himself when talking with his wife, whom he really loved; but now he started to his feet.

"If they dare to breathe a whisper against you, my wife, Lady Mary, I will blow the whole concern to perdition! Confound it, Madam, there are limits to everything!"

She went up to him and put her arm around his neck and kissed him. "I thought that before they touched me, they would have to chain the lion that lies at my door," she said proudly and affectionately; for, notwithstanding these little tiffs, she really was fond of her husband, and proud of his romantic career.

But—coming back to our sheep—Dulcibel not having the same amount of wealth and influence behind her as Master English had, was very well contented at being allowed a room in Keeper Arnold's house; and was on the whole getting along very comfortably. Master Raymond had seen her soon after his arrival, but it was in company with the jailer; the principal result being that he had secretly passed her a letter, and had assured himself that she was not in a suffering condition.

But things of late were looking brighter, for Master Raymond had made the acquaintance of Lady Mary through a friend to whom he had letters from England, and Lady Mary had begun to take an interest in Dulcibel, whom she had seen on one of her visits to Mistress English.

Through Lady Mary, in some way, Dulcibel hoped to escape from the prison; trusting that, if once at large, Master Raymond would be able to provide for her safety. But there was one great difficulty. She, with the others, had given her word to the Keeper not to escape, as the price of her present exemption from confinement in an exposed, unhealthy cell. How this promise was to be managed, neither of them had been able to think of. Keeper Arnold might be approached; but Dulcibel feared not—at least under present circumstances. If brought to trial and convicted then to save her life, Dulcibel thought he might be persuaded to aid her. As to breaking her word to the Keeper, that never entered the mind of the truthful maiden, or of her lover. Death even was more endurable than the thought of dishonor—if they had thought of the matter at all. But as I have said, they never even thought of a such thing. And therefore how to manage the affair was a very perplexing question.

CHAPTER XXXVII.

The First Rattle of the Rattlesnake.

One day about this time Master Raymond was sitting in the porch of the Red Lion, thinking over a sight he had just seen;—a man had passed by wearing on the back of his drab coat a capital I two inches long, cut out of black cloth, and sewed upon it. On inquiry he found the man had married his deceased wife's sister; and both he and the woman had been first whipped, and then condemned to wear this letter for the rest of their lives, according to the law of the colony.[3]

Master Raymond was puzzling over the matter not being able to make out that any real offence had been committed, when who should walk up to the porch but Master Joseph Putnam. After a hearty hand-shaking between the two, they retired to Master Raymond's apartments.

"Well, how are things getting along at Salem?"

"Oh, about as usual!"

"Any more accusations?"

"Plenty of them, people are beginning to find out that the best way to protect themselves is to sham being 'afflicted,' and accuse somebody else."

"I saw that a good while ago."

"And when a girl or a woman is accused, her relatives and her friends gather around her, and implore her to confess, to save her life. For they have found that not one person who has been accused of being a witch, and has admitted the fact, has been convicted.

"And yet it would seem that a confession of witchcraft ought to be a better proof of it, than the mere assertion of possible enemies," responded Master Raymond.

"Of course—if there was any show of reason or fairness in the prosecutions, from first to last; but as it is all sheer malice and wickedness, on the part of the accusers, from the beginning to the end, it would be vain to expect any reasonableness or fairness from them."

"We must admit, however, that there is some delusion in it. It would be too uncharitable to believe otherwise," said Master Raymond thoughtfully.

"There may have been at the very first—on the part of the children," replied Master Putnam. "They might have supposed that Tituba and friendless Sarah Good tormented them—but since then, there has not been more than one part of delusion to twenty parts of wickedness. Why, can any sane man suppose that she-wolf sister-in-law of mine does not know she is lying, when she brings such horrible charges against the best men and women in Salem?"

"No, I give up Mistress Ann, she is possessed by a lying devil," admitted Master Raymond.

"It is well she does not hear that speech," said Joseph Putnam.

"Why?"

"Because, up to this time, you seem to have managed to soften her heart a little."

"I have tried to. I have thought myself justified in playing a part—as King David once did you know."

"It is that which brings me here. I met her at the house of a friend whom I called to see on some business a day or two ago."

"Ah!"

"She said to me, in that soft purring voice of hers, 'Brother Joseph, I hear that your good friend Master Raymond is still in Boston.' I answered that I believed he was. 'When he took leave of me,' she continued, 'I advised him not to stay long in that town—as it was often a bad climate for strangers. I am sorry he does not take wise counsel.' Then she passed on, and out of the house. Have you any idea what she meant?"

Master Raymond studied a moment over it in silence. Then he said:—"It is the first warning of the rattlesnake, I suppose. How many do they usually give before they spring?"

"Three, the saying goes. But I guess this rattlesnake cannot be trusted to give more than one."

"I was convinced I saw your brother Thomas as I came ashore from the Storm King the other day."

"Ah, that explains it then. She understands it all then. She understands it all now just as well as if you had told her."

"But why should she pursue so fiendishly an innocent girl like Dulcibel, who is not conscious of ever having offended her?"

"Why do tigers slay, and scorpions sting? Because it is their nature, I suppose," replied Master Putnam philosophically. "Because, Mistress Dulcibel openly ridiculed and denounced her and the whole witchcraft business. And you will note that there has not been a single instance of this being done, that the circle of accusers have not seemed maddened to frenzy."

"Yes,—there has been one case—your own."

"That is true—because I am Thomas Putnam's brother. And, dupe and tool as he is of that she-wolf, and though there is no great amount of love lost between us—still I am his brother! And that protects me. Besides they know that it is as much any two men's lives are worth to attempt to arrest me."

"And then you think there is no special enmity against Dulcibel?"

"I have not said so. Jethro Sands hates her because she refused him; Leah Herrick wants her driven away, because she herself wants to marry Jethro, and fears Jethro might after all, succeed in getting Dulcibel; and Sister Ann hates her, because—"

"Well, because what?"

"Oh, it seems too egotistical to say it—because she knows she is one of my dear friends."

"She must dislike you very much then?"

"She does."

"Why?"

"Oh, there is no good reason. At the first, she was inclined to like me—but I always knew she was a cold-blooded snake and she-wolf, and I would have nothing to do with her. Then when brother Thomas began to sink his manhood and become the mere dupe and tool of a scheming woman, I remonstrated with him. I think, friend Raymond, that I am as chivalrous as any man ought to be. I admire a woman in her true place as much as any man—and would fight and die for her. But for these men that forget their manhood, these Marc Antonies who yield up their sound reason and their manly strength to the wiles and tears and charms of selfish and ambitious Cleopatras, I have nothing but contempt. There are plenty of them around in all ages of the world, and they generally glory in their shame. Of course brother Thomas did not enjoy very much my mean opinion of his conduct—and as for sister Ann, she has never forgiven me, and never will."

"And so you think she hates Dulcibel, mainly because you love her?"

"That is about the shape of it," said Master Putnam drily. "That Dulcibel feels for me the affection of a sister, only intensifies my sister-in-law's aversion to her. But then, you see, that merely on the general principle of denouncing all who set themselves in opposition to the so-called afflicted circle, Dulcibel would be accused of witchcraft."

"Well, for my part, I think the whole affair can only be accounted for as being a piece of what we men of the world, who do not belong to any church, call devilishness," said Master Raymond hotly.

"You see," responded Master Putnam, "that you men of the world have to come to the same conclusion that we church members do. You impute it to 'devilishness' and we to being 'possessed by the devil.' It is about the same thing. And now give me an idea of your latest plans. Perhaps I can forward them in some way, either here or at Salem."

[3] See Drake's History of Boston

CHAPTER XXXVIII.

Conflicting Currents in Boston.

All this time the under-current of opposition to these criminal proceedings against the alleged witches, was growing stronger, at Boston. The Reverend Samuel Willard and Joshua Moody both ministers of undoubted orthodoxy from the Puritan stand-point, did not scruple to visit the accused in the keeping of jailer Arnold, and sympathize openly with them. Captain Alden and Master Philip English and his wife especially, were persons of too great wealth and reputation not to have many sympathizing friends.

On the other hand, the great majority of the Puritans, under the lead of the Reverend Cotton Mather, and the two Salem ministers, Parris and Noyes were determined that the prosecution should go on, until the witches, those children of the Evil One, were thoroughly cast out; even if half of their congregations should have to be hung by the other half.

At a recent trial in Salem, one of the "afflicted" had even gone so far as to cry out against the Rev. Master Willard. But the Court, it seemed, was not quite ready for that; for the girl was sent out of court, being told that she must have mistaken the person. When this was reported to Master Willard, it by no means tended to lessen his growing belief that the prosecutions were inspired by evil spirits.

Of course in this condition of things, the position of the Governor, Sir William Phips, became a matter of the first importance. As he owed his office mainly to the influence of the Rev. Increase Mather, and sat under the weekly ministrations of his learned son, Cotton Mather, the witch prosecutors had a very great hold upon him. With a good natural intellect, Sir William had received a very scanty education; and was therefore much impressed by the prodigious attainments of such men as the two Mathers. To differ with them on a theological matter seemed to him rather presumptuous. If they did not know what was sound in theology, and right in practise; why was there any use in having ministers at all, or who could be expected to be certain of anything?

Then if Sir William turned to the law, he was met by an almost unanimous array of lawyers and judges who endorsed the witchcraft prosecution. Chief-Justice Stoughton, honest and learned Judge Sewall—and nearly all the rest of the judiciary—were sure of the truth in this matter. Not one magistrate could be found in the whole province, to decide as a sensible English judge is reported by tradition to have done, in the case of an old woman who at last acknowledged in the feebleness of her confused intellect that she was a witch, and in the habit of riding about on a broomstick: "Well, as I know of no law that forbids old women riding about on broomsticks, if they fancy that mode of conveyance, you are discharged." But there was not one magistrate at that time, wise or learned enough to make such a sensible decision in the whole of New England.

Thus with the almost unanimous bar, and the great preponderance of the clergy, advising him to pursue a certain course, Sir William undoubtedly would have followed it, had he not been a man whose sympathies naturally were with sea-captains, military officers, and other men-of-the-world; and, moreover, if he had not a wife, herself the daughter of a sea-captain, who was an utter disbeliever in her accused friends being witches, and who had moreover a very strong will of her own.

Of course if the Governor should come to Lady Mary's opinion, the prosecution might as well be abandoned—for, with a stroke of his pen, he could remit the sentences of all the convicted persons. Left to himself and Lady Mary, he doubtless would have done this; but he wished to continue in his office, and to be a successful Governor; and he knew that to array himself against the prosecution and punishment of the alleged witches was to displease the great majority of the people of the province; including, as I have shown, the most influential persons. In fact, it was simply to retire from his government in disgrace.

All this the Reverend Cotton Mather represented to Sir William, with much else of a less worldly, but no doubt still more effective character, based upon various passages of the old Testament rather than upon anything corresponding to them in the New.

And so the prosecutions and convictions went on; but the further executions waited upon the Governor's decision.

CHAPTER XXXIX.

The Rattlesnake Makes a Spring.

It was a Thursday afternoon, and the "afflicted circle" was having one of its informal meetings at the house of Mistress Ann Putnam. At these meetings the latest developments were talked over; and all the scandal of the neighborhood, and even of Boston and other towns, gathered and discussed. Thus in the examination of Captain Alden in addition to the material charges of witchcraft against him, which I have noted, were entirely irrelevant slanders of the grossest kind against his moral character which the "afflicted girls" must have gathered from very low and vulgar sources.

The only man present on this occasion was Jethro Sands; and the girls, especially Leah Herrick, could not but wonder who now was to be "cried out against," that Jethro was brought into their counsels.

It is a curious natural instinct which leads every faculty—even the basest—to crave more food in proportion to the extent in which it has been already gratified. In the first place, the "afflicted" girls no doubt had their little spites, revenges, and jealousies to indulge, but afterwards they seemed to "cry out" against those of whom they hardly knew anything, either to oblige another of the party, or to punish for an expressed disbelief in their sincerity, or even out of the mere wantonness of power to do evil.

Mistress Ann Putnam opened the serious business of the afternoon, after an hour or so had been spent in gossip and tale-bearing, by an account of some recent troubles of hers.

"A few nights ago," said she, "I awakened in the middle of the night with choking and strangling. I knew at once that a new 'evil hand' was upon me; for the torment was different from any I had ever experienced. I thought the hand that grasped me around the throat would have killed me—and there was a heavy weight upon my breast, so that I could hardly breathe. I clutched at the thing that pressed upon my breast, and it felt hard and bony like a horse's

170

hoof—and it was a horse. By the faint moonlight I saw it was the wild black 'familiar' that belongs to the snake-marked witch, Dulcibel Burton. But the hand that grasped my throat was the strong hand of a man. I caught a sight of his face. I knew it well. But I pity him so much that I hesitate to reveal it. I feel as if I would almost rather suffer myself, than accuse so fine a young man as he seemed to be of such wicked conduct."

"But it appears to me that it is your duty to expose him, Mistress Putnam," said Jethro Sands. "I know the young man whose spectre you saw, for he and that black witch of a mare seem to be making their nightly rounds together. They 'afflicted' me the other night the same way. I flung them off; and I asked him what he meant by acting in that way? And he said he was a lover of the witch Dulcibel; who was one of the queens of Hell—I might know that by the snake-mark on her bosom. And she had told him that he must afflict all those who had testified against her; and she would lend him her 'familiar,' the black mare, to help him do it."

By this time, even the dullest of the girls of course saw very plainly who was being aimed at; but Mistress Putnam added, "upon learning that Master Jethro had also been afflicted by this person, I had very little doubt that I should find the guilty young man had been doing the same to all of you; for we have seen heretofore that when these witches attack one of us, they attack all, hating all for the same reason, that we expose and denounce them. I may add that I have also heard that the young man in question is now in Boston doing all he can in aid of the snake-witch Dulcibel Burton; and representing all of us to Lady Mary Phips and other influential persons, as being untruthful and malicious accusers of innocent people." Here she turned to one who had always been her right-hand as it were, and said:—"I suppose you have been tormented in the same way, dear Abigail?"

Ann Putnam, her daughter, however, that precocious and unmanageable girl of twelve, here broke in: "I think my mother is entirely mistaken. I was treated just the same way about a week ago; but it was not the spectre of Master Raymond at all—it was the spectre of another man whom I never saw before. It was not at all like Master Raymond; and I, for one, will not join in crying out against him."

In those old times, parents were treated with a much greater show, at least, of respect and veneration than they are at present; and therefore Mistress Putnam was greatly shocked at her daughter's language; but her daughter was well known to all present as an exceptional child, being very forward and self-willed, and therefore her mother simply said, "I had not expected such unkind behavior from you, Ann."

"Master Raymond has been very kind to all of us, you know—has given us pretty things, and has promised to send us all presents when he gets back from England; and I have heard you and father both say, that the Putnams always stand up for their friends."

This reference to the promised presents from England, evidently told all around the circle. They had nothing to gain by "crying out" against Master Raymond, they had something to gain by not doing it; besides, he was a very handsome young man, who had tried to make himself agreeable to almost all of them as he had opportunity. And though Dulcibel's beauty went for nothing in their eyes, a young man's good looks and gallant bearing were something entirely different.

And so Abigail Williams, and Mary Walcot, and Mercy Lewis, and Leah Herrick, and Sarah Churchill, and Elizabeth Hubbard all had the same tale to tell with suitable variations, as young Ann Putnam had. They were certain that the face of the "spectre" was not the face of Master Raymond; but of some person they had never before seen. Mercy Lewis and Sarah Churchill, in fact, were inclined to think it was the face of Satan himself; and they all wondered very much that Mistress Putnam could have mistaken such an old and ugly face, for that of the comely young Englishman.

As for Leah Herrick, she did not care in her secret heart if Master Raymond were in love with Dulcibel—so that he would only take her out of the country, where there was no danger of Jethro's seeing her any more. All her belief that Dulcibel was a witch was based upon jealousy, and now that it was utterly improbable that Jethro would ever turn his thoughts in that direction again, she had no hard feeling towards her; while, as she also had reason to expect a handsome present from England, she did not share in the least Jethro's bitterness against the young Englishman.

But although Mistress Putnam was thus utterly foiled in her effort to enlist the "afflicted circle" in her support, she was not the woman to give up her settled purpose on that account. She knew well that she was a host in herself, so far as the magistrates were concerned. And, having Jethro Sands to join her, it made up the two witnesses that were absolutely necessary by the law of Massachusetts as of Moses. The "afflicted circle" might not aid her, but it was not likely that they would openly revolt, and take part against her in public; and so she went the very next morning in company with that obedient tool, her husband and Jethro Sands, to the office of Squire Hathorne, and got him to issue a warrant for the arrest of Master Ellis Raymond, on the usual charge of practicing witchcraft.

CHAPTER XL.

An Interview with Lady Mary.

Master Raymond, having obtained an introduction to the Governor's wife, Lady Mary, lost no time in endeavoring to "cultivate the amenities of life," so far as that very influential person was concerned. He had paid the most deferential court to her on several occasions where he had been able to meet her socially; and had impressed the Governor's lady very favorably, as being an unusually handsome, well-bred and highly cultivated young man. A comely and high-spirited lady of forty, she was better pleased to be the recipient of the courteous and deferential attentions of a young Englishman of good connections like Master Raymond, than even to listen to the wise and weighty counsel of so learned a man as Master Cotton Mather.

Only in the last minutes of their last meeting however, when handing her ladyship to her carriage, did Master Raymond feel at liberty to ask her if he could have a short private interview with her the next morning. She looked a little surprised, and then said, "Of course, Master Raymond."

"At what hour will it suit your ladyship?"

"At twelve, precisely, I have an engagement at one;" and the carriage drove off.

A minute or two before twelve, Master Raymond was at the Governor's house in Green lane; and was duly admitted, as one expected, and shown into her ladyship's boudoir.

"Now, come right to the point, Master Raymond; and tell me what I can do for you," said her ladyship smiling. "If I can help you, I will; if I cannot, or must not, I shall say so at once—and you must continue to be just as good a friend to me as ever."

"I promise that to your ladyship," replied the young man earnestly. He really liked and admired Lady Mary very much.

"Is it love, or money?—young men always want one of these."

"Your ladyship is as quick-witted in this as in everything else."

"Well, which is it?"

"Love."

"Ah—who?"

"Mistress Dulcibel Burton."

"What!—not the girl with the snake-mark?"

Raymond bowed his head very low in answer.

Lady Mary laughed. "She is a witch then, it seems; for she has bewitched you."

"We were betrothed to each other only a few days before that absurd and lying charge was made against her."

"And her horse—her black mare—that upset the Reverend Master Parris into the duck pond; and then went up into the clouds; and, as Master Cotton Mather solemnly assured me, has never been seen or heard of since—what of it—where is it, really?"

"In an out-of-the-way place, up in Master Joseph Putnam's woods," replied the young man smiling.

"And you are certain of it?"

"As certain as riding the mare for about ten miles will warrant."

"Master Mather assured me that no man—except perhaps Satan or one of his imps—could ride her."

"Then I must be Satan or one of his imps, I suppose."

"How did you manage it?"

"I put a side-saddle on the beast; and a woman's skirt on myself."

The lady laughed outright. "Oh, that is too good! It reminds me of what Sir William often says, 'Anything can be done, if you know how to do it!' I must tell it to him he will enjoy it so much. And it will be a good thing to plague Master Mather with."

"Please do not tell anyone just now," protested the young man earnestly. "It may bring my good friend, Joseph Putnam, into trouble. And it would only make them all angrier than they are with Dulcibel."

"Dulcibel—that is a strange name. It is Italian—is it not."

"I judge so. It is a family name. I suppose there is Italian blood in the family. At least Mistress Dulcibel looks it."

"She does. She is very beautiful—of a kind of strange, fascinating beauty. I do not wonder she bewitched you. Was that serpent mark too from Italy?"

"I think it very likely."

"Perhaps she is descended from Cleopatra—and that is the mark left by the serpent on the famous queen's breast."

"I think it exceedingly probable," said Master Raymond. My readers will have observed before this, that he was an exceedingly polite and politic young man.

"Well, and so you want me to get Mistress Dulcibel, this witch descendant of that famous old witch, Cleopatra, out of prison?"

"I hoped that, from the well-known kindness of heart of your ladyship, you would be able to do something for us."

"You see the difficulty is simply here. I know that all these charges of witchcraft against such good, nice people as Captain Alden, Master and Mistress English, your betrothed Dulcibel, and a hundred others, are mere bigotry and superstition at the best, and sheer spite and maliciousness at the worst—but what can I do? Sir William owes his position to the Reverend Increase Mather—and, besides, not being a greatly learned man himself, is more impressed than he ought to be by the learning of the ministers and the lawyers. I tell him that a learned fool is the greatest fool alive; but still he is much puzzled. If he does not conform to the wishes of the ministers and the judges, who are able to lead the great majority of the people in any direction they choose, he will lose his position as Governor. Now, while this is not so much in itself, it will be a bar to his future advancement—for preferment does not often seek the men who fail, even when they fail from having superior wisdom and nobleness to the multitude."

It was evident that Sir William and Lady Mary had talked over this witchcraft matter, and its bearing upon his position, a good many times. And Master Raymond saw very clearly the difficulties of the case.

"And still, if the robe of the Governor can only continue to be worn by dyeing it with innocent blood, I think that a man of the natural greatness and nobility of Sir William, would not hesitate as to his decision."

"But a new Governor in his place might do worse."

"Yes, he might easily do that."

"When it comes to taking more lives by his order, then he will decide upon his course. So far he is temporizing," said the lady.

"And Dulcibel?"

"She is not suffering," was the reply. "Oh, if I only could say the same of the poor old women, and poor young women, now lying in those cold and loathsome cells—innocent of any crime whatever either against God or against man—I should not feel it all here so heavily," and Lady Mary pressed her hand against her heart. "But we are not responsible for it! I have taken off every chain—and do all I dare; while Sir William shuts his eyes to my unlawful doings."

"Will you aid her to escape, should her life be in danger? You told me to speak out frankly and to the point."

The lady hesitated only for a moment. "I will do all I can—even to putting my own life in peril. When something *must* be done, come to me again. And now judge me and Sir William kindly; knowing that we are not despots, but compelled to rule somewhat in accordance with the desires of those whom we have been sent here to govern."

Lady Mary extended her hand; the young man took it, as he might have taken the hand of his sovereign Queen, and pressed it with his lips. Then he bowed himself out of the boudoir.

CHAPTER XLI.

Master Raymond is Arrested for Witchcraft.

As Master Raymond walked up the street toward the Red Lion, he felt in better spirits. He had secured the aid, if things should come to the worst of a very influential friend—and one who, woman-like, would be apt to go even farther than her word, as noble spirits in such cases are apt to do. Therefore he was comparatively light-hearted.

Suddenly he felt a strong grasp upon his shoulder; and turning, he saw a couple of men beside him. One he knew well as deputy-marshall Herrick, of Salem.

"You are wanted at Salem, Master Raymond," said Marshall Herrick gravely, producing a paper.

Raymond felt a sinking of heart as he glanced over it—it was the warrant for his arrest, issued by Squire Hathorne.

"At whose complaint?" he asked, controlling his emotions, and speaking quite calmly and pleasantly.

"At the complaint of Mistress Ann Putnam and Master Jethro Sands," replied the officer.

"Of witchcraft? That is very curious. For as Dr. Griggs knows, just before I left Salem Farms, I was suffering from 'an evil hand' myself."

"Indeed!" said the officer.

"When am I to go?"

"Immediately. We have provided a horse for you."

"I should like to get my valise, and some clothes from the Red Lion."

The officer hesitated.

Master Raymond smiled pleasantly. "You must be hungry about this time of day, and they have some of the best wine at the Lion I ever tasted. You shall drink a bottle or two with me. You know that a man travels all the better for a good dinner and a bottle of good wine."

The officers hesitated no longer. "You are a sensible man, Master Raymond, whether you are a witch or not," said the deputy marshall.

"I think if the wine were better and plentier around Salem, there would be fewer witches," rejoined Master Raymond; which the other officer considered a very witty remark, judging by the way he laughed at it.

The result of this strategic movement of Master Raymond's, was that he had a couple of very pleasant and good-humored officials to attend him all the way to Salem jail, where they arrived in the course of the evening. Proving that thus by the aid of a little metaphorical oil and sugar, even official machinery could be made to work a good deal smoother than it otherwise would. While the officers themselves expressed their utter disbelief to the people they met, of the truth of the charges that had been brought against Master Raymond; who in truth was himself "an afflicted person," and had been suffering some time from an "evil hand," as the wise Dr. Griggs had declared.

The Salem keeper, Uncle Robie, true to his accustomed plan of action, received Master Raymond very gruffly; but after he had got rid of the other professionals, he had a good long talk, and made his cell quite comfortable for him. He also took him in to visit Antipas, who was delighted to see him, and also to hear that Mistress Dulcibel, was quite comfortably lodged with Keeper Arnold.

Then the young man threw himself upon his bed, and slept soundly till morning. He did not need much study to decide upon his plans, as he had contemplated such a possibility as that, ever since the arrest of Dulcibel, and had fully made up his mind in what manner he would meet it. If, however, he had known the results of the conference of the "afflicted circle" two days previous, he would have felt more encouraged as to the probable success of the defence he meditated. The constable that had aided the deputy-marshall in making the arrest, had agreed however to send word to Joseph Putnam of what had occurred; and comforted by the thought of having at least one staunch friend to stand by him, Master Raymond had slept soundly even on a prison pallet.

The next morning, as early as the rules of the jail would admit, Joseph Putnam came to see him. "I had intended to come and see you in Boston to-day," said Master Joseph, "but the she-wolf was too quick for me."

"Why, had you heard anything?"

"Yes, and I hardly understand it. Abigail Williams called to see Goodwife Buckley yesterday, and told her in confidence that it was probable you would be cried out against by Sister Ann and Jethro Sands; and to warn me of it."

"Abigail Williams!"

"Yes; and she also dropped a hint that none of the other 'afflicted girls' had anything to do with it—for they looked upon you as a very nice young man, and a friend."

"Well, that is good news indeed," said Master Raymond brightening up.

"And I called upon Doctor Griggs on my way here, and he says he is confident there was an 'evil hand' upon you when you were suffering at my house; and he will be on hand at the examination to give his testimony, if it is needed, to that effect."

"But that terrible sister-in-law of yours! If she could only be kept away from the examination for half-an-hour; and give me time to impress the magistrates and the people a little."

"It might be done perhaps," said Joseph Putnam musing.

"Do not be too conscientious about the means, my dear friend," continued Master Raymond. "Do not stand so straight that you lean backward. Remember that this is war and a just war against false witnesses, the shedders of innocent blood, and wicked or deceived rulers. If I am imprisoned, what is to become of Dulcibel? Think of her—do not think of me."

Joseph Putnam was greatly agitated. "I will do all I can for both of you. But my soul recoils from anything like deceit, as from wickedness itself. But I will think over it, and see if I cannot devise some way to keep Sister Ann away, for a time or altogether."

"Give me at least fifteen minutes to work on the Magistrates, and to enlist the sympathies of the people in my behalf. For me, so far as my conscience is concerned, I should not hesitate to shoot that Jezebel. For the murder of the twenty innocent men and women who have now been put to death, she is mainly responsible. And to kill her who surely deserves to die, might save the lives of fifty others."

Joseph Putnam shook his head. "I cannot see the matter in that light, Friend Raymond."

"Oh," replied Raymond, "of course I do not mean you should kill Mistress Ann. I only put it as giving my idea of how far *my* conscience would allow me to go in the matter. Draw her off in some way though—keep her out of the room for awhile—give me a little time to work in."

"I will do all I can; you may be sure of that," responded Master Putnam emphatically.

Here further confidential conversation was prevented by the entrance of the marshall.

CHAPTER XLII.

Master Raymond Astonishes the Magistrates.

The examination was to commence at three o'clock in the afternoon, and to be held in the Court House in the town, as being more convenient to Squire Hathorne than the meeting-house in the village.

As Master Thomas Putnam's house and farm were several miles beyond the village, it made quite a long ride for them to attend the examination. He had arranged with his wife, however, to start immediately after their usual twelve o'clock dinner, taking her behind him on a pillion, as was customary at that day—his daughter Ann being already in town, where she was paying a visit to a friend. He had received however a message about ten o'clock, requesting his immediate presence at Ipswich, on a matter of the most urgent importance; and though he was greatly puzzled by it, he concluded to go at once to Ipswich and go from there direct to Salem town, without coming home again, as it would be very much out of his road to do so.

According to this new arrangement, Mistress Ann would take the other horse, and a lady's saddle, and ride to town by herself. They had still a third horse, but that was already in town with her daughter.

The Court House was but a short distance from the prison; and, as it was a good Puritan fashion to be punctual to the minute, at three o'clock precisely Squires Hathorne and Corwin were in their arm-chairs, and Master Raymond standing on the raised platform in front of them. As the latter looked carefully around the room, he saw that neither Thomas Putnam nor his mischievous wife, nor his own best friend Joseph Putnam, was present. Squire Hathorne also observed that Mistress Ann Putnam was not present; but, as she was usually very punctual, he concluded that she would be there in a few minutes, and after some whispered words with his colleague, resolved to proceed with the examination.

Turning to the young Englishman, he said in his usual stern tones: —
"Ellis Raymond, you are brought before authority, upon high
suspicion of sundry acts of witchcraft. Now tell us the truth of this
matter."

But no answer came from the accused. Then, when all eyes were
intently regarding him, he gave a wild shriek, and fell outstretched
upon the platform.

"Let me to him!" said Dr. Griggs, elbowing his way through the
crowd. "I said a month ago that an 'evil hand' was upon him; and
now I am certain of it."

Master Raymond had not been an attentive observer of the recent
trials for nothing; and he now gave the audience an exhibition which
would compare favorably with the best, even with Mistress Ann
Putnam's and Abigail William's. His face became shockingly
contorted, and he writhed and twisted and turned convulsively. He
tore imaginary spectral hands from around his neck. He pushed
imaginary weights from off his breast. He cried, "Take them away!
Pray, take them away!" until the whole company were very much
affected; and even the magistrates were greatly astounded.

Dr. Griggs loosened his collar and unbuttoned his doublet, and had
water brought to sprinkle his face keeping up a running fire of
words at the same time, to the effect that he knew, and had said, as
least a month before, that Master Raymond had an "evil hand" upon
him.

"Who is it hurts you?" at length asked credulous Squire Hathorne.

"See, there is the yellow bird!" cried the young man, staring into
vacancy. "He is coming to peck my eyes out! Kill it! kill it!" dashing
his hands out from his face violently. "Has no one a sword — pray do
try to kill it!"

Here an impetuous young villager, standing by, drew his rapier, and
stabbed violently in the direction of the supposed spectral bird.

"Oh! Oh! You almost killed it! See, there are some of its feathers!"
And three yellow feathers were seen floating in the air; being small

chicken feathers with which he had been provided that very morning by Uncle Robie, the jailer; and which the adroit Master Raymond rightly thought would have a prodigious effect.

And the result was fully equal to his expectations. From that moment, it was evident that he had all the beholders with him; and Squire Hathorne, disposed as he had been to condemn him almost without a hearing, was completely staggered. He had the feathers from the "yellow bird" carefully placed upon his desk, with the purpose of transmitting them at once to Master Cotton Mather who, with these palpable proofs of the reality of the spectral appearance would be able utterly to demolish all the skeptical unbelievers.

Finding that such an effect had been produced, Master Raymond allowed himself to regain his composure somewhat.

"Mistress Ann Putnam, who is one of the two complainants, unaccountably is not here," said Squire Hathorne. "Master Jethro Sands, what have you to say against this young man? You are the other complainant."

"Probably my mother has come to the conclusion that she was mistaken, as I told her; and therefore she has remained at home," said Ann Putnam, the daughter; who was delighted with the feather exhibition, and was secretly wondering how it was done.

"Well, what have you to say, —Jethro Sands?"

The audience looked around at Jethro with scornful faces, evidently considering him an imposter. What did he know about witches— compared to this rich young man from over the seas?

"Tell him you find you were mistaken also," whispered Leah Herrick.

"After seeing what we have seen, I withdraw my charges, Squire. I think that Mistress Putnam and myself must have been visited by the spectre of somebody else, and not by Master Raymond."

"I hope that next time you will wait until you are quite certain," replied Squire Hathorne gruffly. "Do you know that Master

Raymond can have his action against you for very heavy damages, for slander and defamation?"

"I certainly am very sorry, and humbly beg Master Raymond's pardon," said Jethro, very much alarmed. He had never thought that the affair might take this turn—as indeed it did in many cases, some six months afterward; and which was a very effective damper upon the spirits of the prosecutors.

Then the magistrates could do nothing less than discharge the prisoner; and Master Raymond stepped down from the platform a free man, to be surrounded by quite a circle of sympathizing friends. But his first thanks were due to Dr. Griggs for his professional services.

"Doctor, those things you did for me when in the convulsions, relieved me greatly," and he took out his purse. "Yes, Doctor, I insist upon it. Skill like yours is always worth its recompense. We must not muzzle the ox, you know, that treads out the corn." And he put a gold piece into Dr. Grigg's palm—which was not often favored with anything but silver in Salem.

Dr. Griggs was glad that he had been able to render him a little service; and said that, if there had been the least necessity for it, he would have gone on the platform, and testified as to the complete absurdity of the charge that that excellent woman, Mistress Ann Putnam, evidently in mistake, had brought against him.

Then the "afflicted circle" had to be spoken to, who this afternoon did not appear to be in the least afflicted, but in the very best of spirits. They now felt more admiration for him than ever; and greeted him with great cordiality as he came to where they were standing. "When are you going back to England?" was a frequent question; and he assured them he now hoped to go before many weeks; and then, smiling, added that they would be certain to hear from him.

As the crowd thinned out a little, Abigail Williams called him aside; "and did you really see the yellow bird, Master Raymond?" said she archly.

"The yellow bird!" replied he dreamily. "Ah! you know that when we that are 'afflicted' go into trances, we are not conscious of all that we see."

"For it seemed to me," continued the girl in a low tone, "that those feathers looked very much like chicken feathers." Then she laughed cunningly, and peered into his face.

"Indeed!" replied the young man gravely; "well, a chicken's bill, pecking at your eyes, is not a thing to be made light of. I knew of a girl, one of whose eyes was put entirely out by her pet canary."

And as he moved at once toward the rest of the group, the quick-witted and precocious child was compelled to follow.

The magistrates had left the Court House, with the majority of the people, including Jethro Sands, when who should come in, walking hastily, and his face flushed with hard riding, but Thomas Putnam.

"Am I too late? What was done?" he said quickly to Leah Herrick, who was standing near the door.

"Oh, the charge broke down, and Master Raymond was discharged."

"Ah! Where is my wife?"

"She did not come. It was said by your daughter, that she probably found she was mistaken in the person, and stayed for that reason."

"I do not believe it—she would have told me. What did Jethro Sands do?"

"Oh, he withdrew the charges, so far as he was concerned. There was a great deal more danger that Master Raymond would prove him to be a witch, than he Master Raymond."

"I see—it is a case of conspiracy!" exclaimed Master Putnam hotly. "Had you any hand in this, Master Raymond?" turning to the young Englishman, who had drawn near, on his way to the door.

"Ah, Master Putnam, glad to see you. You did get here early enough however to witness my triumphant vindication. Here is learned Dr.

Griggs, and young Mistress Williams, and your own gifted daughter, and handsome Mistress Herrick, and half-a-dozen others of my old friends who were ready to testify in my behalf, if any testimony had been needed. Make my compliments to Mistress Putnam; and give her my best thanks for her noble course, in confessing by her absence that she was mistaken, and that she had accused the wrong person."

The cool assurance with which this was uttered, quite confused Thomas Putnam. Could his wife have stayed away purposely? Perhaps so, for she was accustomed to rapid changes of her plans. But why then had he been lured off on a wild-goose chase all the way to Ipswich?

While he was standing there musing, his daughter came up. "I think, father, you and mother, next time, had better take my advice," said that incorrigible and unmanageable young lady; just about as opposite a character to the usual child of that period as could well be imagined. But these witchcraft trials, in which she figured so prominently had utterly demoralized her in this as in certain other respects.

CHAPTER XLIII.

Why Thomas Putnam Went to Ipswich.

What young Master Joseph Putnam undertook to do, he was apt to do pretty thoroughly. When he had once made up his mind to keep both his brother's wife and his brother himself, away from the examination, he had rapidly thought over various plans, and adopted two which he felt pretty certain would not fail. They all involved a little deceit, or at least double dealing—and he hated both those things with a righteous hatred—but it was to prevent a great injustice, and perhaps to save life.

As he rode rapidly homeward, turning over various plans, in his mind, he had passed through the village, when he saw some one approaching on what seemed to be the skeleton of an old horse. He at once recognized the rider as an odd character, a carpenter, whom he at one time had occasion to employ in doing some work on a small property he owned in Ipswich. Reining up his horse, Master Putnam stopped to have a chat with the man—whose oddity mainly consisted in his taciturnity, which was broken only by brief and pithy sentences.

"A fine day Ezekiel—how are things in Ipswich?"

"Grunty!"

"Ah! I am sorry to hear it. Why, what is the matter?"

"Broomsticks, chiefly."

"You mean the witches. That is a bad business. But how shall we mend it?"

The old carpenter was too shrewd to commit himself. He glanced at Master Putnam, and then turning his head aside, and giving a little laugh, said, "Burn all the broomsticks."

"A good idea," replied Master Putnam, also laughing. "Oh, by the way, Ezekiel, I wonder if you could do a little errand for me?" and the young man took out his purse and began opening it. "You are not in a great hurry, are you?"

"Hurry, is for fools!"

"You know where my brother Thomas lives? Up this road?" They were just where two roads joined, one leading by his own house, and the other past his brother's.

"I wish I knew the road to heaven as well."

"You know how to keep silent, and how to talk also, Ezekiel—especially when you are well paid for it?"

The old man laughed. "A little bullet sometimes makes a big hole," he said.

"I want you to go to my brother Thomas, and say simply these words:—Ipswich Crown and Anchor. Very important indeed. At once. Wait till he comes."

"All right." And he held out his hand, into which Master Joseph put as much silver as the old man could make in a whole week's work.

"You are not to remember who sent you, or anything else than those words. Perhaps you have been drinking rather too much cider, you know. Do you understand?"

The old man's face assumed at once a very dull and vacant expression, and he said in that impressive manner which rather too many glasses is apt to give, "Ipswich. Crown and Anchor. Very important indeed. At once. Wait till he comes."

"That will do very well, Ezekiel. But not a word more, mind!"

"Tight as a rat-trap," replied the old man—and he turned his skeleton's head, and went up the road towards Thomas Putnam's.

Joseph felt certain that this would take his brother to Ipswich. Both of them were greatly interested in a lawsuit with certain of the Ipswich people, regarding the northern boundary of the Putnam farms. Thomas was managing the matter for the family; and was continually on the look-out for fresh evidence to support the Putnam claim. In fact, bright Master Raymond had once said that, between the Salem witches and the Ips-witches, Master Thomas seemed to have no peace of his life. But this was before the witch persecutions had assumed such a tragical aspect.

When Ezekiel had found Thomas Putnam and delivered his brief message, without dismounting from his skeleton steed, Master Putnam asked at once who sent the message.

"Ipswich. Crown and Anchor. Very important indeed! At once. Wait till he comes," repeated the old man, with a face of the most impassive solemnity, and emphasizing every sentence with his long fore-finger.

And that was all Master Thomas could get out of him. That much came just as often as he wished it; but no more—not a word.

Mistress Ann Putnam had come out to the gate by that time. "He has been drinking too much cider," she said.

This gave a suggestion to Ezekiel.

"Yes, too much cider. Rum—steady me!"

Mistress Putnam thought that it might produce an effect of that kind, and, going back into the house, soon reappeared with a rather stiff drink of West India rum; which the old man tossed off with no perceptible difficulty.

He smiled as he handed back the tin cup which had held it. "Yes— steady now!" he said.

"Who gave you the message?" again asked Master Putnam.

Ezekiel looked solemn and thoughtful. "Who gave 'im the message," replied Ezekiel slowly.

"Yes—who sent you to me?"

"Who sent yer—to—me?" again repeated Ezekiel. "Ipswich. Crown and Anchor. At once. Wait till he comes." Then the old man's countenance cleared up, as if everything now must be perfectly satisfactory.

"Oh there is no use in trying to get any more out of him—he is too much fuddled," said Mistress Putnam impatiently.

"More rum—steady me!" mumbled Ezekiel.

"No, not a drop more," said Thomas Putnam peremptorily. "You have had too much already."

The old man frowned—and turning the skeleton steed after considerable effort, he gave his parting shot—"Crown and anchor— wait till he comes!" and rode off in a spasmodic trot down the lane.

"I shall have to go to Ipswich, and see about this, it may supply the missing link in our chain of evidence!"

"But how about this afternoon?" queried his wife.

"Oh, I can get to Salem by three o'clock, by fast riding. I will leave the roan horse for you."

"Saddle the grey mare, Jehosaphat."

And thus it was that his brother Joseph, looking out of his sitting-room window, about an hour after his arrival at home, saw Master Thomas Putnam, on his well-known grey mare, riding along the road past his house on the most direct route to Ipswich.

"He is out of the way, for one—if he waits an hour or two for any person to meet him on important business at the Crown and Anchor," thought the young man. "It is important indeed though that he should go, and keep himself out of mischief; and from helping to take any more innocent lives. And when he comes to his senses—in the next world, if not in this—he will thank me for deceiving him. Now let me see whether I can do as good a turn for that delectable wife of his."

CHAPTER XLIV.

How Master Joseph Circumvented Mistress Ann.

About an hour afterwards, Master Joseph saw one of his farm-hands coming over the fields from the direction of his brother's house, which was about two miles almost directly to the west of his own house. Going out to meet him, he said—

"Well, Simon Peter, I see that you got the rake."

"Yes, Master Joseph; but they wish me to return it as soon as we can."

"That is right. Finish your job in the garden this afternoon, and take it back early tomorrow morning. You can go to work now."

The man walked off toward the garden.

"Wait a moment!" his master cried. The man stopped. "Anything new at brother Thomas's? Are they all at home?"

"No, indeed! Master Thomas has gone off to Ipswich—and little Ann is at Salem town."

"I could not borrow a horse, then, of them, you think?"

"No, indeed, sir. There is only one left in the stable; and Mistress Putnam means to use that to go to the trial this afternoon."

"Oh, well, I do not care much;" and his master walked off to the house, while Simon Peter went to his work.

Then, after a somewhat earlier dinner than usual, Master Joseph ordered his young horse, Sweetbriar, saddled; and after kissing his wife "in a scandalous manner"—that is, out of doors, where some one might have seen him do it—he mounted, and cantered off down the lane.

The young man loved a good horse and he claimed that Sweetbriar, with a year or two more of age and hardening, would be the fastest horse in the Province. As to temper, the horse was well named; for he could be as sweet, when properly handled, as a rose; and as sharp and briary as any rose-stalk under contrary conditions. A nervous, sensitive, high-mettled animal; Mistress Putnam, though a good rider, said it was too much work to manage him. While her husband always responded that Sweetbriar could be ridden by any one, for he was as gentle as a lamb.

Just as Mistress Ann Putnam had got through her dinner, she saw her brother-in-law Joseph riding up the lane. The brothers, as has been seen, differed very widely relative to the Witchcraft prosecutions; but still they visited one another, as they were held together by various family ties, and especially by the old lawsuit against certain of the Ipswich men, to which I have alluded.

Therefore Mistress Putnam opened the door and went out to the garden gate, where by this time the young man had dismounted, and fastened his horse.

"Is brother Thomas at home, Sister Ann?"

"No—he had a call to Ipswich this morning."

"Ah—the lawsuit business."

"I suppose so. But the messenger was so overcome with liquor, that he could not even remember who sent him."

"Why, how could Thomas know where to go then?"

"Oh, the man managed to say that his employee would be waiting for Thomas at the "Crown and Anchor," where he usually stops you know."

"Well, I am glad that Thomas went. I stopped to see if Jehosaphat could do a little errand for me—I might have sent one of my own men, but I forget matters sometimes."

"You will find him at the barn," replied Mistress

Putnam, a little anxious to cut short the conversation, as she wished to get ready for her ride to Salem.

Going to the barn, Master Joseph soon found Jehosaphat. "How do, Fatty!" this was the not very dignified diminutive into which Jehosaphat had dwindled in common use. "How are you getting along?"

"Fair to middlin, sir. Not as well though as on the old place, Master Joseph."

"I do not want to interfere with my brother, remember; but if at any time he should not want you any more, remember the old place is still open for you. It was your own fault, you know, that you went."

"I did not know when I was well off, Master Joseph. I was a fool, that was all."

"I thought so," replied Master Joseph pithily. "But no matter about that now—can you do an errand for me?"

"Of course I can—the mistress willing."

"Well, I said I wished to send you on an errand, and she told me where to find you."

"That is all right then."

"Go to Goodman Buckley's, in Salem village, and ask him for a bundle I left—bring it to my house, you know, you can take the roan horse there. And, by the way, Fatty, if you want to stop an hour or two to see the widow Jones's pretty daughter, I guess no great harm will be done."

Jehosaphat giggled—but then his face clouded. "But Mistress Putnam wants to take the roan herself this afternoon. The trial comes off, you know."

"Oh, it is not a trial—it is only an examination. And it is all fiddlesticks, anyhow. My sister-in-law is ruining her health by all this witch business. But if she insists upon going, I will lend her one of my horses. Therefore that need not keep you."

So Jehosaphat, in high glee at having an afternoon's holiday, with the roan horse, threw on the saddle and mounted.

195

As he rode at a rapid canter down the lane, Mistress Ann heard the noise, but supposed it was Master Joseph riding off again,—and did not even trouble herself to look out of the window, especially as she was just then changing her gown.

Not long after, coming into the family room, who should she see there, sitting demurely, reading one of the Reverend Cotton Mather's most popular sermons, but the same Master Joseph Putnam whom she had thought she was well rid of.

"I thought you had gone. I surely heard you riding down the lane," she said in a surprised tone.

"Oh, no, I wanted to speak with you about something."

"Who was it then?—I surely heard some one."

"Perhaps it was one of those spectral horses, with a spectral rider. As Master Mather says: These are very wonderful and appalling times!" And the young man laughed a little scornfully.

"Brother Joseph, I do not care to talk with you upon this question. I greatly regret, as do your brothers and your uncles, that you have gone over to the infidels and the scoffers."

"And I regret that they are making such fools of themselves," replied Joseph hotly.

"I have no time to discuss this question, brother Joseph," said Mistress Ann with dignity. "I am going to Salem town this afternoon, very much in the cross, to give my testimony against a young friend of yours. Would that I could have been spared this trial!" and his sister-in-law looked up to the ceiling sanctimoniously. As Joseph told his young wife that night, her hypocrisy hardened his heart against her; so that he could have kept her at home by sheer force, if it were necessary, and at all expedient—in fact he would have preferred that rough but sincere way.

"If you testify to anything that throws doubt upon Master Raymond's perfect innocency and goodness, you will testify to a lie," replied Master Joseph severely.

"As I said, I have no time for argument. Will you be good enough to tell Jehosaphat to saddle the roan for me."

"You know that I had your permission to send Fatty off on an errand—and he is not back yet."

Mistress Putnam started and bit her lip. She had made a mistake. "I suppose he will be back before long."

"I doubt it. I sent him to the village."

"Well, I suppose I can put on the saddle myself. Your conscience probably would not allow you to do it—even if common courtesy towards a woman, and that woman your sister, demanded it."

"Without deciding the latter point, I should think it almost impossible for me to put a saddle on the roan just now."

"Why? I do not understand you."

"Because he is doubtless miles away by this time."

"Jehosaphat did not take the horse!"

"It is precisely what he did do."

"He knew I wanted the roan to ride to Salem town this afternoon."

"He told me you did; but I said that I thought you would have too much sense to go. Still, if you would go, that I would lend you one of my horses."

"Well, where is your horse?"

"There, at the door. You can take off my saddle, and put on your side-saddle, and, if you are in a hurry, Sweetbriar can do the distance in half the time that the roan could."

Mistress Putnam could have cried with anger and vexation. Like many people of strong and resolute will, she was a good deal of a coward on horseback; and she knew that Sweetbriar was what the farmers called "a young and very skittish animal." Still her determined spirit rose against thus being outdone; besides, she knew well that in a case like this, where none of the "afflicted circle," not even her own daughter, would aid her, the whole thing might fall through if she were not present. So she said, "Well, I will saddle your horse myself."

Here Master Joseph relented—because he now felt certain of his game. "I have conscientious scruples against lifting even my little finger to aid you in this unholy business," he said more placidly, "but under the circumstances, I will saddle Sweetbriar for you."

So saying, he took off his saddle from the horse, and substituted the side-saddle which he brought from the barn. Then he led Sweetbriar to the horse-block, and his sister-in-law mounted.

She glanced at his spurs. "You ride him with spurs, I see. Hand me my riding-whip," she said, pointing to where she had laid it, when she first came out.

"I would not strike him, if I were you. He is not used to the whip—it might make him troublesome."

Mistress Putnam made no reply; but gathered up the reins, and the horse started down the lane.

A singular smile came across the young man's features. He went back and closed the door of the house, and then started in a rapid walk across the field towards his own home. Neither of them thought it mattered that the house was left for a time unprotected. Mistress Putnam knew that a couple of farm-hands were at work in a distant field, who would be back at sundown; and there were so few strollers at that time, that no farmer thought of bolting up his doors and windows when he went to meeting, or to see a neighbor.

The way home across the fields was a good deal nearer than to go by the road, as the latter made quite an angle. And, as the young man strode swiftly, on he could see in many places his sister-in-law, riding deliberately along, and approaching the forks of the road, where anyone going to his own house, would turn and ride away from, instead of toward Salem.

"When she gets to the forks of the road, look out for squalls," said Master Joseph to himself. For many had been his own fights with Sweetbriar, when the horse wanted to go towards his stable, after a long ride, and his young master wanted him to go in the opposite direction. Sweetbriar had already gone about twenty miles that day—and, besides, had been given only the merest mouthful for dinner, with the object of preparing him for this special occasion.

The next swell in the ground afforded the young man an excellent view. Sweetbriar had arrived at the turn which led to his stable; where rest and oats awaited him; and it evidently seemed to Him the height of injustice and unreason to be asked to go all the way back to Salem again. Mistress Ann, however, knew nothing of these previous experiences of the animal, but imputed his insubordinate behavior entirely to self-will and obstinacy. And thus, as the great globe moves around the sun in a perpetual circle, as the result of the two conflicting forces of gravitation and fly-off-it-iveness, so Sweetbriar circled around and around, like a cat chasing his tail, as the result of the conflicting wills of himself and his rider.

Master Joseph watched the progress of the whole affair with decided pleasure. "No woman but a witch could get Sweetbriar past that turn," he said to himself, laughing outright, "And no man, who had not a pair of spurs on."

At last, getting out of all patience, Mistress Putnam raised her whip and brought it down sharply on her horse's shoulder. This decided the struggle; for, unused to such punishment, the fiery animal reared, and then turning, sprang up the road that led to his stable at a wild gallop.

His rider as I have said, was not a very good horse-woman, and she now took hold of the horn of the saddle with her right hand, to enable her to keep her seat; and tried to moderate the gait of the horse with the reins and the voice, abandoning all further resistance to his will as useless.

Setting off at a run, Master Joseph was able to reach home just about the same time as his sister-in-law did.

"Ah! I am glad you changed your mind, Sister Ann, about going to Salem. It is a great deal more sensible to come and spend the afternoon with Elizabeth."

"Very glad to see you, Sister Ann," said Mistress Joseph, coming out to the horse-block, at which Sweetbriar, from force of habit, had stopped.

Mistress Ann looked offended, and replied coldly, "I had no intention of coming here this afternoon, Sister Elizabeth; but this vile brute, which Joseph lent me, after sending away my own horse, would neither obey the reins nor the whip."

"You rascal!" said Master Joseph severely, addressing the horse. "You do not deserve to have a lady ride you."

"Can you not lend me another horse—say the one Elizabeth always rides?"

"All the other horses are out at work," replied Master Joseph; "and before I could get one of them in, and at all groomed up, ready for the saddle, I am afraid it would be too late for your purpose."

"So I must be compelled to do as you wish, and stay away from the examination?" said Mistress Ann bitterly.

"Oh, if you choose, I will put a pillion on Sweetbriar, and see how that works?" replied Master Joseph with a meek and patient expression of countenance, as of one upbraided without cause. "To be sure, Sweetbriar has never been asked to carry double; but he might as well learn now as ever."

"That seems to be the only thing that can be done now," and the expression of Mistress Ann's face resembled that of a martyr who was about to be tied to the stake; for riding on a pillion brought the lady always into the closest proximity with the gentleman, and she was now cherishing towards Master Joseph a temper that could hardly be called sisterly.

There was necessarily a great waste of time in getting the pillion on Sweetbriar. He never had carried double, and he evidently felt insulted by being asked to do it. Master Joseph glanced at the sun, and knew it must be now full two o'clock. Only by fast riding, would it be possible to get to Salem court-house by three; and the roads, as they then were, did not admit of fast riding except in a few places.

It was no easy thing for Mistress Ann to get on Sweetbriar, for the horse backed and sidled off from the horse-block whenever she attempted it—all his sweetness seemed gone by this time, and the briars alone remained. At least fifteen minutes more were lost in this way. But at last the difficult feat was accomplished.

"Hold on to me tightly," said the young man, "or you will be thrown off—" for the irritated animal began to curvet around in all directions, manifesting a strong determination to go back to his stable, instead of forward towards Salem.

"I think we had better try the other road, and not pass the forks where you had so much trouble with him," said Master Joseph, as the horse went more quietly, going up the first hill.

"As you think best," said his sister-in-law, in a sharp tone, "If I had a horse like this I would shoot him!"

"Oh, Sweetbriar is good enough usually. I never saw him so violent and troublesome as he is to-day. And I think I know the reason of it."

"What is the reason?"

"I fear he has an 'evil hand' upon him," said Master Joseph with great solemnity.

"Nonsense," replied Mistress Ann sharply.

"He has got the wicked One in him; that is the matter with him."

"That is about the same thing," said Master Joseph.

Now they were at the top of the hill, and the horse broke into tantrums again; requiring all of Master Joseph's skill to prevent his toppling himself and his two riders over one of the many boulders that obstructed the road.

"If you do not hold on to me more tightly, Sister Ann, you will be thrown off," said Master Joseph, putting back his right hand to steady her. And Mistress Ann was compelled to lock her arms around him, or take the chance of serious injury from being dashed to the rough highway. The young man would have liked to relieve his feelings by a hearty burst of laughter, as he felt her arms embracing him so warmly, but of course he dared not.

They soon came near the main road, running due north and south, and which it was necessary to take, as it led directly down to Salem. Sweetbriar knew that road well—and that he never stopped when once turned to the south on it, short of a six mile ride. He remembered his recent victorious struggle at the Forks, and now resolved upon another battle. All of Master Putnam's efforts—or what seemed so—could not get him headed southward on that road. In truth, burdened as he was, the young man really could not do it, without incurring too much risk to the lady behind him. Those who have ever had such a battle with a wilful, mettlesome horse, know that it often requires the utmost patience and determination on the part of his rider, to come out victorious. The best plan—the writer speaks from some experience—is to pull the animal round in a circle until his brain becomes confused, and then start him off in the right direction.

But Sweetbriar evidently had a better brain than usual, for when the whirl came to an end, it always found his pointing like the magnetic needle to the north. It had been Master Joseph's plan to pretend a good deal of earnestness in the struggle which he was certain would come in this place; but he was pleased to find that there was no need of any pretence in the matter. The horse, under the circumstances, the young man having a lady's safety to consult, was the master. Repeated trials only proved it. Whenever the fierce, final tug of war came, Mistress Ann's safety had to be consulted, and the horse had his own way. So, as the result Sweetbriar started off in a sharp canter up, instead of down, the road.

"Take me home then," said his sister-in-law—"if you will not take me to Salem."

"If I *will* not," repeated Master Joseph. "I give you my honest word, Sister Ann, that I could not make this horse go down the road, with us two on his back, if I stayed here all the afternoon trying. I should think you must have seen that."

"No matter. Take me home."

"Besides, we could not get to Salem before four o'clock now, if Sweetbriar went his best and prettiest."

"I give it up. Let us turn and go home."

"If we turn and go back the way we came, I do not think I shall be able to get this self-willed animal past my own gate."

"Well, what do you mean to do?" said the lady bitterly. "Ride on up to Topsfield?"

Master Joseph laughed. "No—there is a road strikes off towards your house a short distance above here, and I think I can get you home by it, without any further trouble."

"Very well—get me home as soon as you can. I do not feel like any further riding, or much more talking."

"Of course it is very aggravating," replied Master Putnam soothingly, "but then you know as Master Parris says, that all these earthly disappointments are our most valuable experiences—teaching us not to set our hopes upon worldly things, but upon those of a more enduring and satisfying character."

His sister-in-law's face, that he could not see, she being behind him, wore a look as she listened to this, which could be hardly called evangelical.

"You wished very much I know to go this afternoon to Salem," continued Master Joseph, in the same sermonizing tone; "but doubtless your wish has been overruled for good. I think, as a member of church, you should be willing to acquiesce patiently in the singular turn that affairs have taken, and console yourself with the thought that you have been innocently riding these peaceful roads instead of being in Salem, doing perchance an infinite deal of mischief."

"No doubt what you are saying seems to you very wise and edifying, Joseph Putnam, but I have a bad headache, and do not care to converse any further."

"But you must admit that your projected visit has been frustrated in a very singular, if not remarkable manner?" Master Joseph knew that he had her now at an advantage; she was compelled to listen to everything he chose to say. His saddle was even better in that respect than the minister's pulpit—you might leave a church, but she could not leave the horse.

"I do not see anything very miraculous, brother Joseph, in a young man like you having a self-willed and unprincipled horse. In truth, the wonder would be if you had a decent and well-governed animal," replied his sister-in-law wrathfully.

The young man smiled at the retort, but she could not see the gleam of sunshine as it passed rapidly over his face; lingering a moment in the soft depths of his sweet blue eyes. There was no smile however in his voice, but the previous solemnity, as he continued:—

"And yet if Balaam's ass could see the angel of the Lord, with his drawn-sword, standing in the way, and barring his further progress in wrongdoing, why might not this horse—who is much more intelligent than an ass—have seen a similar vision?"

The young man had begun this speech somewhat in sport; but as he ended it, the assumed tone of solemnity had passed into one of real earnestness. For, as he asked himself, "Why should it not be? This woman with him was bound on a wicked errand. Why should not the angel or the Lord stand in her way also—and the horse see him, even if his riders did not?"

Mistress Putnam made no answer. Perhaps now that the young man was really in earnest, what he said made some impression upon her, but, more probably it did not.

He, too, relapsed into silence. It seemed to him a good place to stop his preaching, and let his sister-in-law think over what he had said.

"Thank Heaven we are here at last!" said the baffled woman, as they rode up to the horse-block at her own door. Sweetbriar stood very quiet, and she stepped on the block, Master Joseph keeping his seat.

"Will you dismount and stay to supper, brother Joseph?" said Mistress Ann, in a soft purring tone. Master Joseph fairly started with his surprise, and looked steadily into her dark, inscrutable eyes—eyes like Jael's as she gazed upon sleeping Sisera.

"No, I thank you—I expect a friend to supper. I hope brother Thomas heard some good news at Ipswich. Come and see us when you feel like it." And he rode off.

As he told his wife afterwards, he would not have taken supper with his sister Ann that evening as he valued his life.

And yet perhaps it was all imagination—and he did not see that thing lurking in the depths of his sister-in-law's cold, unfathomable eyes that he thought he did. And yet her testimony against Rebecca Nurse, reads to us, even at this late day, with all the charity that we are disposed to exercise towards things so long past, as cold-blooded, deliberate murder.

CHAPTER XLV.

The Two Plotters Congratulate Each Other.

When Master Joseph arrived home, he told his wife of what a perverse course things had taken, amid his own and her frequent laughter. And then he could do nothing else than walk up and down impatiently, glancing at frequent intervals towards the road, to see if anybody were coming.

In the course of an hour or so, nobody appearing and Sweetbriar being sweetened up again by a good feed, he ordered the horse brought out. Then he was persuaded by his wife to recall the order, and wait patiently till sundown.

"What impatient creatures you men are!" said Mistress Elizabeth with feminine superiority. "Doubtless he will be along. Give him sufficient time. Now, do not worry, husband mine, but take things patiently."

So Master Joseph was induced to control his restlessness and just as soon as he could have been reasonably expected, Master Raymond was seen riding up the lane at a light canter.

"Hurrah!" cried Master Joseph, running to meet him. "And is it all over?"

"We have smitten Ammon, hip and thigh, from Aroer even till thou come to Minnith!" answered Master Raymond, laughing. "It was you that kept the she-wolf away, I know. How did you do it?"

"Come in and I will tell you all about it. And I want to hear how all went off in Salem."

After a couple of hours' conversation, broken frequently by irresponsible bursts of laughter, the young men were mutually enlightened; and complimented each other upon the success with which they had worked out their respective schemes—while young Mistress Elizabeth complimented them both, thinking honestly in her innocent heart that two such wonderful young men certainly had never before existed.

"How I should like to have seen you astonishing old Squire Hathorne," said Master Joseph.

"I am afraid you would have spoiled all by laughing," said his young wife. "You know you never can control your merriment, Joseph."

"I cannot? You should have seen me preaching to sister Ann this afternoon. I kept my face all the time as sober as a judge's. You know she had to take it all quietly—she could not even run away from it."

"I would have given one of your five-pound Massachusetts notes to see it," said Master Raymond. "And five pounds more to see your brother Thomas stamping up and down the bar-room of the 'Crown and Anchor,' waiting for that Ipswich man to meet him."

"I was very careful all through not to tell a direct falsehood," said Master Joseph; "it is bad enough to deceive people, without being guilty of downright lying."

"Oh, of course," replied Master Raymond. "I do not know that I told a downright lie either, all day; although I must admit that I acted a pretty big one. But you must deal with fools according to their folly—you know we have Scripture for that."

"I do not think I would have done it merely to save myself," said Master Joseph, evidently a little conscience-smitten. "But to save you, my friend, that seems to be different."

"And Dulcibel," added Master Raymond. "If I were imprisoned what would become of her?"

"Yes, I am glad I did it," responded his friend, regaining his confidence. "I have really hurt neither brother Thomas nor Sister Ann; on the contrary, I have prevented them from doing a great wrong. I am willing to answer for this day's work at the Last Day—and I feel certain that then at least, both of them will thank me for it."

"I have no doubt of it," said Mistress Elizabeth who herself brought up in the rigid Puritan school, had felt the same misgivings as her husband, but whose scruples were also removed by this last consideration.

As for Master Raymond, he, being more a man of the world, had felt no scruples at playing such a deceitful part. I am afraid, that to save Dulcibel, he would not have scrupled at open and downright lying. Not that he had not all the sensitiveness of an honorable man as to his word; but because he looked upon the whole affair as a piece of malicious wickedness, in defiance of all just law, and which every true-hearted man was bound to oppose and defeat by all means allowable in open or secret warfare.

"I suppose you go back to Boston to morrow?" said his host, as they were about to separate for the night.

"Yes, immediately after breakfast. This affair is a warning to me, to push my plans to a consummation as soon as possible. I think I know what their next move will be—a shrewd man once said, just think what is the wisest thing for your enemies to do, and provide against that."

"What is it?"

"Remove the Governor."

"Why, I understood he was a mere puppet in the hands of the two Mathers."

"He would be perhaps; but there is a Lady Phips."

"Ah!' the gray mare is the better horse,' is she, as it is over at brother Thomas's?"

"Yes, I think so. Now mark my prediction, friend Joseph; the first blow will be struck at Lady Mary. If Sir William resists, as I feel certain that he will—for he is, if not well educated, a thoroughly manly man—then he will be ousted from his position. You will note that it has been the game all through to strike at any one, man or woman, who came between these vampires and their prey. I know of only one exception."

"Ah, who is that?"

"Yourself."

Master Joseph smiled grimly. "They value their own lives very highly, friend Raymond; and know that to arrest me would be no child's play. Besides, Sweetbriar is never long unsaddled; and he is the fastest horse in Salem."

"Yes, and to add to all that, you are a Putnam; and your wife is closely connected with Squire Hathorne."

"There may be something in that," said his friend.

"Yes, even Mistress Ann has her limits, which her husband— submissive in so many things—will not allow her to pass. But we are both a little tired, after such an eventful day. Good night!"

CHAPTER XLVI.

Mistress Ann's Opinion of the Matter.

While the foregoing conversation was taking place, one of a very different kind was passing between Mistress Ann and her worthy husband. He had gathered up all the particulars he could of the examination and had brought them home to his wife for her instruction.

After listening to all that he had to tell, with at least outward calmness, she said bitterly: "The whole thing was a trick, you see, to keep you and me away from Salem."

"Do you think so? Do you think then, that no man really wanted to see me at Ipswich?"

"It is as plain as the nose on your face," replied his wife. "You were to be decoyed off to Ipswich, my horse sent out of the way, and then Joseph's madcap horse offered to me, they knowing well that the worthless creature would not behave himself with any woman on his back."

"Oh, pshaw, Ann; you do not mean that my simple-hearted brother, Joseph Putnam, ever planned and carried out a subtle scheme of that kind?" said honest Thomas, with an older brother's undervaluation of the capabilities of a mere boy like Joseph.

"I do not say that Joseph thought it all out, for very probably he did not; doubtless that Master Raymond put him up to it—for he seems cunning and unprincipled enough for anything, judging, by what you have told me of his ridiculous doings."

"You may call them ridiculous, Ann; but they impressed everybody very much indeed. Dr. Griggs, told me that he had no doubt whatever that an 'evil hand' was on him."

"Dr. Griggs is an old simpleton," said his wife crossly.

"And even Squire Hathorne says that he never saw a stronger case of spectral persecution. Why, when one of the young men thrust the point of his rapier at the yellow bird, some of its feathers were cut off and came fluttering to the ground. Squire Hathorne says he never saw anything more wonderful."

"Nonsense—it is all trickery!"

"Trickery? Why, my dear wife, the Squire has the feathers!—and he means to send them at once to Master Cotton Mather by a special messenger, to confute all the scoffers and unbelievers in Boston and Plymouth!"

A scornful reply was at the end of his wife's tongue but, on second thought, she did not allow it to get any farther. Suppose that she did convince her husband and Squire Hathorne that they had been grossly deceived and imposed upon—and that Master Raymond's apparent afflictions and spectral appearance were the result of skilful juggling, what then? Would their enlightenment stop there? How about the pins that the girls had concealed around their necks, and taken up with their mouths? How about Mary Walcot secretly biting herself, and then screaming out that good Rebecca Nurse had bitten her? How about the little prints on the arms of the "afflicted girls," which they allowed were made by the teeth of little Dorcas Good, that child not five years old; and which Mistress Ann knew were made by the girls themselves? How about the bites and streaks and bruises which she herself had shown as the visible proof that the spectre of good Rebecca Nurse, then lying in jail, was biting her and beating her with her chains? For Edward Putnam had sworn: "I saw the marks both of bite and chains."

Perhaps it was safer to let Master Raymond's juggling go unexposed, considering that she herself and the "afflicted girls" had done so very much of it.

Therefore she said, "I have no faith in Master Raymond nevertheless; no more than Moses had in King Pharaoh's sorcerers, when they did the very same miracles before the king that he had done. I believe him now to be a cunning and a very bad young man, and I think if I had been on the spot, instead of his being at this very moment as I have very little doubt, over at brother's, where they are congratulating each other on the success of their unprincipled plans, Master Raymond would now be lying in Salem jail."

"Probably you are correct, my dear," responded her husband meekly; "and I think it not unlikely that Master Raymond may have thought the same, and planned to keep you away—but it was evident to me, that if the 'afflicted girls' had taken one side or the other in the matter, it would not have been yours. Why, even our own daughter Ann, was laughing and joking with him when I entered the court room."

"Yes," said his wife disdainfully—"that is girl-nature, all over the earth! Just put a handsome young man before them, who has seen the world, and is full of his smiles and flatteries and cajolements, and the wisest of women can do nothing with them. But the cold years bring them out of that!" she added bitterly. "They find what they call love, is a folly and a snare."

Her husband looked out of the window into the dark night, and made no reply to this outburst. He had always loved his wife, and he thought, when he married her, that she loved him—although he was an excellent match, so far as property and family were concerned. Still she would occasionally talk in this way; and he hoped and trusted that it did not mean much.

"I think myself," he said at length, "that it is quite as much the pretty gifts he has made them, and has promised to send them from England, as his handsome face and pleasant manners."

"Oh, of course, it all goes together. They are a set of mere giggling girls; and that is all you can make of them. And our daughter Ann is as bad as any of the lot. I wish she did not take so much after your family, Thomas."

This roused her husband a little. "I am sure, Ann, that our family are much stronger and healthier than your own are. And as to Ann's being like the other girls, I wish she was. She is about the only delicate and nervous one among them."

"Well, Thomas, if you have got at last upon that matter of the superiority of the Putnams to everybody else in the Province, I think I shall go to bed," retorted his wife. "That is the only thing that you are thoroughly unreasonable about. But I do not think you ever had a single minister, or any learned scholar, in your family, or ever owned a whole island, in the Merrimack river as my family, the Harmons, always have done, since the country was first settled—and probably always shall, for the next five hundred years."

To this Thomas Putnam had no answer. He knew well that he had no minister and no island in his family—and those two things, in his wife's estimation, were things that no family of any reputation should be without. He had not brought on the discussion, although his wife had accused him of so doing, and had only asserted what he thought the truth in stating that the Putnams were the stronger and sturdier race.

"I do not wish to hurt your feelings, Thomas, in reminding you of these things," continued his wife, finding he was not intending to reply; "I will admit that your family is a very reputable and worthy one, even if it is not especially gifted with intellect like the Harmons, else you may be sure that I should not have married into it. But I have a headache, and do not wish to continue this discussion any longer, as it is unpleasant to me, and besides in very bad taste."

And so, taking the hint, Master Putnam, like a dutiful husband, who really loved his somewhat peevish and fretful wife, acknowledged by his silence in the future that the Harmons were much superior to any family that could not boast of possessing a minister and an island; the latter for five hundred years!

CHAPTER XLVII.

Master Raymond Visits Lady Mary.

When Master Raymond returned to Boston, he found that an important event had taken place in his absence. Captain Alden and Master Philip English and his wife, had all escaped from prison, and were nowhere to be found. How Captain Alden had managed things with the jailer the young man was not able to ascertain—probably however, by a liberal use of money. As for Master English and his wife, they were, as I have already said, at liberty in the day time, under heavy bonds; and had nothing to do but walk off sometime between sunrise and sundown. As Master English's ship, "The Porcupine," had been lying for a week or two in Boston harbor, and left with a brisk northwest wind early in the morning of the day when they were reported missing, it was not difficult for anyone to surmise as to their mode of escape. As to Captain Alden, he might or might not have gone with them.

As was natural, there was a good deal of righteous indignation expressed by all in authority. The jailer was reprimanded for his carelessness in the case of Captain Alden, and warned that if another prisoner escaped, he would forfeit his, of late, very profitable position. And the large properties of both gentlemen were attached and held as being subject to confiscation.

But while the magistrates and officials usually were in earnest in these proceedings, it was generally believed that the Governor, influenced by Lady Mary, had secretly favored the escaping parties. The two ministers of South Church—Masters Willard and Moody— were also known to have frequently visited the Captain and Master English in their confinement, and to have expressed themselves very freely in public, relative to the absurdity of the charges which had been made against them. Master Moody had even gone so far as to preach a sermon on the text, 'When they persecute you in this city, flee ye into another,' which was supposed by many to have a direct bearing on the case of the accused. And it is certain that soon afterwards, the Reverend Master Moody found it expedient to resign his position in South Church and go back to his old home in Portsmouth.

Anxious to learn the true inwardness of all this matter, Master Raymond called a few days after his return to see Lady Mary. Upon sending in his name, a maid immediately appeared, and he was taken as before to the boudoir where he found her ladyship eagerly awaiting him.

"And so you are safely out of the lion's den, Master Raymond," said she, laughing. "I heard you had passed through securely."

The young man smiled. "Yes, thanks to Providence, and to a good friend of mine in Salem."

"Tell me all about it," said the lady. "I have had the magisterial account already, and now wish to have yours."

"Will your ladyship pardon me if I ask a question first? I am so anxious to hear about Mistress Dulcibel. Have you seen her lately — and is she well?"

"As well and as blooming as ever. The keeper and his wife treat her very kindly—and I think would continue to do so—even if the supply of British gold pieces were to fail. By the way, she might be on the high seas now—or rather in New York—if she had so chosen."

"I wish she had. Why did she not go with them?"

"Because your arrest complicated things so. She would not go and leave you in the hands of the Philistines."

"Oh, that was foolish."

"I think so, too; but I do not think that you are exactly the person to say so," responded the lady, a little offended at what seemed a want of appreciation of the sacrifice that Dulcibel had made on his account.

But Master Raymond appeared not to notice the rebuke. He simply added: "If I could have been there to counsel her, I would have convinced her that I was in no serious danger—for, even if imprisoned, I do not think there is a jail in the Province that could hold me."

"Well, there was a difficulty with the Keeper also—for she had given her word, you know, not to escape, when she was taken into his house."

"But Captain Alden had also given his word. How did he manage it?"

"I do not know," replied the lady. "But, to a hint dropped by Dulcibel, the jailer shook his head resolutely, and said that no money would tempt him."

"The difficulty in her case then remains the same as ever," said the young man thoughtfully, and a little gloomily. "She might go into the prison. But that would be to give warning that she had planned to escape. Besides, it is such a vile place, that I hate the idea of her passing a single night in one of its sickening cells."

"Perhaps I can wring a pardon out of Sir William," said the lady musing.

"Oh, Lady Mary, if you only could, we should both forever worship you!"

The lady smiled at the young man's impassioned language and manner—he looked as if he would throw himself at her feet.

"I should be too glad to do it. But Sir William just now is more rigid than ever. He had a call yesterday from his pastor, Master Cotton Mather, and a long talk from him about the witches. Master Mather, it seems, has had further evidence and of the most convincing character, of the reality of these spectral appearances."

"Indeed!" said Master Raymond showing great interest for he had an idea of what was coming.

"Yes, in a recent examination at Salem before Squire Hathorne, a young man struck with his sword at a spectral yellow bird which was tormenting an afflicted person; and several small yellow feathers were cut off by the thrust, and floated down to the floor. Squire Hathorne writes to Master Mather that he would not have believed it, if he had not seen it; but, as it was, he would be willing to take his oath before any Court in Christendom, that this wonderful thing really occurred."

Master Raymond could not help laughing.

"I see you have no more faith in the story than I have," continued Lady Mary. "But it had a great effect upon Sir William, coming from a man of such wonderful learning and wisdom as Master Cotton Mather. Especially as he said that he had seen the yellow feathers himself; which had since been sent to him by Squire Hathorne, and which had a singular smell of sulphur about them."

The young man broke into a heartier laugh than before. Then he said scornfully, "It seems to me that no amount of learning, however great, can make a sensible man out of a fool."

"Why, you know something about this then? Did it happen while you were in Salem?"

"I know everything about it," said Master Raymond, "I am the very man that worked the miracle." And he proceeded to give Lady Mary a detailed account of the whole affair, substantially as it is known to the reader.

"By the way, as to the feathers smelling of sulphur," concluded the young man, "I think that it is very probable, inasmuch as I observed the jailer's wife that very morning giving the younger chickens powdered brimstone to cure them of the pip."

"I think you are a marvelously clever young man," was the lady's first remark as he concluded his account.

"Thank your ladyship!" replied Master Raymond smiling. "I hope I shall always act so as to deserve such a good opinion."

"I would have given my gold cup—which the Duke of Albemarle gave me—to have been there; especially when the yellow bird's feathers came floating down to Squire Hathorne's reverential amazement," said Lady Mary, laughing heartily. "You must come up here tomorrow morning at noon. Master Mather is to bring his feathers to show the Governor, and to astound the Governor's skeptical wife. You are not afraid to come, are you?"

"I shall enjoy it very much—that is, if the Governor will promise that I shall not suffer for my disclosures. I am free now, and I do not wish to be arrested again."

"Oh, I will see to that. The Governor will be so curious to hear your story, that he will promise all that you desire as to your safety. Besides, he will not be sorry to take down Master Mather a little; these Puritan ministers presume on their vocation too much. They all think they are perfectly capable of governing not only Provinces, but Kingdoms; while the whole history of the world proves their utter incapacity to govern even a village wisely."

"That is true as the gospel, Lady Mary. But one thing I have always noticed. That while every minister thinks this, he would himself far rather be governed even by one of the world's people, than by a minister of any other belief than his own. So you see they really do think the same as we do about it; only they do not always know it."

"You are a bright young man," Lady Mary replied pleasantly, "and I think almost good enough to wear such a sweet rose next your heart as Mistress Dulcibel."

CHAPTER XLVIII.

Captain Tolley's Propositions.

That evening as Master Raymond was standing in the bar-room of the Red Lion, Captain Tolley came in, and after tossing off a stout glass of rum and water, went out again, giving the young Englishman a nod and the agreed-upon-signal, a smoothing of his black beard with the left hand. After the lapse of a few minutes, Master Raymond followed, going towards the wharves, which in the evening were almost deserted. Arrived at the end of one of the wharves, he found the Captain of the Storm King.

"So you got out of the clutches of those Salem rascals safely?" said the Captain. "I was afraid I should have to go all the way to Salem for you."

"You would not have deserted me then, Captain?"

"That is not the kind of a marlinespike I am," replied the Captain quaintly. "I'd have got you out of Salem jail, unless it is a good deal stronger than the Boston one."

"Thank you, Captain, but I am glad there was no need of your trying."

"You heard of course that Captain Alden was off, and Master and Mistress English?"

"Yes—and very glad I was too."

"Why did not your sweetheart go with the Englishes?"

"There were several reasons—one, a rather foolish one, she would not leave me in prison."

"She would not?"

"No."

"D— — me! Why that girl is fit to be a sailor's wife! When we get her off safely I intend to have her as the figure-head of the Storm King."

"I am afraid that would be a very unhealthy position—she might catch a bad cold," replied Master Raymond.

"Oh, of course I mean in wood, painted white with red cheeks," said Captain Tolley. "It brings good luck to have a fine woman for a figure-head—pleases old Nep, you know."

"But we must get her off first," rejoined Master Raymond. "Now to keep out of that hateful jail, she has given her word to Keeper Arnold not to escape. You know she cannot break her word."

"Of course not," replied the Captain; "a lady is like a sailor, she cannot go back on her promise."

"And there is where the trouble comes in."

"Buy Keeper Arnold over."

"I am afraid I cannot—not for a good while at least. They are all down upon him for Captain Alden's escape. They might give him a terrible whipping if another prisoner got off."

The Captain shrugged his shoulders. "Yes, I saw them whip some Quakers once. It was not a good honest lash, but something the hangman had got up on purpose, and which cut to the very bone. I have seen men and women killed, down on the Spanish main, but I never saw a sight like that! Good, harmless men and women too! A little touched here, you know," and the Captain tapped his forehead lightly with his fore-finger.

"Yes—I should not like to hear that Master Arnold had been tortured like that on our account."

"Suppose we carry her off some night by force, she having no hand in the arrangements? She can even refuse to go, you know, if she pleases—we will handle her as gently as a little bird, and you can come up and rescue her, if you choose, and knock down two or three of us. How would that do? Half-a-dozen of the Storm King's men could easily do that. Choose a night with a brisk nor'wester, and we would be past the castle's guns before the sleepy land-lubbers had their eyes open."

Master Raymond shook his head dubiously. "I do not like it—and yet I suppose it must do, if nothing better can be found. Of course if we carry her off bodily, against her will, it would neither be a breaking of her pledge nor expose Keeper Arnold to any danger of after punishment, though he might perhaps get pretty seriously hurt in resisting us, and she would not like that much."

"I suppose then we must wait a while longer," said the Captain. "I am ready any time you say the word—only be careful that a good west or a nor'west wind is blowing. When once out on the high seas, we can take care of ourselves."

"Many French privateers out there?"

"Thick as blackberries. But they are of no account. Those we cannot fight, we can easily run away from. There is no craft on these seas, that can overhaul the Storm King!"

With a hearty shake of the hand the two parted, the Captain for the vessel of which he was so proud; Master Raymond for his room in the Red Lion.

CHAPTER XLIX.

Master Raymond Confounds Master Cotton Mather.

The next day, a little before noon, Master Raymond knocked at the door of the Governor's Mansion, and was at once conducted to Lady Mary's boudoir. "The Reverend Master Mather is already with the Governor," said her ladyship, "and I expect to receive a summons to join them every moment." And in fact the words were hardly out of her mouth, when Sir William's private secretary, Master Josslyn, appeared, with a request for her ladyship's presence.

"Come with me," said she to Master Raymond; "but do not say anything—much less smile or laugh—until I call upon you for your testimony."

As they entered, the courteous Governor handed his lady to a seat on the sofa; and Master Mather made a dignified obeisance.

"I have brought along a young friend of mine, who was with me, and would also like to hear of all these wonderful things," said her ladyship; and Master Raymond bowed very deferentially to both the high dignities, they returning the bow, while Sir William politely requested him to be seated.

"I was just on the point of showing to Sir William the most remarkable curiosities of even this very remarkable era—and he suggested that you also doubtless would like to see them," said the minister; at this time a man of about thirty years of age. He was a rather comely and intelligent looking man, and Master Raymond wondered that one who appeared so intellectual, should be the victim of such absurd hallucinations.

Lady Mary bent her head approvingly, in answer to the minister. "I should like very much to see them," she replied courteously; and Master Mather continued:—

"In the work I have been preparing on the "Wonders of the Invisible World," several of the sheets of which I have already shown to Sir

William, I have collected many curious and wonderful instances. Thus in the case of the eldest daughter of Master John Goodwin, whom I took to my own house, in order that I might more thoroughly investigate the spiritual and physical phenomena of witchcraft, I found that while the devils that tormented her were familiar with Latin, Greek and Hebrew, they seemed to have very little knowledge of the various Indian dialects."

"That certainly is very curious," replied Sir William, "inasmuch as those heathen are undeniably the children of the devil, as all our wisest and most godly ministers agree."

"Yes," continued the minister, "it is true; and that makes me conjecture, that these devils were in fact only playing a part; to deceive me into thinking that the red heathen around us were not really the children of Satan, as they undoubtedly are."

"I think that the most reasonable view," responded the Governor.

"As to the reality of this new assault by Satan upon this little seed of God's people in the new world," continued Master Mather, fervently, "I have now no doubt whatever. Proof has been multiplied upon proof, and the man, or woman, who does not by this time believe, is simply one of those deplorable doubters, like Thomas, who never can be convinced. For my part, I consider Witchcraft the most nefandous high treason against the Majesty on High! And a principal design of my book is to manifest its hideous enormity, and to promote a pious thankfulness to God that Justice so far is being inflexibly executed among us."

Lady Mary's face flushed a little, for she saw the drift of the minister's censure. It was well known in all the inner circles, that she had neither faith in the reality of witchcraft, nor the least sympathy with the numerous prosecutions, and the inflexible justice which the minister lauded. The Governor knew his wife's temper, and hastened to say:—

"Still we must admit, Master Mather, that some persons, with tender conscience, require more convincing proofs than do others. And therefore I was anxious that Lady Mary should see these feathers you spoke of, cut from the wings of one of those yellow birds which appear to be used so frequently as familiars by the Salem witches."

"Oh, yes, I had forgotten them for the moment." And putting his hand into his breast pocket, Master Mather produced a small box, which he opened carefully and called their attention to a couple of small yellow feathers placed on a piece of black cloth within. "I would not take a hundred pounds for these spectral feathers," said the minister exultingly. "They are the only positive proof of the kind, now existing in the whole world. With these little feathers I shall dash out the brains of a host of unbelievers—especially of that silly Calef, or Caitiff, who is all the time going around among the merchants, wagging his vile tongue against me."

Sir William and Lady Mary had been looking upon the feathers very curiously. At last Lady Mary gave a low, incredulous laugh. Her husband looked at her inquiringly.

"They are nothing but common chicken feathers which could be picked up in any barn yard," she said scornfully.

"Your ladyship is very much mistaken, you never saw chicken feathers like those," said the minister, his face now also flushing.

"Who was the yellow bird afflicting, when these feathers were cut?" the lady asked.

"A young man was on his examination for witchcraft, Squire Hathorne writes me; but he was found to be himself a victim, and was released—which proves, by the way, how careful the worshipful magistrates are in Salem, lest any who are innocent should be implicated with the guilty. The young man began to cry out that an 'evil hand' was on him, and that a yellow bird was trying to peck out his eyes. Whereupon one of the by-standers pulled out his rapier, and smote at the spectral bird—when these feathers were cut off; becoming visible of course as soon as they were detached from the bird and its evil influence. It is one of the most wonderful things that I ever heard of," and Master Mather gazed on the feathers with admiring and almost reverential eyes.

"Sir William," said his lady, "you have, I hope, a little common sense left, if these Massachusetts ministers and magistrates have all gone crazy on this subject. You know what a chicken is, if they do not. Are not those simply chicken feathers?"

"Why, my dear," replied the Governor, wriggling in his great arm-chair, "I grant that they certainly do look like chicken feathers; but then you know, the yellow bird the witches use, may have feathers like unto a chicken's."

"Nonsense!" replied Lady Mary. "None are so blind as those that will not see. I suppose that if I were to bring that afflicted young man here, and he were to acknowledge that the whole thing was a trick, got up by him to save his life, you would not believe him?"

"Indeed I should," replied Sir William.

"Yes, Lady Mary, find the young man, and question him yourself," said Master Mather. "None are so certain as those that have never informed themselves. I have made inquiry into these marvelous things; I even took that afflicted girl, as I have told you, into my own house, in order to inform myself of the truth. When you have investigated the matter to one-tenth the extent that I have, you will be prepared to give a reasonable opinion as to its truth or falsehood. Until then, some modesty of statement would become a lady who sets up her crude opinion against all the ministers and the magistracy of the land."

This was a tone which the leading ministers of that day among the Puritans, did not hesitate to take, even where high dignitaries were concerned and Master Mather had the highest ideas of the privilege of his order.

"Then I suppose, Master Mather, that if the afflicted young man himself should testify that these feathers were simply chicken feathers, that he had artfully thrown up into the air, you would not acknowledge that he had deceived you?"

"If such an impossible thing could happen, though I know that it could not, of course I should be compelled to admit that Squire Hathorne and a hundred others, who all saw this marvelous thing plainly, in open day, were deceived by the trick of an unprincipled mountebank and juggler."

"I shall hold both you and Sir William to your word," replied Lady Mary emphatically. Then, turning to the young Englishman, who had remained entirely silent so far, paying evident attention to all that was spoken, but giving no sign of approval or disapproval, she said, "Master Raymond, what do you think of this matter?"

Master Raymond rose from his chair and stepped a pace or two forward. Then he said, "If I answer your ladyship's question freely, it might be to my own hurt. Having had my head once in the lion's mouth, I am not anxious to put it there again."

The lady looked significantly at Sir William.

"Speak out truly, and fear nothing, young man," said the Governor. "Nothing that you say here shall ever work you injury while I am Governor of the Province."

"What do you wish to know, Lady Mary?"

"You, I believe, were the afflicted young man, to whom Master Mather has referred?"

Master Raymond bowed.

"Was there any reality in those pretended afflictions?"

"Only a bad cold to begin with," said the young man smiling.

"How about the yellow bird?"

"It was all a sham. I dealt with credulous and dangerous fools according to their folly."

"How about those feathers?"

"They are feathers I got from the wings of one of the Salem jailor's chickens."

Sir William laughed,

"How about the smell of sulphur which Squire Hathorne and Master Mather have detected in the feathers?"

"I think it very probable; as I observed Goodwife Foster that morning giving her chickens powdered brimstone for the pip."

Here the Governor laughed loudly and long until Master Mather said indignantly, "I am sorry, Sir William, that you can treat so lightly this infamous confession of falsehood and villainy. This impudent young man deserves to be set for three days in the pillory, and then whipped at the cart's tail out of town."

"Of course it is a very shameful piece of business," replied the Governor, regaining his gravity. "But you know that as the confession has been made only on the promise of perfect immunity, I cannot, as a man of my word, suffer the least harm to come to the young person for making it."

"Oh, of course not," said the minister, taking up his hat, and preparing to leave the room; "but it is scandalous! scandalous! All respect for the Magistracy and authority seems to be fading out of the popular mind. I consider you a dangerous man, a very dangerous young man!" This last of course to Master Raymond.

"And I consider you tenfold more dangerous with your clerical influence, and credulity, and superstition!" replied the young Englishman hotly. Being of good family, he was not inclined to take such insults mildly. "How dare you, with your hands all red with the blood of twenty innocent men and women, talk to me about being dangerous!"

"Peace!" said Sir William with dignity. "My audience chamber is no place to quarrel in.

"I beg your Excellency's pardon!" said Master Raymond, humbly.

"One moment, before you go," said Lady Mary, stepping in front of the minister. "I suppose you will be as good as your word, Master Mather and admit that with all your wisdom you were entirely mistaken?"

"I acknowledge that Squire Hathorne and myself have been grossly deceived by an unprincipled adventurer—but that proves nothing. Because Jannes and Jambres imitated with their sorceries the miracles of Moses, did it prove that Moses was an impostor? There was one Judas among the twelve apostles, but does that invalidate the credibility of the eleven others, who were not liars and cheats? It is the great and overwhelming burden of the testimony which decides in this as in all other disputed matters—not mere isolated cases. Good afternoon, madam. I will see you soon again, Sir William, when we can have a quiet talk to ourselves."

"Stay!" cried Lady Mary, as the offended minister was stalking out of the room. "You have forgotten something," and she pointed to the little box, containing the chicken's feathers which had been left lying upon the table.

The minister gave a gesture expressive of mingled contempt and indignation—but did not come back for it. It was evident that he valued the feathers now at considerably less than one hundred pounds.

"Young man," said the Governor, smiling, "you are a very bright and keen-witted person, but I would advise you not to linger in this province any longer than is absolutely necessary. Master Mather is much stronger here than I am."

CHAPTER L.

Bringing Affairs to a Crisis.

The next morning a note came to Master Raymond from Joseph Putnam, brought by one of the farm-hands.

It was important. Abigail Williams had called upon Goodwife Buckley, and told her in confidence that it was in contemplation, as she had learned from Ann Putnam, to bring Dulcibel Burton back to Salem jail again. The escape of Captain Alden and the Englishes from the Bridewell in Boston, had caused a doubt in Salem as to its security. Besides, Lady Phips had taken ground so openly against the witch prosecutions, that there was no knowing to how great an extent she might not go to aid any prisoner in whom she took an interest.

Abigail Williams further said that Mistress Ann Putnam had become very bitter both against her brother-in-law Joseph and his friend Master Raymond. She was busy combatting the idea that the latter really ever had been afflicted — and was endeavoring to rouse Squire Hathorne's indignation against him as being a deceiver.

As the young man read this last, he wondered what effect would be produced upon the credulous magistrate, when he received word from Master Mather as to what had occurred in the Governor's presence. Would he be so angry as to take very arbitrary measures; or so ashamed as to let it all pass, rather than expose the extent to which he had been duped? He feared the former — knowing in which way Mistress Ann Putnam's great influence with him would be directed.

Master Joseph advised immediate action — if peaceable means would not serve, then the use of violent ones. If Captain Tolley could not find among his sailors those who would undertake the job, he, Master Joseph, would come down any night with three stout men, overpower the keepers, and carry off Mistress Dulcibel, with the requisite amount of violence to keep her promise unbroken.

Master Raymond wrote a note in return. He was much obliged for the information. It was evident that the time had come for action; and that it was dangerous to delay much longer. Of course peaceable means were to be preferred; and it was possible he might be able either to bribe the keeper, or to get a release from the Governor; but, if force had to be resorted to, Captain Tolley could command his whole crew for such a service, as they were the kind of men who would like nothing better. In fact, they would not hesitate to open fire upon the town, if he ordered it—and even run up the flag of a French privateer.

After dispatching this business, Master Raymond went out on the porch of the Red Lion, and began an examination of the clouds and the weather-cocks. It had been raining slightly for a day or two, with the wind from the southeast; but though the vanes still pointed to the southeast, and the light lower clouds were moving from the same point of the compass, he caught glimpses through the scud of higher clouds that were moving in an entirely opposite direction.

"How do you make it out?" said a well-known voice. He had heard some one approaching, but had supposed it to be a stranger.

"I am not much of a sailor; but I should say it would clear up, with a brisk wind from the west or the northwest by afternoon."

"Aye!" said Captain Tolley, for it was he; "and a stiff nor'wester by night. If it isn't I'll give my head for a foot-ball. Were I bound out of the harbor, I would not whistle for a better wind than we shall have before six hours are over."

Master Raymond glanced around; no one was near them. "Are you certain of that, Captain? Would it do to bet upon?

"You may bet all you are worth, and your sweetheart into the bargain," replied the Captain laughing, with a significant look out of his eyes.

"When are you going, Captain?"

"Oh, to-night, perhaps—if I can get all my live stock on board.

"To-night then let it be," said the young man in a whisper; "by fair means, or by foul. I may succeed by fair means; have a boat waiting at the wharf for me. It will be light enough to get out of the harbor?"

"There is a gibbous moon—plenty. Once past the castle, and we are safe. We can easily break open the keeper's house—and quiet him with a pistol at his head."

"You must not harm him—he has been a good friend to her."

"Of course—only scare him a little. Besides, he is not a good friend, if he makes a noise."

"Well, I will see you by ten o'clock—with her or without her—Yes, I will bet you a gold piece, Captain, that the wind gets around to the west by four o'clock." This last was in Master Raymond's usual tones—the previous conversation having been in whispers.

"You will be safe enough in that, Master Raymond," said the landlord of the Red Lion, whose steps the young Englishman had heard approaching.

"Do you think so? I do not want to take the young man's money, he is only a landsman you know, Mate; but I will bet you a piece of eight that the wind will not get around till a half hour after that time. And we will take it all out in drinks at your bar, at our leisure."

"Done!" said the landlord. "And now let us go in, and take a drink all around in advance."

CHAPTER LI.

Lady Mary's Coup D'Etat.

Master Raymond's next proceeding was to call on Lady Phips. Sending in his name, with a request to see her ladyship on very important business, he was ushered as usual into her boudoir.

"I must be doing something, Lady Mary," he said, after a few words relative to the evident change of weather; "I have news from Salem that the Magistrates are about to send Mistress Dulcibel back to Salem jail."

"That is sad," she answered.

"And, besides, there is no knowing what new proceedings they may be concocting against me. I must take Sir William's advice, and get out of this hornet's nest as soon as possible."

"Well what can I do for you?"

"Get an order from Sir William releasing Dulcibel from prison."

"Oh, that I could! God knows how gladly I would do it."

"You can at least try," said Master Raymond desperately.

The lady hesitated a moment. "Yes, as you say, I can at least try. But you know how impossible it is to carry on the government of this Province without the support of the ministers and the magistrates. Sir William is naturally anxious to succeed; for, if he fails here, it will block his road to further preferment."

"And he will allow the shedding of innocent blood to go on, in order to promote his own selfish ambition?" said the young man indignantly.

"You are unjust to the Governor. He will do all he can to moderate this fanaticism; and, if it comes to the worst, he will order a general jail-delivery, and meet the consequences. But he hopes much from time, and from such developments as those of your chicken feathers"—and the lady smiled at the thought of the minister's discomfiture.

"Some things can wait, but I cannot wait," insisted Master Raymond. "You must acknowledge that."

"Sir William starts this afternoon on a visit to Plymouth, to remain for a day or so; but I will have a talk with him, and see what I can do," replied the lady. "Call here again at six o'clock this evening."

"Such beauty and spirit as yours must be irresistible in the cause of virtue and innocence," said the young man, rising to depart.

"No flattery, Master Raymond; I will do all I can without that;" but Lady Mary being still a very comely woman, as she certainly was a very spirited one, was not much displeased at the compliment, coming from such a handsome young man as Master Raymond. Eulogy that the hearer hopes embodies but the simple truth, is always pleasant alike to men and women. It is falsehood, and not truth, that constitutes the essence of Flattery.

The day dragged on very drearily and slowly to Master Raymond. The waiting for the hour of action is so irksome, that even the approach of danger is a relief. But patience will at last weary out the slowest hours; and punctually at six o'clock, the young man stood again at the door of the Governor's mansion.

Lady Mary evidently was expecting him—for he was shown in at once. She looked up wearily as he entered. "I can do nothing to-day," she said.

"What ground did the Governor take?"

"That sound policy forbade him to move in the matter at present. The persecuting party were very indignant at the escape of Captain Alden and the Englishes; and now for him to grant a pardon to another of the accused, would be to irritate them to madness."

Master Raymond acknowledged to himself the soundness of the Governor's policy; but he only said: "Then it seems that Dulcibel must go back to Salem prison; and I run a good chance of going to prison also, as a self-confessed deceiver and impostor."

"If she were released, could you both get away from Boston—at once?"

Master Raymond's voice sank to a whisper. "I have all my plans arranged. By the third hour after midnight, we shall be where we can snap our fingers at the magistrates of Boston."

"I have been thinking of a plan. It may work—or may not. But it is worth trying."

The young man's face lightened.

"You know that England is ruled by William and Mary, why should not the Province of Massachusetts also be?"

"I do not understand you."

"Upon leaving Sir William, I was somewhat indignant that he would not grant my request. And to pacify me, he said he was sorry that I had not the same share in the government here, that Queen Mary had at home—and then I could do more as I pleased."

Still Master Raymond's face showed that he was puzzled to catch her meaning.

She laughed and rose from her chair; the old, resolute expression upon her spirited face, and, opening the door into the next room, which was the Governor's private office, she said:

"Come here a moment, Master Josslyn."

The private Secretary entered.

"Prepare me," she said to the Secretary, "the proper paper, to be signed by the Governor, ordering Keeper Arnold to release at once Mistress Dulcibel Burton from confinement in the Boston Bridewell."

"But the Governor, you know, is absent, Lady Mary," said the Secretary, "and his signature will be necessary."

"Oh, I will see to that," replied the lady a little haughtily.

Master Raymond sat quietly—waiting for what was to come next. He could not conceive how Lady Mary intended to manage it. As for the lady, she tapped the table with her shapely fingers impatiently.

In a few minutes Master Josslyn reappeared with the paper. "All it now wants is the signature of the Governor," said he.

The lady took up a pen from the table by which she was sitting, and filled it with ink; then with a firm hand she signed the paper, "William Phips, Governor, by Lady Mary Phips."

"But, your ladyship, the keeper will not acknowledge the validity of that signature, or obey it," said Master Josslyn in some alarm.

"He will not? We shall see!" responded her ladyship rising. "Order my carriage, Master Josslyn."

In fifteen minutes, Lady Mary, accompanied by Master Raymond, was at Keeper Arnold's house.

"I bring you good news, Master Arnold," said Lady Mary, "I know you will rejoice, such a tender-hearted man as you are at the release of Mistress Dulcibel Burton. Here is the official document." She flourished it at him, but still kept it in her hand.

Dulcibel was soon informed of the good news; and came flying out to meet her benefactor and her lover.

"Put on a shawl and your veil at once; and make a bundle of your belongings," said Lady Mary, kissing her. "Master Raymond is in a great hurry to carry you off—at which I confess that I do not wonder." Dulcibel tripped off—the sooner she was out of that close place the better.

"Well, what is it, Master Arnold?" said Lady Mary to the keeper, who acted as if he wished to say something.

"It is only a form, my lady; but you have not shown me the Governor's warrant yet?"

"Why, yes I have," said Lady Mary, fluttering it at him as before.

But Keeper Arnold was fully aware of the responsibility of his position; and putting out his hand, he steadied the fluttering paper sufficiently to glance over its contents. When he came to the signature, his face paled. "Pardon me, my lady; but this is not the Governor's writing."

"Of course it is not—why, you silly loon, how could it be when he has gone to Plymouth? But you will perceive that it is in Master Josslyn's writing—and the Governor ought to have signed it before he started."

"This is hardly in regular form, my lady."

"It is not? Do you not see the Governor's name; and there below it is my name, as proof of the Governor's. Do you mean to impeach my attestation of Sir William's signature? There is my name, Lady Mary Phips: and I will take the responsibility of this paper being a legal one. If anybody finds fault with you, send him to me; and I will say you did it, in the Governor's absence from town, at my peremptory order." The lady's face glowed, and her eyes flashed, with her excitement and determination.

"It would be as much as my position is worth to disobey it and me!" rejoined Lady Mary. "I will have you out of this place in three days' time, if you cast disrespect upon my written name."

"There can be no great haste in this matter. Bring the release tomorrow, and I will consult authority in the meanwhile," said the keeper pleadingly.

"Authority? The Governor's name is authority! I am authority! Who dare you set up beside us? You forget your proper respect and duty, Master Arnold."

The keeper was overborne at last. "You will uphold me, if I do this thing, Lady Mary?" said he imploringly.

"You know me, Master Arnold—and that I never desert my friends! I shall accept the full responsibility of this deed before Sir William and the magistrates. And they cannot order any punishment which he cannot pardon."

By this time it had grown quite dark. "Shall I take you anywhere in my carriage?" said Lady Mary, as Dulcibel reappeared with a bundle.

"It is not necessary," replied Master Raymond joyfully, "I will not compromise you any further. God forever bless your ladyship! There is not another woman in New England with the spirit and courage to do what you have done this day—and the reader of our history a hundred years to come, as he reads this page, shall cry fervently, God bless the fearless and generous soul of Lady Mary!"

"Let me know when you are safe," she whispered to the young man, as he stood by her carriage. "Master and Mistress English are now the guests of Governor Fletcher of New York—changing a Boston prison for a Governor's mansion. You will be perfectly secure in that Province—or in Pennsylvania, or Maryland or Virginia." And the carriage drove off.

It was in that early hour of the evening, when the streets in town and city, are more deserted than they are for some hours afterwards; everyone being indoors, and not come out for visiting or amusement. And so the young man and his companion walked towards the north-eastern part of the town, meeting only one or two persons, who took no special notice of them.

"You do not ask where we are going, Dulcibel?" at last said Master Raymond.

She could not see the sweet smile on his face; but she could feel it in his voice.

"Anywhere, with you!" the maiden replied in a low tone.

"We are going to be married."

He felt the pressure of her hand upon his arm in response.

"That is, if we can find a minister to perform the ceremony."

"That will be difficult, I should think."

"Yes, difficult, but not impossible. After getting you out of prison, as Lady Mary did, I should not like to call anything impossible."

"Lady Mary is an angel!"

"Yes, one of the kind with wings," replied her companion laughing. "She has kindly loaned us her wings though—and we are flying away on them."

Before long they were at one of the wharves; then on a small boat— then on the deck of the "Storm King."

"I am better than my word, Captain Tolley."

"Aye! indeed you are. And this is the birdie! Fair Mistress, the "Storm King" and his brood are ready to die to shield you from harm."

Dulcibel looked wonder out of her clear blue eyes. What did it all mean? She smiled at the Captain's devoted speech. "I do not want any one to die for me, Captain. I would rather have you sing me a good sea-song, such as my father, who was also a sea-captain, used to delight me with at home."

"Oh, we can do that too," answered the Captain gaily. "I hope we shall have a jolly time of it, before we reach our destination. Now, come down into the cabin and see the preparations I have made for you; a sailor's daughter must have the best of sailor's cheer."

"One word, Captain," said Master Raymond, as the Captain came up on deck again, leaving Dulcibel to the privacy of her state-room. "It does not seem fitting that a young unmarried woman should be alone on a vessel like this, with no matron to bear her company."

"Sir!" said the Captain, "I would have you know that the maiden is as safe from aught that could offend her modesty on the decks of the "Storm King," as if she were in her father's house."

"Of course she is. I know that well—and mean not the least offense. And she, innocent as she is, has no other thought. But this is a slanderous world, Captain, and we men who know the world, must think for her."

"Oh, I admit that," said Captain Tolley, somewhat mollified, "we cannot expect of mere land's people, who put an innocent girl like that into prison for no offense, the gentle behavior towards women that comes naturally from a seaman; but what do you propose?"

"To send for one of the Boston ministers, and marry her before we leave port."

"Why, of course," replied the Captain. "It is the very thing. Whom shall we send for? The North Church is nearest—how would Master Cotton Mather do?"

The young man stood thoughtfully silent for a moment or two. The ministers of South Church and of King's chapel were more heterodox in all this witchcraft business; but for that very reason he did not wish to compromise them in any way. Besides, he owed a grudge to Master Mather, for his general course in sustaining the persecution, and his recent language in particular towards himself. So his lips gradually settled into a stern determination, and he replied "Master Mather is the very man."

"It may require a little ingenuity to get him aboard at this time of the evening," said the Captain. "But I reckon my first mate, Simmons, can do it, if any one can."

"Here, Simmons," to the first mate, who was standing near, "you look like a pillar of the church, go ashore and bring off Master Cotton Mather with you. A wealthy young Englishman is dying— and he cannot pass away from Boston in peace without his ministerial services."

"Dying?" ejaculated Master Raymond.

"Yes, dying! dying to get married—and you cannot pass out of Boston harbor in peace, without his ministerial services."

"Would it not do as well to ask him to come and marry us?"

"I doubt it," replied the Captain. "Master Mather is honest in his faith, even if he is bigoted and superstitious—and death cannot be put off like marriage till tomorrow. But take your own course, Simmons—only bring him."

"Shall I use force, sir, if he will not come peaceably?" asked the mate coolly.

"Not if it will make a disturbance," said his commander. "We do not want to run the gauntlet of the castle's guns as we go out of the harbor. The wind is hardly lively enough for that."

"I will go down and tell Dulcibel," said Master Raymond. "It is rather sudden, but she is a maiden of great good sense, and will see clearly the necessity of the case. And as she is an orphan, she has no father or mother whose consent she might consider necessary. But Mate"—going to the side of the vessel, which the boat was just leaving, "not a word as to my name or that of the maiden. That would spoil all."

"Aye, aye, sir! Trust me to bring him!" and the boat started for the shore, under the vigorous strokes of two oarsmen.

CHAPTER LII.

An Unwilling Parson.

Not quite an hour had elapsed, when the sound of oars was again heard; and Captain Tolley, peering through the dark, saw that another form was seated opposite the mate in the stern-sheets of the boat.

"I thought that Simmons would bring him," said Captain Tolley to the second mate; "such a smooth tongue as he has. It is a pity he wasn't a minister himself—his genius is half wasted here."

"Glad to see you on board the Storm King, Master Mather," was the greeting of the Captain, as the minister was helped up to the deck by the mates.

"The Storm King! Why I was told that it was an English frigate, just come into port," said the minister in a surprised voice.

"The messenger must have made a mistake," replied the Captain coolly. "You know that landsmen always do get things mixed.

"Well, as I am here, no matter. Show me the dying man."

"Walk down into the cabin," said the Captain politely.

Entering the cabin which was well lighted, Master Raymond stepped forward, "I am happy to see you, Master Mather. You remember me, do you not?"

"Master Raymond, I believe," returned the minister coldly. "Where is the dying man who requires my spiritual ministrations?"

"Dying!" laughed the Captain. "How strangely that fellow got things mixed. I said dying to get married—did I not, Master Raymond?"

"Of course you did—that is, after you had explained yourself."

Master Mather's face looked blank, he did not know what to make of it.

"In truth, Master Mather," said the young Englishman, "I was under the necessity of getting married this evening; and, thinking over the worshipful ministers of Boston town, I singled you out as the one I should prefer to officiate on the happy occasion."

"I decline to have anything to do with it," said Master Mather indignantly, turning on his heel, and going to the door of the cabin. But here a muscular sailor, with a boarding pike, promptly forbade his passage by putting the pike across the door way.

"What do you mean by barring my way in this manner?" said the minister in great wrath to the captain. "Have you no reverence for the law?"

"Not a particle for Boston law," replied Captain Tolley. "The only law recognized on board the Storm King is the command of its Captain. You have been brought here to marry these two young friends of mine; and you will not leave the vessel before you do it—if I have to take you with us all the way to China."

Master Mather pondered the matter for a moment. "This is too informal, there are certain preliminaries that are necessary in such cases."

"Advisable—but I am told not absolutely necessary," replied Master Raymond.

"Wait then for an hour or two; and we shall be on the high seas— and out of any jurisdiction," added Captain Tolley.

"Who is this maiden? Who gives her away?" asked the minister.

"This maiden is Mistress Dulcibel Burton," said Master Raymond, taking her by the hand.

"She is an orphan; but I give her away," added the Captain.

"Dulcibel Burton! the serpent witch!" exclaimed Master Mather. "What is that convict doing here? Has she broken jail?"

"Master Mather," said the Captain in an excited tone, "if you utter another word of insult against this innocent and beautiful maiden, I will have you flung overboard to the sharks! So take care of what you say!" and the indignant seaman shook his finger in the minister's face warningly.

"Master Mather," added Raymond, more coolly, "Mistress Burton has not broken jail. She was duly released from custody by Keeper Arnold on the presentation of an official paper by Lady Mary Phips. Therefore your conscience need not be uneasy on that score."

"Why are you here then—why making this haste? It is evident that there is something wrong about it."

"Boston has not treated either of us so well that we are very desirous of remaining," replied Master Raymond. "And as we are going together, it is only decorous that we should get married. If you however refuse to marry us, we shall be compelled to take you with us—for the mere presence of such a respected minister will be sufficient to shield the maiden's name from all reckless calumniators."

The second mate came to the door of the cabin. "Captain, there is a fine breeze blowing, it is a pity not to use it."

"Make all ready, sir," replied the Captain. Then turning to the minister, "There is no particular hurry, Master Mather. You can take the night to think over it. To-morrow morning probably, if you come to your senses, we may be able to send you ashore somewhere, between here and the capes of the Delaware."

"This is outrageous!" said Master Mather. "I will hold both of you accountable for it."

"It is a bad time to threaten, when your head is in the lion's mouth, Master Mather," returned Captain Tolley fiercely. "No one knows but my own men that you ever came on board the 'Storm King.' How do you know that I am not Captain Kidd himself?"

The minister's face grew pale. It was no disparagement to his manhood. Even Master Raymond's face grew very serious—for did even he know that this Captain Tolley might not be the renowned freebooter, of whose many acts of daring and violence the wide seas rang?

"I would counsel you for your own good to do at once what you will have to do ultimately," said Master Raymond gravely. "I owe you no thanks for anything; but"—and the young man laughed as he turned to Dulcibel—"I never could trap even a fox without pitying the animal."

Dulcibel went up to the minister, and put her hand upon his arm:— "Do I look so much like a witch?" she said in a playful tone.

"We are told that Satan can enrobe himself like an angel of light," replied Master Mather severely. "I judge you by what I have heard of your cruel deeds."

"As you judged the cruel yellow bird that turned out to be only a harmless little chicken," said Master Raymond sarcastically. "Enough of this folly. Will you marry us now—or not? If you will, you shall be put ashore unharmed. If you will not, you shall go along with us. Make up your mind at once, for we shall soon be out of Boston harbor."

Master Mather had a strong will—and an equally strong won't—but the Philistines were, for this time, too much for him. That reference to Captain Kidd had frightened him badly. "Stand up—and I will marry you. Unscrupulous as you both are, it is better that you should be married by legal rites, than allowed to go your own way to destruction."

And then—the important ceremony being duly gone through—he pronounced Master Ellis Raymond and Mistress Dulcibel Burton man and wife. The Captain being allowed by Master Raymond to take the first kiss, as acting in the place of the bride's father.

"No, not a penny!" said the minister, closing his hand against the golden pieces that the groom held out to him. "All I ask is, that you comply with your promise—and put me on shore again as soon as possible."

"Better take a drink of wine first," said the Captain, filling up a glass and handing it to him.

"I will neither break bread nor drink wine on this"—he was going to say *accursed* ship; but the fierce eyes of the possible freebooter were upon him, and he said, "on this unhappy vessel."

Captain Tolley laughed heartily. "Oh well, good wine never goes begging. The anchor is not up yet, and we will put you off just where you came on. Come along!"

Without a word of leave-taking to the two whom he had joined together, Master Mather followed the Captain. In fact though, Master Raymond and Dulcibel scarcely noted his going, for they were now seated on a small sofa, the arm of the young husband around the shapely waist of his newly-made wife, and the minister dismissed from their minds as completely as the wine-glass out of which they had just drank. He had answered their purpose and in the deep bliss of their new relation, they thought no more about him.

As Master Mather turned to descend to the boat again—not wasting any formal words of leave-taking upon the Captain either—the latter grasped him by the arm.

"Wait one moment," said Captain Tolley. "You will speak of what has occurred here this evening Master Mather, or not, at your pleasure. But be careful of what you say—for there is no power on this coast, strong enough to protect you against my vengeance!" And with a scowl upon his face, that would not have done injustice to the dreaded Captain Kidd himself, he added in a hoarse, fierce tone the one impressive word "Beware!"

The minister made no reply. It was a day of fierce men and wild deeds—especially on the high seas. Prudence in some positions is far better than valor.

"Now, my hearties! let us get out of this harbor as soon as possible!" cried the Captain. "I might have held him till we were opposite the castle, and put him ashore there; but it is safer as it is. We have a regular clearance, and he cannot do anything legally under an hour or two at least—while in half-an-hour we shall be outside. With a stiff breeze like this, once on the open seas, I fear neither man nor devil!"

CHAPTER LIII.

The Wedding Trip and Where Then.

Whether Master Mather did make any serious effort to prevent the "Storm King" from leaving the harbor, I am unable to say; but as I find no reference to this affair either in his biography or his numerous works, I am inclined to think that like a wise man, he held his peace as to what had occurred, and resolved never to go on board another vessel after nightfall.

Certainly no cannon ball cut the waves as the "Storm King" sailed swiftly past the castle, and no signal was displayed signifying that she must come at once to anchor.

And the little trip to New York was as pleasant in all respects as a young couple on a bridal tour could desire—even if the mere relief from the anxieties and threatened dangers of the previous long months had not been of itself a cause of happiness.

Arrived at New York, Master Philip English and his wife received them with open arms. Master Raymond had brought letters from England to Governor Fletcher and others, and soon made warm friends among the very best people. There was no sympathy whatever in New York at that time with the witchcraft persecutions in Massachusetts; and all fugitives were received, as in the case of the Englishes, with great sympathy and kindness.

Much to my regret, at this point, the old manuscript book to which I have been so largely indebted, suddenly closes its record of the fortunes of Master and Mistress Raymond. Whether they went to England, and took up their residence there among Master Raymond's friends, or found a home in this new world, I am therefore not able with absolute certainty to say. From what I have been able, however, to gather from other quarters, I have come to the conclusion that they were so much pleased with their reception in New York, that Master Raymond purchased an estate on the east side of the Hudson River, where he and the charming Dulcibel lived and loved to a good old age, leaving three sons and three daughters.

If this couple really were our hero and heroine, then the Raymonds became connected, through the three daughters, with the Smiths, the Joneses and the Browns. In one way, perhaps, the question might be set at rest, were it not too delicate a one for successful handling. There is little doubt that among the descendants of Mistress Dulcibel, on the female side, the birth-mark of the serpent, more or less distinct, will be found occasionally occurring, even now, at the lapse of almost two centuries. Therefore, if among the secret traditions of any of the families I have mentioned, there be one relative to this curious birth-mark, doubtless that would be sufficient proof that in their veins runs the rich blood of the charming Dulcibel Raymond.

CHAPTER LIV.

Some Concluding Remarks.

Perhaps before I conclude I should state that the keeper of the Boston Bridewell, Master Arnold, was summarily dismissed for accepting the validity of the Governor's signature. But he did not take it very grievously to heart for Master Raymond, Captain Alden and others whom he had obliged saw him largely recompensed. Captain Alden, by the way, had fled for concealment to his relatives in Duxbury. Being asked when he appeared there, "Where he came from?" the old captain said "he was fleeing from the devil—who was still after him." However his relatives managed to keep him safely, until all danger was passed, both from the devil and from his imps.

As for Lady Mary, the indignation of "the faithful" was hot against her—and finally against Sir William, who could not be made to see in it anything but a very good joke. "You know that Lady Mary will have her own way," he said to Master Mather.

"Wives should be kept in due gospel subjection!" returned the minister.

"Oh, yes, rejoined the Governor smiling; but I wish you had a wife like Lady Mary, and would try it on her! I think we should hear something breaking."

But when Mistress Ann Putnam and others began "to cry out" against Lady Mary as a witch, the Governor waxed angry in his turn.

"It is time to put a stop to all this," he said indignantly. "They will denounce me as a witch next." So he issued a general pardon and jail delivery—alike to the ten persons who were then under sentence of death, to those who had escaped from prison, and to the one hundred and fifty lying in different jails, and the two hundred others who had been denounced for prosecution.

It was a fair blow, delivered at the very front and forehead of the cruel persecution and it did its good work, though it lost Sir William his position—sending him back to England to answer the charges of his enemies, and to die there soon afterwards in his forty-fifth year.

When Chief-Justice Stoughton, engaged in fresh trials against the reputed witches, read the Governor's proclamation of Pardon, he was so indignant that he left his seat on the bench, and could not be prevailed upon to return to it.

Neither could he, to the day of his death, be brought to see that he had done anything else than what was right in the whole matter.

Not so the jury—which, several years after, confessed its great mistake, and publicly asked forgiveness. Nor Judge Sewall, who rose openly in church, and confessed his fault, and afterward kept one of the days of execution, with every returning year, sacred to repentance and prayer—seeing no person from sunrise to nightfall, mourning in the privacy of his own room the sin he had committed.

Mistress Ann Putnam and her husband both died within the seven years, as Dulcibel in her moment of spiritual exaltation had predicted. Her daughter Ann lived to make a public confession, asking pardon of those whom she had (she said unintentionally) injured, and died at the age of thirty-five—her grave being one that nobody wanted their loved ones to lie next to.

As for the majority of the "afflicted circle," they fell as the years went on into various evil ways—one authority describing them as "abandoned to open and shameless vice."

Master Philip English, after the issue of the Governor's pardon, returned to Salem. Seventeen years afterwards, he was still trying to recover his property from the officials of the Province. Of £1500 seized, he never recovered more than £300; while his wife died in two years, at the age of forty-two, in consequence of the treatment to which she had been subjected.

Master Joseph Putnam and his fair Elizabeth lived on in peace at the old place; taking into his service the Quaker Antipas upon his release from prison. The latter was always quiet and peaceful, save when any allusion was made to the witches. But he had easy service and good treatment; and was a great favorite with the children, especially with that image of his father, who afterwards became distinguished as the Major General Putnam of Revolutionary fame.

As for the presents that had been promised to the "afflicted circle," they came to them duly, and from London too. And they were rich gifts also; but such a collection of odd and grotesque articles, certainly are not often got together. Master Raymond had commissioned an eccentric friend of his in London to purchase them, and send them on; acquainting him with the peculiar circumstances. There were yellow birds, and red dragons, and other fantastic animals, birds and beasts. But they came from London and the "circle" found them just suited to their peculiar tastes; and they always maintained, even in defiance of Mistress Ann, that Master Raymond was a lovely gentleman and an "afflicted" person himself. It will thus be seen that these Salem maidens were in their day truly esthetic—having that sympathetic fondness for unlovely and repulsive things, which is the unerring indication of a daughter of Lilith.

And now, in conclusion, some one may ask, "Did the Province of Massachusetts ever make any suitable atonement for the great wrongs her Courts of Injustice had committed?" I answer Never! Massachusetts has never made any, adequate atonement—no, not to this day!

The General Assembly, eighteen years afterwards, did indeed pass an act reversing the convictions and attainders in all but six of the cases; and ordering the distribution of the paltry sum of £578 among the heirs of twenty-four persons, as a kind of compensation to the families of those who had suffered; but this was all—nothing, or next to nothing!

Perhaps the day will some time come, when the cry of innocent blood from the rocky platform of Witch Hill, shall swell into sufficient volume to be heard across the chasm of two centuries. Then, on some high pedestal, where the world can see it,

Massachusetts shall proclaim in enduring marble her penitence and ask a late forgiveness of the twenty innocent men and women whom she so terribly wronged. And as all around, and even the mariner far out at sea, shall behold the gleaming shaft, standing where stood the rude gallows of two centuries ago, they shall say with softening eyes and glowing cheeks: "It is never too late to right a great wrong; and Massachusetts now makes all the expiation that is possible to those whom her deluded forefathers dishonored and persecuted and slew!"

By the Author of Dulcibel

PEMBERTON;

OR,

ONE HUNDRED YEARS AGO

"A well-told romance of old Philadelphia and its vicinity. The incidents of the story are interwoven with the struggle for independence. The book is intensely American in character and sentiment, and healthful in its stimulation of patriotism." —*New York Observer.*

Lightning Source UK Ltd.
Milton Keynes UK
UKHW010727060722
405454UK00001B/99